JUSTICE

PAMELA MURRAY

ALSO BY PAMELA MURRAY

Murderland

Bloodline

Duplicity

(The Manchester Murders trilogy)

Signs

The Raven

Death is Relative

(Detectives Burton & Fielding trilogy)

In Absentia

The Cross Woman

Bon Voyage

With thanks to

Anita, Ruby and Claudia

for letting me turn you into characters

CHAPTER ONE

Tiss Lawson entered the building which had been her place of work now for the past three years. Three happy years, she reminded herself as she pushed the heavy white handle of the door inwards and walked over towards the reception desk. The girl partially hidden by her computer screen looked up as she heard the door open and greeted Tiss with a wide beaming smile. So, when faced with such joy so early in the morning, why was Tiss feeling so unsettled and more than a little disgruntled this day in particular?

'Morning Tiss,' Denise trilled a greeting, which Tiss felt was a little too cheerily said for it being 8am on a Monday morning and the first day back in work after the ten-day Christmas holiday break. How could anyone be *that* ecstatic to be in work after being off for so long?

'Somebody's happy,' Tiss said a little grumpily as she picked up a pen from the desk to sign herself in. Despite being a new and modern company, the firm of Sanderson and Barnes still upheld the idea that its employees and visitors should print and then sign their names in a ledger when entering and leaving its premises instead of having the same data inputted onto Denise's computer.

'And what's got your back up this morning?' Denise asked with a little laugh. 'You're usually as chipper as I am first thing.'

It was true. The two girls normally exchanged spritely pleasantries every single morning, had done since they'd known one another, but today felt just that little bit different. 'I don't know,' Tiss admitted, settling the pen back down onto the crease of the open book. 'Just a feeling, I guess.'

'Just a feeling?'

'Yes. Oh, I don't know. You know when you get the feeling that something's not quite right?'

Denise nodded.

'Well, that.'

'That's normally not like you, though,' the receptionist continued with a slight frown. 'Anything on your mind got you thinking that?'

'No, nothing. Just-'

'Just a feeling,' Denise gave another gently laugh as she completed the sentence for her.

Tiss couldn't help but smile at that. Yes, it was unusual for her to be this out of sorts, and it was certainly *not* like her to be so grumpy about anything. 'Ah, forgive me,' she uttered, 'and don't mind me. Must have slept wrong or something.'

'Well, you know what would help with that,' she said with a raised eyebrow and a slight smirk.

Tiss had heard it all before … many, many times. She should get herself a boyfriend. Or at least Denise thought that she should get herself a boyfriend. Tiss, on the other hand, was not of the same mind as her. She *didn't* want a boyfriend; she was happy with her life and didn't need anyone to make her feel complete. If she wanted companionship, she'd get herself a pet, a cat most likely, but even then, she didn't really want that. So, she smiled an acknowledgement, the same one she always gave her when the subject came up. And it was often, and not only from Denise.

Denise knew the response her remarks always got, so she quickly changed the subject. 'Was Christmas okay?' she asked concerned, detecting something else amiss with her friend. 'Everything okay with the family?'

'Yes, it was lovely, and my parents were great as usual. Ate too much, drank too much, you know how it goes,' she chuckled.

'I certainly do!'

'How was yours?'

'Great,' Denise replied. 'You're probably just fed up that it's January again, and we're back here after having all that lovely time to ourselves. Ten days of absolute freedom from work.'

'Yes, that's probably it,' Tiss agreed with a small smile. She'd had a lovely week at her parents' house. She'd been spoiled rotten and wanted for nothing, and here she was back to the grind again, so that was probably why her mood was a little sour this cold and chilly morning.

'Anyway,' Denise continued, 'just to let you know your 8.30 appointment is here and he's waiting outside your office.'

'Already!' Tiss exclaimed in disbelief, her eyebrows inching closer to her hairline. In her three years with the law firm, nobody with a morning appointment had ever arrived in the building before she had. 'A bit eager, aren't they?'

'I did tell him that. I even suggested he go for a coffee or something, but he insisted on staying until you arrived.'

Tiss let out a long breath, thinking that she wouldn't even have time to grab herself a cup before seeing him. 'Anybody else in yet?'

'Don, Claudia and Lionel. Like you, they don't seem to have a life either.'

'Haha,' Tiss said sarcastically, throwing her friend a mock scowl. At that point the telephone on Denise's desk gave out a shrill ring, echoing throughout the empty reception area. 'My cue to go,' she said as she bent down and picked up her briefcase from the floor where she'd unceremoniously dumped it as she signed in, and started to walk away from the desk.

'Lunch at half-twelve at *The Daily Grind*?' Denise asked as she made a move to pick up the persistent phone from its cradle.

'Okay, see you later then,' Tiss called over her shoulder as she headed towards the door leading to the stairs. Her heels made a click clicking sound on the treads as she climbed them, loud enough to give anybody advance warning that she was coming. As she was making her way up, she fished around for a bunch of keys out of her handbag, the one she kept separate from her own house and car keys. Her "work bunch", as she called it. When she reached the first floor landing and looked right, she saw her client sitting in a chair directly across from her office. He was a middle-aged man, late fifties she thought, nicely dressed in a navy blue suit with a matching tie. A businessman from the look of him, probably on an early appointment so that he can get back to work. He politely stood up as she approached, something not many of her clients did, if ever, and smiled softly at her.

'Ms Lawson?' he asked.

'Yes, that's me,' Tiss replied as she reached down and put her key into the lock to open up. 'If you can just give me a few moments to get myself settled in and turn on my computer, then I'll be with you.'

'Yes, of course,' he replied nodding his head in acknowledgement before sitting back down on the chair.

'Thank you. I shan't be long,' she smiled as she entered her office and closed the door behind her. She had to admit to herself that even though she knew she had an early appointment, she couldn't for the life of her remember what his name was, thinking that she'd be able to check it out before he arrived. So much for that.

Despite the office being closed for the ten days over Christmas and the New Year, the room was already warm thanks to Denise's diligence in turning on the central heating every day as soon as she arrived, something which was greatly appreciated by everyone, especially in the colder months. Winter had already settled in, with snow having fallen over the Christmas period and more predicted within the next week, and as someone who disliked the cold in all its forms, she liked the cold edge to be taken off by any means possible. Putting her briefcase down by her desk, she quickly pressed the button on her computer to start it up before taking off her coat and hanging it up on the coat rack. After the screen came to life telling her, somewhat redundantly, that the company's name was Sanderson and Barnes, she logged in and went straight to her diary, which is where she found the name of the person who was waiting outside to see her: Frank Marshall. There were no further notes than that as he was a new client who hadn't previously seen anyone else at the law firm.

'Okay then,' she said to herself, 'time to go to work,' as she slipped from her seat in readiness to begin.

'Mr Marshall,' she said warmly with a welcoming smile as she opened the door wide for him to enter, and he rose from his chair to eagerly make his way in.

'Please take a seat,' she offered, indicating the chair across the desk from her own as she returned to hers. She waited for him to sit before continuing. 'Now, what can I do for you?'

He smiled. 'Well, it's a bit of an odd one,' he began almost hesitantly, biting his bottom lip as he said it. 'It's about my wife.'

'Okay.' She poised her pen above the blank page of the A4 notebook as she waited for him to elaborate. Most of her colleagues preferred to make notes directly onto the computer screen as the client was talking, but she liked to do it the old fashioned handwritten way to be transferred onto the client's file after they'd gone. Truth was, she liked to doodle as she was listening, making scrolling flower designs or small box-shaped houses. She'd no idea why, but that's what she had done so for as long as she could remember and found it to be strangely soothing.

'You see,' he continued, 'I think she's having an affair.' This was not new to Tiss' ears as far more clients than Mr Marshall here had come to the company for that very same reason, usually to draw up separation papers. 'And I think she's hankering after a divorce,' he continued. 'You see, I followed her the other day as she's been acting a bit suspiciously, and she came here-'

'She came here?' Tiss interrupted. If his wife was already one of the firm's clients then that would make things difficult, both for both him and for the company. Usually, if a husband and wife were either separating or divorcing then the stipulation was that they don't use the same law firm. This could definitely be a problem.

'Yes. I'm presuming that she saw somebody about it.'

'You know I can't tell you about that,' she insisted, the laws surrounding confidentiality obviously forbidding it.

'I know,' he nodded, and she was grateful that he at least he knew that much.

'Then I don't understand why you've come here yourself,' she said.

He suddenly seemed nervous and rubbed the back of his neck. 'Well,' he continued, although Tiss could sense he was uncomfortable about it. 'I think that she might be seeing one of your solicitors.'

That piece of news hit Tiss like a full-on body punch, leaving her unable to respond for a few moments. She had to think on her feet, and quickly. Of course, Mr Marshall might have got it all wrong, probably had in fact, but she would have to find out who his wife saw when she came to the practice and have a very, *very* discreet conversation with them. There were no rules that she knew of regarding solicitor/client relationships, especially as they were so few and far between, but she'd have to be sure. In any case, that was one aspect of a working life she disagreed with – the powers that be frowning over a workplace romance. If two people were attracted to one another, she could see no reason whatsoever to keep them apart. Her only concern about this was the fact that a married couple seeking divorce couldn't engage the same legal firm. Chances were that Marshall had got himself so worked up about the possibility that his wife might – and it's a big might – be having an affair, that he'd pretty much convinced himself that anybody she spoke to could possibly be having an illicit relationship with her.

'What's your wife's name, Mr Marshall?' she eventually asked, ready to make a note of it. His face perked up a bit when she asked, but then changed again when she told him quite emphatically that she wouldn't be able to disclose anything to him. 'I'll tell you what I'll do, though,' she added, 'I'll write to you to let you know if we'll be able to take you on as a client-'

'But-' he interrupted, and as soon as he did Tiss put up a hand to prevent him from going any further.

'That's all I can do under the circumstances, and I certainly can't tell you if she has engaged the services of the company on any matter. I can, however, give you the name of a private investigator that we use on occasions when we think it may help a client, unless you'd prefer to hire one of your own?'

'No,' he looked dejected. 'I mean, yes, I'd like the name of the person you use.'

Tiss quickly looked through the card holder on her desk and pulled the appropriate one free from it. 'Here,' she said handing it over. 'I'm sure she'll be able to help if needed.'

Marshall reciprocated by bringing out his wallet and giving her one of his own. 'It's my work address; you can contact me here.'

'Thank you,' she said as she took it from him. 'However, do wait until I get a letter out to you first to confirm yes or no.'

'Okay,' Marshall said making a move to get up. Tiss rose with him. He held out a hand and she took it. His palms were slightly sweaty but he had a firm handshake.

'I'll be in touch,' she said as she walked him to the door before returning to her computer and typed in the name *Miriam Marshall.*

CHAPTER TWO

'Leonard, can I have a word with you?' Tiss asked after he picked up his extension. She knew he was in as Denise had already told her when she'd arrived, and she'd also checked to see if he was currently with a client or not.

'Sure, what it is?' he asked chirpily.

'Mind if I come along and see you; it's a bit personal.'

'O-kay,' he said with a questioning voice. 'Everything alright?'

'Yes, yes, but I've just got a quick query for you.'

'Come right along then. I don't have a client for another fifteen minutes or so.'

'See you soon.' And with that she put her computer on standby and locked her room before heading to his downstairs office.

The reception area was starting to fill up, with two clients already waiting to be seen. They both raised their heads as she passed by, but seeing she wasn't who they had an appointment with they resumed looking at their phones. Denise was sorting out the day's post and gave her a quick nod as she passed through to the ground level offices. After knocking on Leonard's door his voice called her in.

'Hey, Leonard,' she said as she took the seat across from him and got straight into it. 'It's a confidential thing, but I need to know the answers,'

'Okay.' He gave her a quizzical look and put both elbows on the desk and steepled his fingers together waiting for her to continue.

'I've just had a potential client come and see me, but it seems his wife is already one of ours so I can't in all honesty take him on.'

'I see. Who is it?'

'Miriam Marshall.' Tiss replied.

'Yes, she's one of mine, but I'm guessing you already know that.'

'I do. He wasn't sure if she'd hired us or had just come in for some information though.'

'She's definitely hired us. It's for a will re-write.'

Tiss frowned as it was not what she was expecting. 'He seems to think that it was for a divorce.'

'Most certainly not,' Leonard continued with shake of his head and the hint of a laugh. 'Do all men think their wives are unfaithful to them? No, she's actually updated her will to make more things available to him if she should go before he does.'

'Ah, I see. And you know what else he thought?' she added with a twinkle in her eyes.

'No, what?'

When Tiss found out which solicitor had seen her she'd laughed to herself. If there anyone Mrs Marshall was going to have an affair with it certainly wasn't Leonard as he was gay ... and he had a fiancé to boot. 'Well, he thought that she might be having an affair with her solicitor.'

Leonard snorted before full-on laughing. 'I don't think she's my type somehow, Tiss!'

'I know she's not. Okay, I'll get going then,' she said rising from the chair. 'I'll send him a letter saying we can't take him on as his wife's already one of our clients. I won't say anything other than that, and I did warn him as such if she'd hired anyone. I've also given him Lily Singer's card in case he wants to pursue the PI route, but I'm suspecting he won't need it.'

'Just an over-suspicious middle-aged gentleman then?'

'Looks like.'

'Do married couples *never* talk to one another?'

'Wrong person to ask here,' she retorted with a smile.

***

The rest of the day went without a hitch or any further excitement. At midday, Tiss and Denise had lunch in the little café across the street, the one they always frequented a couple of times a week. Then she had three more clients in the afternoon before the clock finally crawled around to five. None of them were exciting: a couple of wills and an argument between neighbours regarding one parking across the other's driveway. Routine stuff, really, but it was work she enjoyed; all of it was, every single aspect of it. For Tiss, or to give her her full name, Justice, the law was in her blood, and not just in her name, and it had been for as long as she could remember. Her parents were something of a legend in their own right in the legal profession, the well-known and revered barristers Paul and Sarah Lawson, and she'd always known from a very young age that she would be following their footsteps into a legal career when the time came. Unlike most children who'd been given unusual names by their parents, she actually loved hers, and it was fitting on so many levels. She'd grown up in a household surrounded by law books and box files with legal cases in them, and two parents who lived and breathed every aspect of the law. When she was old enough to understand, it had both excited and terrified her to think that a solicitor was the only person able to speak up for and defend someone who was innocent, thereby stopping them from going to prison for something they didn't do and allowing them to be free. At the time she couldn't see her future self being anything other than that person. So she studied for a law degree, gaining invaluable help and knowledge from both her parents along the way, and after passing her exams with distinction she settled happily into working for the company she's currently with. Everyone knew from the outset who her parents were, such was their fame in legal circles, but there was no nepotism in her gaining the position as she did that on the back of her own qualifications and determination.

The rest of the working week continued without any hitches and Friday came around again as it always did. It was the day when she and her two besties would celebrate their friendship by going out for a meal followed by spending the remaining evening dancing the night away in a club. One of her friends was Claudia Romano, was another solicitor from the office who was originally from Italy but had settled down in the country following a visit a few years back and loved it so much that she hadn't wanted to leave, and Ruby Duran, her constant companion from her university days who had pursued a career in nursing but had progressed to the administrative side of things at the local hospital. Thanks to her degree and proven talent, she had quickly risen to the ranks of Head of Medical Administration. Claudia was single like herself but had just started seeing someone, and Ruby was engaged to her long-time boyfriend, Joshua Scott, and the pair were planning to tie the knot later in the year. He usually worked late on a Friday, and wasn't the jealous type who would begrudge his fiancée going out with her friends for a few hours. Tiss knew many who would be, but Josh was very understanding on that score. In the same way, Ruby wouldn't begrudge him if he likewise wanted a night out with his friends. They fit together so easily, had done from the start, and Tiss was thrilled for their upcoming nuptials.

The Uber called at Tiss' house a couple of minutes before 7pm. While she was locking her front door she turned her head around towards the car and could see Claudia smiling and waving to her from the back seat. She smiled back and slipped her keys into a zipped inside pocket of her handbag and hurried over towards the waiting vehicle to join her, opening the back door and quickly sliding in. She could see the driver looking at her in the rear view mirror and she acknowledged him by telling him she'd secured the seat belt. Satisfied both passengers were safely strapped in, he began to pull away from the kerb. From there it was a relatively short journey to Ruby's place and then on to the restaurant in the middle of town.

The Olive Garden was one of the town's more popular restaurants and had been a firm favourite of theirs for just over a year now. They'd tried out a variety of others in the beginning, but this one had stood out above the rest and become their regular Friday night eatery. They'd even gone so far as to secure a standing weekly reservation. The place was already buzzing with customers and ambiance when they entered, and the girl on the reception desk greeted them in a warm and familiar way like she always did every Friday evening she was on relief. With a friendly smile and a hearty "follow me, please", she quickly escorted them to their private little haven some way back from the main area where their regular table was situated. They'd chosen it as it was the perfect secluded spot for chatting and catching up without the sound of other voices and background music overpowering their conversation. In short, it was idyllic and peaceful, and also quite private. Beside the table was a large picture window, and beyond that a patio area with a sturdy-looking pergola, perfect for dining outside on warmer nights. The restaurant held barbeque evenings and other special events when the weather was more pleasant and they'd spent more than their fair share of evenings out there. But the nights were far too cold for that now and the tables were put away into storage until the finer weather came around again. Fairy lights, twisted around the wooden structure and twinkling in the gentle breeze caught Tiss' eye. They always delighted her, giving the area a special magical feel to it even without diners present. In the heat of the summer the pergola would be draped with gloriously colourful hanging baskets, and the deck strewn with planters of all shapes and sizes, making it almost like sitting in some faraway foreign location instead of in the middle of a busy town. That was why they all loved it so much, that and the fact that the food was second to none.

Over dinner the girls chatted about how their respective week had gone, but before long the conversation turned somewhat expectedly to Ruby's upcoming nuptials in a few months' time. She was excited, of course she was, who wouldn't be, as it was promised to be the best day of her life according to all the wedding magazines she'd amassed along the way. And there'd been more than a few of them. But she knew that it was going to be a very special day regardless of what any magazine told her. Josh was the love of her life, and she his, so their joining together was something special for the pair of them. They'd been together now for two years. Both were in good jobs and well-off financially, and she admitted that she wanted to start a family as soon as they were married, so from an affordability aspect there was no reason not to. Ruby jokingly said that she knew Josh was definitely fertile enough!

'So should the gifts be joint wedding and baby shower ones?' Claudia joked as Ruby continued to gush about the thought of a wedding followed by the sound of the patter of tiny feet running around the place.

'Oh shush!' she chided, making everyone laugh. 'A girl can be dream about being happy, can't she?' And Claudia and Tiss *were* so very happy for her, having found the man of her dreams with the prospect of them soon entering parenthood together. What could be better? Tiss only wished that she could be so lucky in love. Up until now, finding a life partner, a soul mate, and becoming a mother hadn't bothered her, but hearing her friend talk and seeing the look in her eyes was making her have second thoughts. Not that she thought there was anything missing at present, but perhaps there was, and that's what she needed in her life after all. She'd only had one regular boyfriend, Joe who she met whilst at university, but all that had fizzled out when they'd gone their separate ways after graduating. She'd felt upset by it at first, but her blossoming career had helped her get over it in that respect. Since then she didn't think she needed a man in her life.

'Penny for them.' Ruby's voice brought her out of her thoughts and back into the here and now.

'Oh,' she gasped, 'nothing; just thinking.'

'Be careful,' Claudia laughed. 'I hear it's bad for you at times.'

Tiss joined in with the laughter, but it had indeed given her food for thought, no pun intended.

Following their meal they headed off to *Lux*, a new nightclub which had only opened a month previously. As it was only a couple of blocks at most from where they were, they walked rather than call for a ride. Just like the restaurant they'd chosen, they'd been looking for a nightclub to make it their regular one for quite some time, and *Lux* had been on their radar ever since its opening. Everybody had been raving about it, the press, their friends, hailing it as *the* place to be, but they had yet to visit themselves in order to make up their own minds. They'd decided, however, that this was going to be the night they would.

They'd expected a queue to get in judging by all the publicity that was out there for the place, and when they turned the corner and onto the street where it was located they weren't surprised by the long one that had already formed. They tagged on at the end behind what appeared to be a hen night party of six women, all dressed in inappropriate clothing for the coolness of the night. Strangely enough none of them appeared to notice it, but judging by their loud voices and laughter, and their overall demeanour, Tiss suspected that the alcohol they'd already consumed elsewhere was what was keeping them warm. Gradually the queue lessened, bringing them nearer to the door to go in. After paying their statutory entrance fees at the desk they descended the flight of stairs which would take them down into the bowels of the building where the main body of the club was. The thrumming beat of the music became louder the further they went down, assaulting their ears and reverberated throughout them when they finally entered the cavernous space of the dancefloor. They were met with a sea of bodies gyrating to the sound of the techno beats; flashing multicolour lights washing over them as they all moved seductively in time to the music. It was quite hypnotic to watch.

'Wow!' Claudia exclaimed, shouting loud enough for the girls to hopefully hear her. Even then they barely could as she was easily outdone by the sheer volume of the club's speakers.

Tiss could already feel trickles of sweat running down her back from both the temperature of being below ground and the body heat of everyone currently surrounding them. She loved the vibrant atmosphere of a club, which was very much at odds with her quiet and restrained lifestyle, but perhaps that was why. This was her one day a week to let all the tension of her often stressful work seep out of her, and what could be better than to just let it all go like this. She could already sense that the place was living up to all her expectations and proving that it could be a keeper for them, even perhaps become their regular one. As she'd seen the show a couple of times, she recognised the name *Lux* from the tv series *Lucifer,* and the connection between the two had already been mentioned in the opening press reports she'd read in the papers and online. True to its name there was a distinct devilish theme running throughout, from the almost decadent decorative colour scheme of reds and blacks to the complimentary symbols and prints of a more supernatural nature covering the walls. And then there was the bar, which ran the entire length of one of the walls; she'd never seen one quite like it. It was fully stocked with all kinds of wines and spirits, with attentive bartenders doing their thing with cocktail shakers while wearing headbands with flashing red horns. In any other situation it would have been cheesy, but somehow it wasn't the case here. She found the whole thing captivating and exciting, and something of a contrast to her almost boring lifestyle above ground in the real world. It was as if she'd stepped into an alternative reality, more so than their usual club nights.

'I love this!' she shouted to her friends as she followed them to the bar, but doubted if they could even hear her at that moment above the noise. How the bartenders were hearing anybody above this said a lot about their aural integrity, and she wondered if perhaps they were hired on that requirement alone. Once the drinks were in the front of them they found a table on one of the raised seating areas which, strangely enough, seemed less noisy than the dancefloor.

'Great acoustics,' Ruby said without the need to raise her voice for the others to hear her. 'I can actually hear myself speak up here.' Tiss and

Claudia nodded their agreement as they took a welcome sip of their drinks, an assortment of different cocktails each with a plastic red pitchfork sticking out of the glass. Despite being suddenly thirsty due to the heat of the enclosed space that was the club, Tiss didn't want to rush hers because of its alcoholic content. She knew that if she did that she'd be well and truly sloshed within the next half hour, especially as she'd already had a large glass of wine at the restaurant. Drinking to excess just wasn't her thing, neither were the after effects of consuming copious amounts of alcohol. She just didn't like the sensations of feeling or being physically sick, so she always paced herself wherever she was.

They sat like that for a while, just chatting watching what was happening all around them and taking it all in.

'I think you have an admirer,' Claudia suddenly said, nudging Tiss' arm gently.

'What?' Tiss looked around her in surprise.

'Over there.' Claudia nodded over to her left and Tiss' eyes followed to over where the bar was. 'He's been looking over at you for a while,' she added before Ruby got involved in the action, straining her neck to see what they were both looking at.

The man nodded and held up his drink in a salutary fashion when he saw they were looking but didn't take his eyes away from their table, and from Tiss in particular.

'Oh, yes, definitely an admirer!' Ruby joked. 'I think you're in there girl.'

'I don't think I want to be "in", as you put it,' Tiss returned, sipping nonchalantly on her drink and trying to avoid the unexpected attention.

'Oh, come on,' came the reply. 'You know you could do with a bit of relief. When was the last time you were on a date? You don't have to answer that because I know it's been ages. So why not?'

'Look, he might be looking over but that doesn't mean anything,' Tiss insisted. But at that point the man pushed himself away from the bar and started to make a move towards them. 'Oh,' she said quietly, lowering her head.

'See,' Ruby crowed triumphantly. 'Carpe Diem, Tiss. Seize the day!'

All eyes were on him as he made his approach, stopping just beside their table. His eyes scanned all of them before settling on Tiss, making her feel somewhat uncomfortable at the attention and, if she admitted it, the intrusion. All she wanted was to be on a night out with her two friends, not attract the attention of an unwanted admirer. An attractive admirer, if she admitted it to herself, but still an unwarranted one, nevertheless.

'Hi,' he said, his eyes never leaving hers.

'Um ... hi,' she returned, feeling more than a little out of the game.

'Can I get you a drink?' he asked.

'I've already got one,' Tiss replied holding her glass up for him to see, and he laughed gently at her action.

'I mean another one,' he added. 'After you've finished the one you've got there.'

Tiss was about to go into all-out solicitor mode and argue the case against her doing so when Ruby elbowed her a little too strongly in the ribcage causing her to react rather loudly.

'Ouch!' she looked venomously at her friend which garnered another laugh from this mystery man.

'I think your friends are trying to tell you something.' He gave her a broad smile, obviously designed to disarm anyone in his vicinity. Tiss, however, was still not biting.

'Look,' she began firmly. 'I'm just not interested, sorry. Now if you don't mind I'd like to continue to enjoy my drink in peace with my friends.'

Despite the rebuff, his smile didn't waver. 'Okay then, I can get the hint. Your loss, though,' he chuckled as he turned around and started to walk away.

'What are you doing?' Ruby attacked her almost immediately. 'The man was drop-dead gorgeous, and there you are sending him away with his tail between his legs.'

'And whatever else is there!' Claudia smirked. She, too, knew of her friend's prolonged abstinence when it came to men.

'This could have been a chance to get yourself out of that rut you're in,' Ruby continued, casually ignoring the remark.

'For one thing, I'm not in a rut,' Tiss said petulantly. 'And another, he's just not my type.'

'Not your type? Listen to me, anybody's your type when you've gone this long without.'

'Hey, come on, Ruby,' Tiss said, sticking to her decisions. 'I'm not like that, you know I'm not. I'm not going to get on my back when the first person with a dazzling smile comes along. I'm just too … picky, I guess.'

'Well, you don't have to get on your back-' Claudia began, but was immediately cut off by both girls at the same time.

'Claudia!' the others both said loudly, which ended up with all three getting the giggles.

'Seriously, though,' Tiss continued when the laughter subsided. 'That's not what I need right now. When the time's right I'll know it, and right now I've got all this extra studying I need to get in for my next exam in two weeks' time.' Although more than fully qualified for her current position, she'd decided to go for an extra notch to her belt by taking a counselling course. In her mind she thought it to be a good idea as that way she could give personal advice to clients in addition to legal. It made sense to her as she'd always had an interest in psychology, and at one point even thought that interest might supersede the law, but nature took its course in the end. That didn't stop her, though, from still being invested in it. In her mind, the two of them went hand in hand as both entailed giving advice, legal and personal.

'Okay then,' Ruby said, 'I'll let you off.'

'Gee, thanks,' Tiss laughed. 'Maybe I'll meet Mister Right at your wedding later in the year.'

'It's a while off yet. Are you sure you can hang on that long?'

'I've hung on this long, I'm sure I can go a bit longer!'

After that little interlude, the three of them took to the dancefloor again and spent the next few hours just indulging themselves, soaking up the music and the atmosphere. For each of them, the freedom just to let go was the perfect end to the working week, as come Monday morning they'd be back to the grindstone again. Tiss did notice that man looking at her again during the course of the evening, but simply dismissed it.

CHAPTER THREE

When Tiss got into the office on Monday morning and logged onto her computer, she found a curious email message waiting for her in her inbox. It was from Lily Singer, her go-to private investigator when the occasion warranted it. Lily didn't usually contact her again once the recommendation to a client had been sent out, so it immediately sparked her interest. Opening it, Lily began with her thanks for the work, and confirmed that she'd been hired by the client to investigate his wife's behaviour. Tiss felt like replying to explain what the situation was, but that would have breached confidentiality, so she didn't. She was curious, however, as to Mr Marshall's insistence in continuing with this, as she had written to him to confirm his wife was a client of the firm and suggested that he discuss the matter with her instead of resorting to hiring an investigator. She tried to make it as plain as she could without going against all regulations that the matter wasn't one of infidelity, but perhaps he hadn't picked up on that even though she'd gone out of her way to stress it without actually saying it. Going by Lily's email, it seemed that he hadn't picked up on it. Tiss let out a long sigh. She'd tried, but that was all she could do. If he wanted to waste his money hiring Lily, then that was his own business. But then as she read further, the next thing Lily wrote made her even more puzzled. She had insisted on a meeting with her, at her office or privately outside of work, the time and place left up to her and at her own convenience. Why had Lily requested that as she'd never done it before in the past, so why now; what was so different about this case? With her interest was piqued, Tiss felt like calling her, but sent a quicky reply saying she could squeeze her in that afternoon at 3pm if that was suitable. A message came back almost immediately, simply saying *yes.*

At ten to three, Denise rang up from reception to say that Lily had arrived, and as Tiss was clientless at that moment she asked for her to be sent up straight away.

'Hi,' she said after Lily had knocked and entered the room, gesturing to her that she take a seat opposite.

'I'm sorry this is a bit sudden,' Lily replied sitting herself down as instructed.

'I have to admit I'm a bit puzzled,' Tiss looked at her associate. 'Especially as you didn't say anything in your email.'

'I know. I wanted to keep it private between the two of us.'

'But emails are priv'-' Tiss began to explain, but Lily cut in.

'I know they are, but I wanted to do this face to face.'

'Okay.'

'It's just … well, it's Mr Marshall.'

'What about him?'

Lily frowned for a moment before answering. 'How did he come across to you?'

'In what way?'

'Well … I get the feeling there's something not quite right about all this.'

'I'm not sure what you mean, Lily.'

The private detective sat back in the chair. 'I'm not really sure how to describe it. It's just that … oh, I don't know, just a feeling I guess, but I knew I needed to come and speak to you about it.'

'You've sparked my interest.' Admittedly, Tiss didn't meet with her go-to PI very often, but on the occasions that she had, she was never this indecisive about anything. Tiss knew a great deal about feelings, though.

'I've got a very funny feeling about this, and not in a good way.'

'Do you think he's dangerous?'

'To be honest with you, I don't know.'

Now it was Tiss' turn to sit back in her chair and rock it slowly back and forth for a few moments. She had no idea where this was going, or where it was coming from, but she needed to find out for her own curiosity if nothing else. 'Tell me what you're thinking,' she insisted, leaning forward again and resting her elbows on her desk.

'Well, it's going to sound odd, but his wife *did* meet someone, a young man, but I don't think it was on the lines of what he was thinking.' She reached insider her bag and brought out two photographs then handed them over to Tiss.

'This is them?' Tiss asked as she took them from her and scrutinised both people carefully. The man in question looked to be much younger than Mrs Williams, and one of the pictures had been taken inside a café and the other as the pair of them were approaching the front steps of a building. It appeared that Lily was nothing if not thorough.

'Go on,' she said, putting them down.

'I followed them as I thought he was going to be right about everything. But then ...' Lily hesitated for a second, something Tiss immediately caught onto.

'Then what?'

'Firstly they met inside a café on the high street, the first photo I handed you, and stayed for around thirty minutes. Then they went to a club.'

'A club? What, in the middle of the afternoon?'

'Yes, but not that kind of club. And here's where it becomes somewhat inexplicable. He actually took her to a gentleman's club.'

'To a what?' Tiss picked up the second photo and looked at it again. It seemed innocuous enough, nondescript even, with nothing to give that away.

'Yes, I know. I don't know what to make of it; I've no idea what it all means.'

'Me neither. Well, that wasn't something I was expecting,' Tiss confessed. If they were having an affair she'd have expected them to go off to a hotel or something, but a gentleman's club? 'Which one?' she asked at last.

'The Regency.'

'Give me the address, will you? And did she get in; I mean, it's supposed to only be for men, right?' Despite Tiss' view on that, from a legal standpoint it was still okay to allow men only in an establishment of that nature.

'She did. But here's another thing. When I got back to the office and checked the club out, it seems that it doesn't exist.'

'What ... how?'

'I don't know,' Lily said, and Tiss could see her frustration at this. 'I tried everything, absolutely everything, and even got my tech guy involved. And that's what really bothers me about this. It just doesn't officially exist.'

***

Tiss was feeling apprehensive as she approached the outside of the building, but felt it was something she needed to do if she wanted to get any answers. She looked around anxiously, but she'd turned her phone's location on and Lily would be able to find her should something untoward happen. Exactly what she thought might happen she didn't know. Like Lily, she'd scoured the internet for something, anything, to do with the Regency Gentleman's Club, and had found nothing. She'd even tried Companies House, but again, nothing was forthcoming. Every company was supposed to be registered with it, so the only reason she could think was that it was registered in another name. Although what that was was anybody's guess. Even so, the address should have yielded something for her to work with, but that was also a dead end. It wasn't her job to do this, investigate clients as that was more Lily's line of work, but now that it had got under her skin she found she couldn't let go. Like at all.

It was 6.15pm and there were already people entering the place. The doorman looked at her strangely as she walked in past him but he didn't challenge her or stop her from entering. Tiss decided that was a plus. Once inside she looked around and found herself in some kind of alternate reality, as if she'd stepped straight out of the 21st century and into the past. The décor had a distinct Victorian feel to it; mahogany wood reception desk with a high shelf shielding anyone who might be sitting behind it, red floral wallpaper and heavy green velvet curtains framing the windows. She walked up to and stood behind a small queue of two elderly men while they were signing a thick red ledger on the top of the shelf. Then it was her turn to speak. The man behind the desk was standing, and his eyebrows shot up when he saw her, obviously not expecting a woman, and especially not one dressed in a smart business suit.

'Can I help you?' he asked to which Tiss asked if she could speak to the manager. 'He isn't in yet,' came the reply. 'He's not in until around nine o'clock.'

'Is there something I can help with, George?' a voice behind Tiss asked, and she swivelled around to face the source of it head on. 'I'm the relief manager,' he said to her. 'Perhaps I can be of assistance to you in his absence.'

'Oh, right, maybe,' Tiss replied taken off guard. For one fleeting moment she thought he looked a bit familiar somehow, like someone she'd seen in passing, maybe at the office, but before she could place him he began to speak again.

'You do know that this is a *gentleman's* club?' he asked, somewhat stating the obvious. At that point Tiss delved into her bag and produced her trump card – the photo Lily had taken of Mrs Marshall and her unknown friend entering the building. He took it from her and looked unamused at it.

'And?' he asked, seemingly disregarding what he'd just said regarding the club's gender policy.

'You can see that that's a woman, can't you?'

'Of course I can, I'm not blind,' came the rather testy reply.

'So, she's going in.'

'I'm sorry, but who are you exactly?'

Tiss went into her bag again and brought out one of her business cards to hand to him. Again, as with the business card, he looked at it then back to her with a stoic expression on his face.

'And?' Was that all the man could say?

'I'd like to know what she was doing here?'

'And this has to do with?'

Tiss could tell that she was getting nowhere with this person so said that it would probably be best if she spoke to the actual manager. 'It's a legal matter,' she added, although if questioned about it at that moment she had no idea what she was going to say.

'Well, as George here said, he isn't in until nine this evening.'

'That's a bit late for a manager to be in a business, isn't it?'

'That's why I'm here.'

Tiss knew she wasn't going to win with this one so decided to walk away from it. 'Okay then, I'll come back at nine.' And with that she turned around and made her way to the door.

Once outside Tiss rang Lily to tell her what had happened. She knew she'd be anxiously waiting to hear what had transpired so didn't waste a second to get her phone out and let her know.

'That's an odd time to come into work,' was the first thing she said, to which Tiss agreed.

'I know, right? Plus, I got a very odd vibe from the place.'

'Like what?'

'I don't know, like a lot of secrecy.'

'Well, it is a men's club; I can only imagine all the secrets that go on in there. Boys on their own left to their own devices and all that.'

'I guess. But what's still bugging me is the fact that neither you nor I can find out a damned thing about them.'

'Yeah, and there's that. Maybe it's some secret government establishment,' Lily suggested ironically, laughing as she did so, and in that moment the thought crossed Tiss' mind that it might be a possibility.

'You know, that's a good point,' she said, not taking the notion as lightly as her friend had.

'I *was* joking, you know,' came the retort with a huff.

'Yes, I know you were, but what if it is? It's completely off the radar, and what kind of establishments can you say that about ... covert ones.'

'But that doesn't make sense,' Lily argued.

'I think that's the only thing about this that does make sense.'

'Well, I'm coming with you,' Lily declared on hearing that. 'If you are indeed heading into one of the country's best-kept secrets, then I'm not having you go in there all alone. I was the one who alerted you to this, so it's only fair that I go with you.'

Tiss couldn't find it in her to disagree, nor did she really want to. Having a second person as backup was a very good idea.

The two of them entered the club at exactly nine on the dot. As she was entering, Tiss noticed something on the brickwork next to the club's name plate. Interesting, she thought as she recognised it. No George this time behind the reception desk, but another man, an elderly gentleman, who was there in his place. Fortunately there was no sign of the relief manager this time, something Tiss was grateful for. She strode towards the man with determination.

'Ladies,' he said on their arrival. 'What can I do for you?'

'Firstly you can tell us just what's up with this club?' Before Tiss could open her mouth to speak, Lily jumped straight in with it, and Tiss turned around to stare at her with a *really?* expression on her face. It may have been direct and to the point, a little *too* direct, but even if it was the ultimate goal, it still had to be approached more delicately.

'I'm sorry?' he asked, a little taken back by her forthrightness.

'I mean,' she continued, 'is it some kind of secret spy establishment, or is there like an S & M sex dungeon downstairs?'

'Lily!' Tiss hissed at her, not wishing her to continue this line of conversation, especially not the way she was heading with it. 'Sorry,' she said turning back to the man behind the desk, 'my friend here is just joking with you.'

Lily was about to speak up but Tiss elbowed her in the ribs to keep her from saying anything more than she already had. She ignored the *ouch* she heard come from her.

'Ah,' was all he said as if it was an everyday occurrence to have two women in the club, one of whom was trying to be a comedienne at best. 'I gather you're the young lady from earlier, the one who spoke to the relief manager,' he said looking towards Tiss. 'I was told to make the manager aware of your arrival should you return.' Tiss thought his posh accent made him sound like a butler in an episode of a period drama. She nodded, hoping that Lily would refrain from saying anything further. He picked up a telephone from below her line of vision. Tiss was half expecting to see an old fashioned one, a candlestick-type where the earpiece was attached to a cord and you spoke directly into the mouthpiece on the stick, but it was a modern cordless one which seemed completely out of place with the surroundings.

'Ms Justice Lawson is here to see you, sir, the legal lady from earlier,' he said into the phone. Adding, 'yes, of course,' before replacing the phone back where he'd retrieved it. 'He'll be down for you both in a minute,' he informed them.

As he went back to work behind the desk, Tiss and Lily stood off to one side, and the latter looked through the leaflets on the console desk.

'Find something you're interested in?' Tiss asked her, to which the reply came that she wasn't really looking but merely passing the time. After a while a man came in through the entrance door and looked at them before heading towards the desk. At first they both thought it was the manager, but it appeared he was only a member gaining admittance. He cast them both a glance as he signed his name in the ledger, but once done he thanked "Timothy" before heading through another door to goodness knows where. Tiss could only assume it was through to the main body of the club itself. A few moments more passed until a gentleman dressed in a smart pinstripe suit came through an internal door this time. He glanced briefly at the individual attending the desk, now identified as Timothy, then proceeded to approach the girls when Timothy nodded in their direction.

'Matthew Ford,' he said holding out his hand. Tiss took it first, then Lily. The man had a very firm handshake. 'Sorry to keep you waiting, but if you'd like to follow me we can go up to my office.'

'Of course,' Tiss said with a smile. At this point she was trying to work out in her mind what to say to him regarding why they were there. She thought about just coming out and asking about Mrs Marshall and her young gentleman friend, but knew was breaching client confidentiality. If it had been left to Lily she would have just come out and said it, but she had to be professional about it all if they were to find anything out. After all, the manager could be a close personal friend of Mrs Marshall, which would make the whole questioning difficult and probably end up with her having to explain herself to her bosses. So in the end, an idea occurred to her which she hoped Lily would back her up on.

Ford led them through a corridor to the rear of the reception desk and up a flight of wooden stairs to the first floor. Tiss was curious to see that the style and décor of the building was not confined to the ground floor entrance, and the Victorian theme was indeed carried beyond it. Perhaps the building itself was of that era, like many on the side streets were, and the owners decided to maintain its uniqueness and preserve it in the tasteful way they had. They could have gone all modern, but somehow that wouldn't have suited an old building like this. To Tiss, modern buildings were the ones which should have modern exterior and interiors, not the architectural wonders of years gone by which were steeped in history.

Ford's office was at the end of the corridor, and once they were all in he invited them to sit on the two leather bucket chairs in front of his desk. It was mahogany like the finish of the one in the reception area, and polished to an equally high standard of sheen that you could see your own reflection in. It made Tiss think that she would like one in her own office instead of her old teak one. But she digressed, delaying the moment when she would need to give the man a decent explanation for why she and her friend were making enquiries about two people who had visited the premises.

'So,' he began, resting his elbows on the desk and steepling his fingers, his eyes flitting between the two of them then back onto Tiss. 'What's this all about?'

Moment of truth. Tiss brought the photo Lily had given her out of her bag, the one that showed the two of them about to enter the club, and handed it over to him. As he looked at it his brows furrowed.

'We were wondering what you could tell us about these two people,' she said, all the while watching his reaction. Apart from the initial frown, she couldn't see any sign of recognition in his eyes.

'I can't say I either know or recognise them,' he admitted. 'Is this in some way related to a legal case you're working on?'

Tiss then had the way out she was searching for and simply told him that, yes, it was, but she wasn't in a position of being able to discuss it with him.

'Ah, I see.' Then added, 'Do you happen to know what day and time this took place, because if need be I think I might be able to help you out with it.'
It was going better than expected, and Tiss didn't either have to lie or make up a story on the spot. Surely it wasn't going to be *this* easy.

'I can help with that,' Lily chirped up, opening up her bag and pulling out a red backed journal. She opened it and searched for what she was after, then announced the exact date and time the photograph was taken.

'That's pretty accurate,' Ford asked with a smile as he looked at her. The man was nothing if not charming and hospitable.

'Because I'm the one who took it,' she said proudly.

'I see,' was all he said, continuing to gaze at her. Such scrutiny would have made Tiss feel a little uncomfortable, buy Lily was taking it all in her stride. And if Tiss knew her, which she did, she'd say that she was actually enjoying it.

'Well then, let me see if I can help you both.' Ford picked up the phone on his desk, this one being of the more modern kind than the one downstairs, and punched in a three digit number. 'Timothy, do you think you could bring the signing in ledger up to me as soon as possible,' he asked, ending the call as soon as he'd begun it, not even waiting for a response. 'It shouldn't take long,' he continued, rocking back in his chair and looking towards the two women in front of him again.

'So,' he turned to Tiss, 'I get that you're the solicitor, but who are you?' The latter question being directed towards her companion when he settled on her.

'I'm a private investigator,' she said without hesitation. Tiss would have preferred her to keep quiet on that score, but Lily being the impetuous person that she always is, had her reply out before she could stop her.

'A private investigator, eh?' Ford stared at her, not out of malice, but something akin to admiration. Did he actually have a thing for her friend? If Tiss' judgment was anything to go by, then she'd say yes, he did.

'Yes, I work with Ms Lawson on occasion.'

'And the occasion of this being?' he pushed for information, but before Tiss could stop her friend from saying anything she shouldn't, there was a knock on the door before it opened. Tiss thanked her lucky stars for the interruption.

'Ah, Timothy. Thank you,' Ford said taking the large ledger from him.

'Will there be anything else, sir?' he very politely asked, to which he was told no. The man then turned around and exited the room. Yes, most certainly a butler from *Upstairs Downstairs.*

'So, let me see,' the manager said as he opened up the book and searched for the date and time he'd been given. Both girls watched as his index finger went up and down a page without settling on anything specific. 'Hmm,' he muttered to himself. 'Strange.'

'Strange?' Tiss echoed. 'How do you mean?'

'According to the ledger, nobody entered the building for an hour either side of the time you say.'

'No, that can't be right,' Lily insisted. 'I was there; I took the photograph.'

'Look for yourself,' Ford said turning the book around and pushing it forward towards the edge of the desk for them both to see.

'And everybody has to sign in?' Tiss asked him as she leaned forward.

'Yes.'

'And there's nowhere they could have gone before getting to the reception desk?'

'No. Everyone who comes in through the main door has to sign in.'

'Do you have security cameras?' Lily cut in.

'No, we don't. We don't need them. All our members are upstanding members of the community, so there's no need for such intrusion.'

***

'He's lying, I know he is!' Lily spluttered once they'd left the building. 'I saw them both go in there, so they had to end up somewhere inside.'

'It seems so, but why? And why is there no record of it either?'

'I don't know,' came the reply, 'but I'm definitely going to check Ford out; find out all I can about him.' The rising tone of Lily's voice was a sure indicator to Tiss that she was annoyed about the whole interaction in there.

'This is becoming personal for you, isn't it?'

'Damn right it is!'

'Look then, you do some digging and I'll have a word with my colleague, the one who saw Mrs Marshall, and try to find out a bit more about it. I know he said it was for one thing, but maybe there was more to it than he put in the client notes.'

'Okay.' The reply was sharp, harsh even, but Tiss knew how to try and get her friend to relax.

'Come on,' she said, linking her arm in Lily's, 'Let's get you to a café and get some caffeine inside you. Maybe some food as well. Dinner, even, if you'd like it.'

'I'm just so fired up,' she said, exasperated.

'I can tell,' Tiss laughed gently, easing her friend away from the building. It wasn't doing her any good to be standing outside and raging about it, especially now as she could see Timothy gazing through the window at them. Tiss just wanted Lily out of the way before storming the building for answers, because she knew she would do it if left there long enough. Lily had always been an impulsive kind of person, and was the complete opposite to Tiss in so many ways. She couldn't really explain why, but felt it was the reason why she liked her so much. Perhaps it was the old idea of chalk and cheese, and opposites attracting.

They walked a couple of streets before spying a quiet little Italian restaurant tucked away just off the main thoroughfare, and Tiss immediately pulled them both into it. As they stood at the door they were approached by an enthusiastic-looking waiter with menus in hand who walked them through the tables and seated them at a quiet spot near the back. After handing them both the menus, he asked if they'd like a drink, and after saying what they would, he hurried off to get them.

'Seems keen,' Tiss laughed, watching him scuttle away.

'Unlike Mr Ford,' Lily snarked before looking at what was on offer for them to eat.

'Although I do think he seemed quite keen on you.'

'Who, the waiter?' Lily looked up in shock.

'No, Mr Ford. I saw the way he was looking at you,' but Lily just waved it off and continued to peruse the menu. She finally settled on a house lasagne and Tiss on mushroom fettucine. The attentive waiter took their order when he returned with their drinks, saying to give him a wave if they needed anything else in the meantime.

'He's after a tip,' Lily quipped as she picked up her Jack and Coke and took a hefty swig of it.

'Whoa, steady,' Tiss urged, not wishing to have to take a drunken friend back home later in the evening.

'What? I need this,' she huffed.

'Maybe you do. Just not all at once though.'

When their meals arrived they ate in silence, neither wishing to have to go over the events of the club once again. Tiss knew that Lily would do her utmost to investigate anything there was about the manager now that they had his name, hoping that something would come up about him when it hadn't about the club itself. She couldn't understand how somewhere would yield up absolutely nothing when searched for. In this digital age information was just a fingertip away, and something put in a search box on a computer would result with an answer being brought up in mere seconds. But not the Regency Club it seemed. That was shrouded in mystery, which made think Lily's suggestion was true – that it was somehow affiliated with the government. And if that was the case, what was both it and Mr Ford hiding?

CHAPTER FOUR

The first thing Tiss did the next morning was to send Lionel an email. She wanted to talk to him about Miriam Marshall in more detail. 'You know I can't talk about it,' he said to her after he'd responded to it and invited her down to his office.

'You also know that I could just look at her file,' she replied. She, too, knew the rules and regulations, but after her visit to the Regency Club with Lily, she felt that there was something unusual going on with Mrs Marshall and the man she was accompanying.

'I think I know you pretty well, Tiss, and I know you're not the kind of person who would go against what's legal and what's not. So what's this all about; what's got you so interested in this woman to the point that you'd risk your career to find out more about her?'

Tiss sighed deeply. 'Call it a feeling, intuition if you like, but there's something bothering me about that club.'

'The Regency, you say?'

'Yes. But the thing is, Lionel, Lily has searched everywhere for information about the place, and it seems that it technically doesn't exist.'

'How do you mean?'

Tiss then went on to explain how her PI friend had tried to find anything, absolutely anything, about the place but there was nothing. She didn't include the fact that Lily had also said she'd asked a tech friend of hers to try a bit of hacking, but again the results were zero. Tiss told Lily at the time that she simply hadn't heard what she'd just said, nor did she want to hear anything else like it again.

Lionel sat back in his chair and rocked it gently, and Tiss could see he was mulling it all over. 'It is unusual,' he said at last.

'Unusual?' Tiss echoed. 'Li, it's unheard of. Okay, so let me ask you a question, and I'd appreciate it if you to answer me honestly.'

He brought his chair back to the upright position and nodded his head.

'Is there anything more to this case than what you've already told me?'

She noticed a slight hesitation before he said, 'No, there isn't.' She eyed him suspiciously but didn't say anything in response to that; there wasn't really any more she could either say or ask on the subject without expecting the same response. She knew about the laws surrounding confidentiality, *of course she knew*, but she considered this to be something the law could be slackened on. However, she didn't push it any further and thanked him as she left to return to her own office. Perhaps she was wrong, but she still felt he was holding something back, something about the case he didn't want to disclose, and that made her all the more determined to find out what that something was.

When Friday morning came around again, neither she nor Lily had made any further headway into finding out anything about the club or its manager, Matthew Ford. Lily was frustrated when she called Tiss to tell her of the development – or lack thereof.

'What do you think we can do?' she'd asked with a strained voice. Tiss knew on instinct that she'd been burning the candle at both ends trying to make headway with her search.

Tiss sighed before replying. 'I think I'm going to give Mr Marshall a call,' she began, but was interrupted by Lily.

'But I thought you said the firm couldn't represent him what with his wife already being a client?'

'I did, and that's true. But I just want to ask him a few more questions, ones which might actually clear all this up for us.'

'Like what?'

'Well, for starters I'd like to show him the photograph you took. By the way, why haven't you got back to him and shown to him it yourself? I know you said you were waiting, but waiting for what?'

'I wanted to find out more about the place before getting back to him. But, as we know, that's drawn a complete blank.'

'So why not just show him it and see what his reaction is?'

'I don't know. I guess I don't like to think I've failed.'

'How have you failed?' Tiss asked. This was so unlike her friend. The Lily she knew was a very confident person, one who would normally let something like this wash over her without giving it a second thought. Had she finally come across a case which she felt challenged her abilities? It wasn't like her to take something so personally, but Tiss could tell by her frustration the night they visited the club that she had.

'I just do,' came the reply.

'We've hit a brick wall, so that's why I want to speak to him, outside the office preferably.'

'Do you want me to come with you? You know, the two of us together?'

'No, not necessarily. Unless you want to, of course.'

'Let me think about it,' Lily replied somewhat pensively. ''Let me know what you arrange and I can let you know.'

Following their conversation, Tiss rang Mr Marshall and asked him if they could meet in person. He was taken a bit taken aback at first, not expecting to hear from her again after receiving her letter and he told her as much, but he agreed to meet her at a café he nominated the following Tuesday. Once that was arranged, Tiss was determined to try and take her mind off the entire situation and concentrate on enjoying the weekend instead. As it was Friday, she couldn't wait for the evening to come around and spend it with her friends. She had three new clients booked in for the rest of the day, and a returning one to sign a document, and once that was over the night was all hers. Being a Friday, she and Diane had their usual twice-weekly lunch out, which really only consisted of a sandwich and a cup of coffee, but it was a habit they'd both got into and were more than comfortable with. However, try as she might, for the rest of the afternoon, Tiss just couldn't get the whole situation with the Marshalls out of her mind. She couldn't for the life of her think what was going on there, both with the pair of them and also with the Regency Club. She knew she'd thought it before, but if it was simply a case of Mrs Marshall taking a younger lover, then surely a hotel tucked away somewhere in the back of beyond would have been more appropriate than some mysterious gentleman's club where women were not usually welcome nor expected to frequent? The whole situation had left both her and her PI pal Lily confused and bewildered. So she hoped her appointment with Mr Marshall the following week would perhaps throw a light on it. If not, then she had no idea what to make of it or how to find any kind of answer to the questions swirling around in both hers and Lily's minds.

***

By the time 5pm came around, Tiss had determined her still burgeoning thoughts weren't going to let this deter her from enjoying her Friday girls' night out. In many ways her life was predictable in that she liked to stick to a regular routine during the week, both at work and at home. It was really only on her weekends that she liked to let loose a bit and veer away from the usual and do something just that little bit different. For example, this weekend she'd planned to attend an evening art exhibition one of her ex-clients was putting on in her home village, and was eagerly looking forward to that, even booking an overnight stay nearby so that she could spend the rest of the weekend enjoying the peace and quiet of the countryside far away from the hustle and bustle of the Monday to Friday working week. She fully intended to buy one of her paintings if one caught her eye, and going by her previous work, Tiss was sure one of them would do just that as she already had another of hers hanging in her dining room. She liked her style, which was predominantly modern, but with her own personal touches and lifestyle woven into it. In other words, it was unique, and trying to categorise it would be difficult.

So, as they sat at their usual reserved table at *The Olive Garden,* they unanimously decided to return back to *Lux* again as they'd enjoyed the ambiance of the place. Fortunately, this time they weren't disturbed by any amorous men looking for potential hook ups, or whatever that had been the last time they were there, and their evening went off without any distractions. As she would be driving the next day, Tiss restricted herself to just a few drinks, not wishing to exceed her limit and end up with a hangover for the journey. That wouldn't have been a good way to spend what she hoped would be a relaxing two days in the peaceful surroundings of the countryside.

'So, have you found a space for it yet?' Claudia asked during the course of the evening.

'Space for what?' Tiss asked, temporarily confused by the question as it had come out of the blue.

'Your next Anita Jazmin painting,' came the reply. 'We know you'll end up buying another one of her works tomorrow.'

Tiss laughed. Her friends knew her so well. 'As a matter of fact I have, as long as it's something I like.'

'I'm sure you will,' Ruby chipped in. 'That one in the dining room is magnificent. Wouldn't mind one of my own if I could afford it.'

'They're not all that expensive,' Tiss responded, 'and besides, I'm sure art appreciates over time and she's already quite big on the scene.'

'Thanks to your company clearing up that little issue with a disgruntled rival artist. She should give you discount on her works for that.'

'You know me,' Tiss responded. 'Always happy to pay for something I really want. And in answer to your question, I'd like something to hang in the living room, in that big open space behind the bigger sofa.'

'Yes, something her style would look good up there. Well I hope you find something to your taste tomorrow.'

'I hope so too.'

CHAPTER FIVE

Even though it was now winter, the weather had taken a sudden turn for the worse, becoming even colder than usual for the time of year. Despite the chill, Tiss awoke to a gloriously sunny day with barely a cloud in the sky. Although the bright sun wasn't ideal for driving, she knew her polarising sunglasses would sufficiently block out the glare for the journey. After a leisurely breakfast, she dressed, grabbed her suitcase at 10.30am, locked the door, and headed to her car. The drive took just over an hour, and she planned to have lunch at the quaint pub she'd visited on her last trip to see one of Anita's exhibitions. Afterwards she would check into the village's one and only hotel, the same one she'd stayed in before. The pub was small and cosy, with an inglenook fireplace and a fire burning fiercely in the grate when she arrived, and she settled herself at a vacant table beside the hearth.

'Cold out today, isn't it?' a voice said beside her as she was reading the menu. She looked up and saw a friendly-looking middle-aged woman with a pad and pen already poised in her hand ready to take her order. 'Oh I remember you,' she said suddenly. 'You were in here a few months back, weren't you?'

Tiss was surprised anybody would remember her from the one time she'd been there. 'You remembered that?' she asked with a smile, to which the lady nodded.

'Don't get many strangers passing through these parts, at least not stopping.'

'I'm surprised, especially with such a beautiful village as this.'

'Not much going on really,' she replied. 'It's only special events that bring people here. So I'm assuming you're back for Anita Jazmin's art exhibition again?'

'Yes, that's right.' How did this woman remember her?

'Are you a friend of hers?' Although some might have found the questioning intrusive, Tiss didn't find this in the slightest. After all, she was the interloper, the one who was intruding on their close-knit village life.

'We met through work.' Tiss simply said, not wishing to go into details of the true nature of how they met.

'Oh, are you an artist too?'

'I wish,' she laughed, 'but no, it was more of a business connection.'

'Ah, I see,' the waitress nodded before holding her pen over the pad again. 'Now, what can I get for you to eat and drink?'

After ordering something vegetarian from the menu, together with a diet soft drink, Tiss sat back and planned out the rest of her day. The exhibition wasn't on until 7.30pm, but the area had some very interesting architectural features and sightseeing attractions she wanted to check out while she was here. She hadn't had time to look around the last time, only coming for the exhibition itself, but had decided that any subsequent visits would include seeing what the area had to offer. And it had plenty. First port of call was going to be the much-lauded 16th century church in an adjoining village, which was still as it had been built all those hundreds of years ago. Many experts considered it the prime example of the era's architecture, at a time when Protestantism was emerging as a viable alternative to Catholicism. The only noticeable difference in church styles was primarily reflected in their internal layouts. This church was one of the very first Protestant ones in both the area and in the country, therefore of great historical significance.

Her second port of call were the gardens adjoining a small stately home, which tour guides stressed was a must see for any lover of all things horticultural. And they weren't wrong. The main garden was the best one of its kind she'd seen outside of Kew Gardens, the conservatory of which was filled with colourful blooms and plants, many of which were non-indigenous to the UK. She found the exotic ones to be the best. And the smell ... ah ... the plants' aromas were indescribable and unique. Her camera had never stopped clicking since she'd arrived, same with the church.

Following her very enjoyable day, she returned to the *Countryman* pub for a meal before heading to the exhibition. While there, she discovered that the lady she had assumed was a waitress was actually Judith Weston, the joint owner of the establishment along with her husband, John.

'We're both going to your friend's exhibition tonight,' she stated when she brought Tiss' meal over. 'Got to support local talent, eh?'

'Indeed. So you're both having a night off then?'

'They're very few and far between these days. We may not get very many tourists passing through the village, what with all the big attractions being in the surrounding ones, but it's a great place for the locals to gather and enjoy themselves. We have themed nights, quizzes and the like, and even have live music from local bands on a Friday.

'A local pub for local people,' Tiss said with a small laugh, remembering a catch phrase in a show a number of years back and her allusion to it.

'Yes, exactly,' Judith said in a serious manner, seemingly unfamiliar with either the phrase or the show.

After she'd finished her delicious meal, Tiss said her farewells to Judith, telling her that she'd see her and her husband later, and left for the hotel in order to change into her outfit for the night. The invitation said that it would be black tie, so she'd brought along one of her favourite evening outfits for the occasion.

At 6.50pm, she arrived at the event location, which was held like before in the spacious local village hall. Even before entering, she could tell it was well-attended; the hall doors were open and she could hear chatter coming from inside. Just inside the door stood a gentleman dressed smartly in a black suit and tie, checking the invitations of the couple in front of her. Tiss held out her invitation for him to check when it was her turn.

'Ah, Ms Lawson,' he said as he read the card she handed him. 'The artist asked that you join her as soon as you arrived.' Tiss hadn't expected any preferential treatment, so wondered why Anita had requested it. He turned around and caught the attention of another man similarly dressed and he waved for him to come over. 'Jim, can you please take Ms Lawson to where the artist is.' It tickled Tiss to hear him keep referring to Anita as "the artist". It all seemed a little pretentious for a small village gathering, that and the whole black tie dress mode. But who was she to make the final decision on such a thing, so she let "Jim" lead her over to her friend.

'Tiss!' Anita declared when she saw her approaching. She'd been talking to a small group of people but broke away with an apology in order to greet her. 'I'm so glad you could make it.'

'I wouldn't have missed it for the world,' she said as they gave each other a quick hug, adding, 'This is a bit of a new theme for you though,' as she looked around at the paintings. The work on display was in complete contrast to what she'd come to expect from her in the past, with more unusual shapes and colours in predominantly red and black. The style hardly seemed like her own.

'You noticed. It was actually a commission, but if you go further back into the hall you'll find more traditional works, the ones you'll be more familiar with.'

'I was actually after buying one, but I don't think the black and red will go very well with my décor. I've got to be honest here, Anita, it's not what I expected. It just doesn't seem to be, well, *you*.'

'I know,' Anita agreed, nodding. 'But, like I said, it was commissioned especially for this show.

However, I couldn't just leave out the kind of work I'm known for, so perhaps you'll find something to your liking back there.'

'I'm sure I will,' Tiss agreed. 'And thank you for inviting me again.'

'I would have invited you anyway, but, I've got to tell you, the person who commissioned this insisted that I ask you to come along.'

'What?' Tiss frowned, taken aback somewhat. 'Somebody specifically asked for me to be here. Why?'

'I don't know, but I can only assume they've heard all about you and wanted to meet you. You do have a very good reputation in the legal world, you know. They're not here yet, but that was the only reason I could think about, that they respect you.'

'That's a bit unusual, isn't it?'

'Tell me about it. I said the same thing when they told me.'

'And who is it exactly?' Tiss asked, her curiosity piqued. But before Anita had a chance to answer, an arriving guest caught her eye.

'Well, now you'll get to know as he's just walked through the door.'

Tiss spun around at hearing that, her eyes focusing on the middle-aged man who had just entered the hall. The man who was checking people's invitations was fussing around him, so he seemed to know exactly who he was.

'Who is he?' Tiss asked, turning back to Anita.

'I'm sure he's about to introduce himself to you,' came the reply.

When she turned back, the man's eyes were on the pair of them standing together, and on Tiss in particular. It made her feel a little uncomfortable if she was being honest.

'Ah, just the person I wanted to see!' the stranger declared, coming forward and reaching for her hand.

'I'm afraid you have me at a disadvantage,' Tiss said, allowing him to shake it with unbidden enthusiasm.

'Of course, of course,' he began as he released her hand from his grasp. 'Do forgive me. My name is Frederick Marshall and I'm a great admirer of your parents. So when the opportunity arose to meet their daughter, well, I couldn't let that pass up now could I?'

'You flatter me.'

'No, my dear. Your blossoming reputation precedes you.'

'Well, thank you,' Tiss replied, not quite knowing what to make of this. 'And are you an art connoisseur?'

He let out a gentle laugh. 'Nothing quite as exotic as that; I'm a businessman, but I do appreciate the beauty of art … in all its forms.'

For some inexplicable reason Tiss felt like the man was flirting with her, especially as his eyes seem to take in every part of her, looking her up and down as if she herself was a piece of art he was appreciating. As he was around the same age as her own father, she felt it to be somewhat inappropriate. But she smiled at him throughout, if only for the sake of her own curiosity and also because this was the person who had commissioned Anita's exhibition.

'I also believe that you've met my brother,' he casually dropped in.

It was then that the name Marshall clicked with her. Surely not? If he was indeed the brother of Frank Marshall, then this was all a bit too coincidental – or was that contrived?

'You're Frank Marshall's brother?' she asked him and he nodded.

'He told me that he'd been to see you, which is when I realised who you were. Your parents are very well-known in their own field, as I'm sure you know well enough. I'd already commissioned the lovely Anita here for an exhibition, but when I found out that you two ladies were friends, then I just had to meet you. I hope you don't mind my forwardness?'

'No, of course not,' Tiss said to be polite. He was, after all, the person who had commissioned Anita's work so she felt civility was necessary, but she was still uncertain about the whole situation. She didn't like coincidences, and she didn't like uncertainty about anything. Something was eating away at the back of her mind, but she just didn't know what it was.

When Marshall bid his farewell and prepared to mingle, Anita turned to Tiss and asked what had just taken place. Tiss explained as best as she could who his brother was, simply stating that he'd come to see her on a legal matter a few weeks back.

'Small world,' Anita responded, but Tiss was still unsure about it. 'Anyway,' she continued, 'did you bring your camera with you, because I'd love some shots of these paintings for my website.'

'Lucky for you I did,' Tiss replied with a chuckle, trying to get past her confused thoughts and delving into her bag for it.

'Good. Well, if you don't mind taking a few shots, I guess I have to go and mingle myself. My fans await!' she added overdramatically as she swept away.

'You go ahead,' Tiss laughed. She didn't know what it was, but any time she was with Anita made her laugh more than usual. They just had a rapport with one another.

As Tiss made her way around the exhibition she half-listened to people's conversations as she passed them by. She wasn't intentionally snooping, but it was difficult not to hear at times, and what came across from everyone present was the fact that they all liked Anita's work, even though the current exhibition was so different from the work she usually produced. She stopped at one point and looked through some of the shots she'd taken, but when she was near the end she saw something on one of them which took her breath away. The photo was admittedly a little bit blurry as she must have taken that one a little too quickly, but just out of shot of the painting she saw a figure who looked a little bit too familiar. Her eyes shot up from the camera screen and looked around her, trying to find them again but to no avail. She looked back at the photo. If she wasn't mistaken, and she most definitely wasn't, the man in the shot looking directly at her was the man who had approached her and her friends in *Lux* a few weeks previously.

CHAPTER SIX

Tiss made her way stealthily through the crowd of people, desperately trying to find the mystery man who had turned up in one of her photos. One would have been bad enough, but two coincidences in one night were two too many for her, and it now appeared that she was being followed by not only one, but by two people: Frederick Marshall and this other mystery person. However, try as she might, she just couldn't find him. At one point she caught up with Anita and pulled her to one side.

'Do you recognise this man at all?' she asked, showing her the photo.

Anita looked carefully at it. 'It's not very clear, so I don't know. I mean, whoever it is he looks like a number of people. Why, what's the matter?'

'It's just … well, he turned up recently when my friends and I were out at a club. He was doing the same thing then, just standing staring at me.'

Anita laughed gently. 'Well I think you might have an admirer there. What's that, two in one night, Tiss? I wish I was that popular!'

'But don't you think it's a little strange?' She wasn't as amused by it as her friend seemed to be.

'Yes, but I don't know.' She waved a hand in a non-committedly in the air and Tiss could tell that perhaps she'd had one glass of wine more than she was used to, that and the excitement of the night. 'Maybe it's nothing. Maybe it's something. I'm not sure what you want me to say.'

'No, it's okay, it's fine. Like you say, it's probably nothing to be concerned about.'

'Okay then. Oh, did you get some other good shots; ones not so blurry and good enough for my website?'

'I did,' Tiss assured her, and I'll send them on to you tomorrow. In the meantime I've seen a painting I like-'

'Oooh,' Anita cheered, interrupting her. 'Which one?' When Tiss showed it to her she said that she would put a reserved sticker onto it for her and ship it out during the week as it was too big to fit in her car.

While Anita went off to do her mingling with the guests, thoughts of the stranger still stuck with Tiss for the rest of the evening. She planned to send the photo to Claudia and Ruby when she got back to her hotel room to see what they made of it all, to get their take on it as she simply wasn't convinced that it was mere coincidence that he was there. It had to mean something. Was he following her for a reason?

***

'Well it *does* look a bit like him, if you squint, that is,' Ruby said when she rang Tiss up as soon as she'd received the photograph. 'But if it is him, why on earth would he be there?'

'That's what's bothering me. Plus, add that to the fact that the brother of a recent potential client commissioned Anita's paintings for the exhibition; I'm not sure what it all means.'

'I don't know either, but I agree that it seems unlikely it's a case of chance. What about Lily; might she be able to find anything out about him?'

'I'm going to contact her on Monday when I get back into work. I doubt it, but she might have had something back about the club or Matthew Ford.'

'It's all a bit of an enigma, isn't it?'

'Tell me about it,' Tiss scoffed.

'You know,' Ruby began. 'I'm looking at the photograph now and don't you think that painting he's standing near to looks a bit like the artwork on the walls of *Lux*?'

'I have to admit I wasn't really taking much notice of the ones that had been commissioned; just snapping them for Anita's website. They're not my kind of thing at all.'

'They are very similar. Has she been doing those as well, as the club's only recently opened?'

'I've no idea,' Tiss began, but then had notification that there was another call waiting. 'Oh, I've got another call coming through. I'll give you a call next week. Got to go.'

'Okay. Bye Tiss, and take care. See you next week.'

The incoming call was from Claudia, who'd also received the photo, and despite also commenting on the quality of it, agreed with Ruby in that it could have been the stranger from *Lux.* She, too, thought that it was a very odd situation that definitely needed to be looked into.

'I feel like I'm being stalked and I've no idea why,' Tiss admitted to her friend, adding that she was going to hire Lily to do a little digging on top of everything else she was looking into for her.

'It's a bit like you've stepped into an episode of *The Twilight Zone.*'

Tiss laughed, thinking how that summed it up completely. 'I only hope I find my way back home.'

'I'm sure you will.'

'You know, Ruby has just said that she thinks that painting in the photo is very similar to the ones in *Lux.*'

'Hmmm, a bit I guess. But wouldn't that make it even weirder?' she asked, and Tiss had already thought that it would. When the call ended, Tiss took some time to look through all the photos from the exhibition. She then brought up *Lux* on the computer and looked at the interior pictures, and could see there was a distinct similarity. Well, they were both predominantly in red and black so were already alike in that respect. Out of curiosity, she must give Anita a call sometime to confirm or deny. That night Tiss had the weirdest dream. She dreamt that she was sitting at her desk at work and the Marshalls, together with Mr Marshall's brother, Matthew Ford, Mrs Marshall's as-yet unknown male friend, and the stranger from both *Lux* and Anita's exhibition were all sitting across the desk and taking photographs of her. All while Anita was hanging some of the curious red and black paintings up in her office. She felt exposed and laid bare before them all, wondering why she was of such specific interest to them. She woke up in the middle of the night soaked in sweat, which was something that never happened. The uncertainty was affecting her even during sleep, and she needed answers promptly to avoid any further distress.

***

Come Monday morning she greeted Denise on the reception desk as was her wont, and found herself actually looking forward to contacting Lily to get her started on the investigation. She was meeting with Frank Marshall the next day, and had to make a list of all the things she now wanted to speak to him about without making him overly suspicious. Although, she wasn't sure if what she was going to ask was going to do that, as she knew so very little about what was going on in the first place. All she wanted to know was if he knew the man in the photo with his wife, and what, if anything he knew about the Regency Club.

The first person she rang in the firm was Lionel again. 'Li, what do you know about a place called the Regency Club?'

'The where?'

'Regency Club. It's in the centre of town just past where the post office used to be.'

'Never heard of it. Why?'

'Oh, just wondering.'

'Wait, why would you think I have anything to do with it; what kind of a club is it?'

'A gentleman's club from what I can gather.'

Tiss heard him snort on the other end of the line. 'You and I both know that the male of the species is my gender of choice, but it's really not my kind of thing. Isn't that somewhere elderly gentlemen go to get away from their overpowering wives? You do know that I'm only twenty-seven and will most likely, no, most positively, never have a wife.'

Tiss chuckled at his response. 'To be honest, I'm not really sure, only what I've seen in old films, but

I wondered if you'd ever heard of it, what with being a man and all!'

'Hate to disappoint, but no.'

'I just can't find anything out about the place, and searches are yielding absolutely nothing.'

'Well, maybe it's one of those Masonic places where everything is shrouded in secrecy.'

'Perhaps it is, but would they let women into such a place?'

'There is such a thing as a woman's version of the Masons.'

'And how would you know something like that?' Tiss asked humorously. Although she *did* know that for a fact, she wondered how Lionel did.

'I know many things, my dear Tiss, and that is just one of them!'

'Okay, super knowledgeable friend of mine, thank you for hearing me out,' she said as a conclusion to their telephone conversation.

'Any time. You know where I am.'

The rest of the day was spent seeing five clients, one of whom was a new one, and quickly dropping Lily an email asking if she could enlist her services. A reply came back just before she saw her final client of the day.

'Yes, of course you can,' she'd written in her response. 'I'm still not getting anywhere with either the club or the manager, so would appreciate something else to get to grips with as this is driving me up the wall. From what you've told me, you may very well have either a stalker or somebody watching you on behalf of someone else, a PI like me perhaps, although I can't for the life of me think why that would be the case. But not to fear, Lily is here to help! Send me all the info and I'll get right onto it. Love Lily xx'

Tiss smiled. Her friend was always reliable, that's why she had no hesitation recommending her to anyone in need of her investigative skills. It was a shame, however, that she now found the need to hire her services herself, never imagining that she ever would. But needs must.

***

That night when she got home, Tiss made the list she'd promised herself of all of the things she wanted to ask Frank Marshall when she met with him the next day, adding the fact that she'd now rather unexpectedly been introduced to his brother. She intended to bring him gradually into the conversation, not wishing to make a big thing of the fact that the Marshall brothers appeared to have some kind of strange interest in her. What that was she had no idea, other than what Fred had told her about admiring her parents and, it seemed, also her as their daughter. It could have been as simple as that, and it very probably was, but the whole thing with Frank's wife and the still-unknown young man, coupled with the elusive and somewhat mysterious Regency Club, the whole business had become a bit too complex and interlinked for her liking. And she didn't like either unfinished business or anything she couldn't define. However, next day when the morning came around and she went downstairs to have her breakfast, she was both taken aback and horrified to find that she had been burgled. Or at least she thought she had. The back door had been damaged which is how whoever it was had got in, and the place was a mess, with furniture and soft furnishings scattered around the living room. But as she looked closer, that was all that was out of place and the only indication that anyone had even been there apart from her. Her TV set was still where it always was, as was her laptop and all her files that she sometimes brought home with her, so like everything else in her life these days the whole thing was a bit of a puzzle. Even so, she spent no time in getting in touch with the police, who arrived thirty minutes later in the form of one young detective constable by the name of James Woodhouse.

'As you can see,' Tiss said as she led him through her house, 'it's only been disturbed in here.'

'Well, that's very odd,' he exclaimed as he couldn't seem to understand what it meant either.

'I know. They haven't even taken the television, which I'll assume is one of the first things burglars go for.'

'Usually, at least at all the break-ins I've attended. It's a bit of a curious one, I must say. You know what it looks like to me,' he continued. 'It looks like someone's just leaving you a message. Something on the lines of we know where you are and where you live. Do you have any enemies that you know of?'

'Enemies? No not at all, at least not that I'm aware of. I mean, I'm a solicitor, but I don't do court cases or anything; that's my parents' field not mine.'

'Your parents are solicitors too?'

'Barristers, both of them, and they've handled a number of criminal cases over the years, and some high-profile ones at that.'

'So maybe they're trying to get to them through you.'

'But that doesn't make any sense!'

'Some crimes don't make any sense at first until we delve deep enough into them and hidden agendas make themselves apparent.'

Tiss let out a long sigh. This was the last thing she wanted this morning, waking up to a burglary that wasn't one, and everything else that was going on in her life just now. Surely they couldn't be related. But she shook that idea off – how could they be? That was ridiculous.

'Okay, so here's what I'll do,' the DC spoke up, bringing Tiss out of her thoughts. 'Don't touch the damaged window and I'll send someone from forensics around to dust it for prints. They'll also have to take your prints as well, just for elimination purposes.'

'Yes, that's okay. I mean, I expected that. This is the first time anything like this has ever happened to me, so it's a bit of a shock.' Then as an afterthought she asked him if he would like something to drink. She was uncertain about proceeding, but she recognized the necessity of discussing recent events with an individual outside her professional and social circles. Speaking with someone unfamiliar with her or her situation could potentially provide a new perspective on the matter. When he agreed to a drink she made him a coffee, then quickly rang Denise at work to tell her what was going on and that she'd be in late, and then she began to give him some details of the events of the past few weeks.

The detective constable sat with her until one of the forensic team arrived to dust the window. To give credit where it was due, it didn't take very long for them to come. By which time he had learned all about Mrs Marshall, her mysterious young man, the equally mysterious gentleman's club, and meeting

Frank Marshall's brother at her friend's art exhibition. She didn't mention any names for confidentiality reasons, which in her mind made it acceptable to talk about. He listened with interest, trying to make some kind of sense of it all – *any* kind of sense of it – but, like her, he was as equally stumped by it.

'You said you already had a private investigator looking into it?'

'Yes, she's a friend and I also sometimes refer clients to her practice.'

'So you collaborate?'

'I suppose you could put it that way, yes,' she confirmed.

'And she hasn't found anything about the club or the manager?'

'Not a thing. The club's not even listed at Companies House, but I suppose that could be down to the fact that that it might be registered as something completely different.'

'True. But it's still an odd one. I'm not even sure we could get involved with that for you.'

'Oh, no, I'm not expecting you to,' Tiss raised both hands in defence. 'The private investigator is working on that, and it's just curiosity at the moment as I'm not saying there's anything illegal going on there or anything like that. It's just so frustrating that there's seemingly nothing to be found. I'm sorry if I used you as a sounding board, it's just that I think I needed somebody out of the loop to talk to about it. I wasn't trying to ask the police to get involved.'

'I understand,' he said softly. 'But what's concerning me right now is that person who following you, or seems to be following you. I could try to find out something about him bearing in mind that you've now been broken into. He could have something to do with it, or he could not, but at least that's something we could work from, something to base an investigation on.'

'Is that possible; you could do that?'

'I believe so.'

Tiss felt a wave of relief flow over her. She never expected to have to get the police involved in this, but then she never expected to find her home had been burgled – even though nothing had been taken. So she agreed, and as soon as both the forensic officer and DC Woodhouse left, she got ready to get herself into work. With all that was going on she'd almost forgotten about her lunch appointment with Frank Marshall, but there was still plenty of time to prepare herself for that.

CHAPTER SEVEN

At 12.30pm on the dot Tiss logged off her computer and grabbed her coat and bag. She informed Denise where she was going as she left, then headed straight to the café Frank Marshall suggested they should meet. She was ten minutes early for their 1pm appointment and he wasn't there when she arrived, so she made her way to a table regardless, ordering a coffee at the counter on the way. He'd find her when he came. She kept checking her watch, nervous about the whole meeting. As far as he was concerned his connection with the firm was at an end, so he'd be wondering exactly why Tiss had asked him to meet her, especially when she hadn't been very forthcoming about the reason.

At two minutes past the hour Marshall appeared in the doorway and looked around. Tiss saw him and raised a hand to catch his attention. When he saw her he nodded and made his way over to where she was sitting.

'Thank you for coming,' she said as he removed his outer coat and hung it over the back of his chair. He nodded again and sat down across from her.

'I've got to say,' he began, 'I'm a little confused as to why you asked me here. I was under the impression that there was nothing you could do for me.'

'There wasn't, and there still isn't, which is why I referred you to a private investigator.'

He looked at her curiously, baffled by what she'd just said to him.

'Then why-' he began, but she quickly added to what she was saying.

'Because there are a couple of things I'd like to ask you about your wife,' she simply said.

'Go on,' he replied, his expression indicating that he'd become more interested.

'What has Lily Singer told you?' Tiss already knew something of what had been said, but wanted to hear it from the man himself.

'Well, I think that's between me and her, Ms Lawson.'

'Yes, of course it is, but a lot of strange things have started to happen since you came into my office.'

'Meaning?'

'As you will appreciate, I'm not at liberty to discuss that.'

'Then why contact me, because from where I'm sitting this just looks like a stalemate?' Tiss could tell that he was beginning to get annoyed by the direction in which the conversation was heading, and in many ways she didn't blame him. Even she wasn't sure why she'd contacted him if she was being honest with herself. 'Look, Ms Lawson, this I will let you know. I asked my wife point blank if she was having an affair and she told me categorically no. She told me about the young man who she was seen in the photograph with, and it was to arrange a meeting place for the members of one of her groups to hold their annual fundraiser. The club he directed her to and showed her around was as good a place as any, and they offered the group a very reasonable hire rate. And that's all there was to it. My wife doesn't tell me every little thing that she does in the same way that I don't tell her.'

'And what about your brother?'

'What about him?'

'He told my artist friend that he was very interested in meeting me. He said that you'd discussed me with him.'

Frank Marshall sat back in his chair and smiled. 'Ah, Ms Lawson you are very suspicious! I did discuss the matter of my wife with him and told him who I'd seen. He knew your parents to be something akin to royalty in the legal world and simply wanted to meet you. He'd already commissioned Ms Jazmin's work by then and quite by chance your name came up in the conversation. She told him that she knew you and that you would be attending. He thought it would be a good opportunity to meet you; it's really as simple as that.'

Tiss had to admit that it all sounded kosher and above board. So had she been mistaken all along and was worrying herself about nothing? But then there was the matter of the break-in that wasn't one. However, she didn't want to bring that to the table; DC Woodhouse was already looking into that for her so there was no need to mention it at all. In the end she had to agree with him, as everything he said seemed to be a reasonable explanation.

'Well, thank you for coming,' she said quietly, hoping that would end the meeting. Thankfully it did.

'Not a problem,' he muttered and began to get up, but not before asking if she thought she'd want to contact him again. It was an odd question, but the intention was clear: he didn't want her to contact him again. She shook her head, and with that he took his coat from the back of the chair and carried it out with him. Only when he left the café did he put it on. *Well, that's me put in my place*, Tiss thought to herself. Not to self: *do not* contact this man again, for any reason, no matter what.

***

The rest of Tiss' working week was busy as there was an unexpected onslaught of new clients to see. She didn't even have time to contact Lily to see what she'd managed, or not managed, to dig up as she'd had to take work home with her just to keep up with it all. While she was away on that art exhibition weekend, a local newspaper had printed an article on the town's businesses, concentrating on the many legal practices and giving them each a star rating. As luck would have it, Sanderson and Barnes had come out on top with a full five stars, which seemed to give people a sudden need for the services of a solicitor. The bosses were naturally happy with both the publicity and the popularity, unlike their suddenly overworked employees. So once again, when Friday came around, Tiss was more ready than usual to spend time with her two girlfriends. Claudia, like herself, had been loaded down with the new-found intake of work and was also glad of the break, only Ruby seemed to have had the easiest workload of the three of them.

'What can I say?' she declared after hearing their woes. 'I'm sure if I had to be out of the office and doing what I originally trained for then I'd be as busy as the two of you.'

'But you love the admin side of the job,' Claudia remarked.

'And you two love the legal side of yours,' came the reply.

'But thank goodness for Fridays and the weekends,' Tiss said chirpily, wanting to hastily change the subject as the sheer amount of work had completely drained her that week.

Tiss mentioned that she'd like to go back to *Lux* again after they'd eaten.

'I thought we were going to make that our go-to place anyway,' Ruby asked.

'Yes,' Tiss agreed, 'but this time I want to ask them about the artwork on their walls. I've been looking at the club online, and it does look very much like the kind of thing Anita was commissioned to paint.'

'But she didn't mention it to you?' Claudia asked her.

'To be honest, I didn't get the opportunity to ask her as almost everyone there was queuing up for her attention,' she admitted. 'Which is why I'd like to take another look.'

'And if it is?'

'I don't really know,' she confessed. 'But in a very strange way everything that's happened over the course of the last couple of weeks seems to be related. And you both know I don't like anomalies I can't find a logical explanation for.'

'And what will you do if you find out that Anita actually did the work?' Ruby continued.

'Again, I really don't know,' she replied. 'But I just feel that I need to know. One thing is certain though, and that is I don't for one minute believe anything that Frank Marshall said to me when I met him on Tuesday.'

'Why is that?'

'Just a feeling. I think I should also ring my parents and find out what they know about his brother, Fred, if anything. He said that he admired them, but I'm even uncertain about that.'

Ruby let out a long exhale. 'Boy, we need you to get out of your head for tonight, and that might include copious amounts of alcohol,' she laughed. 'Okay, we'll go to the club and you can ask whoever you need to about their choice of decoration. I just see it being part of the whole concept of the place, but you need to do what you need to do. After that, though, you're going to get sloshed; you need it!'

***

'I'm just going to find somebody to talk to,' Tiss said once they were inside *Lux*, and with that headed off to speak to someone who looked like they may be a member of staff and decided that the bar was a good starting point.'

'What can I get you,' the smiling bartender asked her with a wink.

'I need to speak to the club's manager, or somebody else in authority.'

His smile faltered at those words, immediately thinking that something was wrong. 'Is there a problem?' he asked, his voice laced with concern. Perhaps he thought that he'd done something wrong and she wanted to make a complaint about him.

'No, no,' she reassured him, making sure to add a smile. 'I just want to ask about the artwork in here.

You see, my friend is an artist, and I'm almost sure that this is her work. I'd just like to have it confirmed before I congratulate her on it.' She hoped it sounded convincing enough for him to contact one of his superiors.

'Ah, I see,' the broad smile returned again. 'That would be David, tonight's duty manager. If you hang on I'll give him a call to come and have a word with you.'

Tiss thanked him and waited until he returned. 'He'll be down in a minute,' he beamed again, playing the part for his customers. 'Can I get you a drink in the meantime?'

'No,' she said, refusing his offer. 'I'm here with some friends; they're getting them and I will be joining them once I've spoken to him. But thank you, though.'

'Well, come back to me when you're all in need of drinks and I'll give you a discount,' he said with another wink. Tiss thought his flirting was perhaps a bit over the top even though it was probably all part of the job, but she'd definitely be taking him up on his offer of a reduction if he was offering!

It didn't take long for the duty manager to arrive. Tiss saw a man who didn't look like a club goer approach the bartender, and the latter pointed over in her direction.

'Dave Telford,' he said, holding out a hand which she took.

'Tiss Lawson,' she returned.

'And what can I do for you? Mark said it was something about the artwork on the walls?'

'Yes, it is. My friend is an artist and I've just been to her exhibition, and a lot of the work she was commissioned to do looked like this. I was just wondering if it was indeed her work?'

'When we opened the local newspaper did an article on us and they mentioned who that artist was.'

'I'm sorry, I didn't see it. Can you tell me who it was?'

'Certainly. It's a lady by the name of Anita Jazmin.'

Tiss smiled and nodded. 'That's her,' she said cheerily. 'And I'm going to assume that it was a commission.'

'That's right. One of the club's shareholders had seen some of her work and liked it.'

'But her usual work is nothing as dramatic; she normally doesn't do anything remotely like this.' Tiss indicated the walls around them as she spoke.

'Well, I can only assume he saw something in her work that he liked.'

'And are you permitted to tell me the name of the shareholder?'

Telford shook his head. 'I'm afraid not. All that kind of thing is confidential, as I'm sure you will appreciate.'

'Of course,' she replied, already trying to figure a way out in her head how she might obtain that information. 'Okay then, thank you for coming out to see me. I just had that feeling that this was her work, and it's good to know that it's been confirmed. I'll have to make a point of telling her I've seen it.' This time she was the one to hold out her hand as a parting gesture. 'Thank you for coming out to tell me.'

'Not a problem,' he said as he smiled at her before leaving. But rather than feeling that his answer had resolved anything, she couldn't help but feel that the opposite was true.

CHAPTER EIGHT

O n Saturday morning Tiss was still mulling over what the duty manager had said to her at *Lux* about Anita's paintings. She wondered why she hadn't mentioned it the weekend she attended the exhibition, but then reminded herself that her friend was tied up with promoting her work that evening so why should she have. In any case, Anita didn't know that she frequented the very same club that she'd done the work for, how could she? But the fact that it *was* her work was another in the long list of current coincidences that didn't sit at all well with her. It was like fate was ganging up against her for some reason. So she decided to ring her parents to ask them what they knew, if anything, about Fred Marshall, businessman and seeming art commissioner.

'And how's work?' was the first thing her mother had asked after greeting her warmly. As ever, her parents were all about work ethics and job satisfaction.

'Work's fine, Mum,' she replied. 'Actually, I was wanting to pick your brain about something, or rather, someone.'

'Oh, really? Who?'

'Have either you or Dad ever come across a businessman by the name of Frederick Marshall?'

'Fred Marshall? To be honest, sweetheart, I couldn't tell you off the bat. But give me a minute and I'll ask your father.' Tiss could hear her moving through the house to where her other parent was. 'Do you know what kind of business he's in?' her mother asked whilst on the move.

'Not really sure, but I think he might also be a shareholder in one of the town's new nightclubs.'

'That's not much to go on. Oh, wait, here's your father. I'll pass you over to him.'

When Tiss heard her father's voice greeting her she asked him the same question that she'd asked her mother: was he aware of someone called Fred Marshall.

'Can you describe him?' her father asked, and when she did she added the name of his brother and his sister-in-law. 'Hmm, can't say that I do. Is it important Tiss?'

'Probably not. It's just that he seemed to know you and Mum, which led him on to want to meet me, so I thought you might be aware.'

'No, sorry, I ... we ... can't help you there.'

'Okay then, it's not a problem.'

After that they talked a bit more with Tiss' mother joining in on the conversation on the extension phone. Once the call ended she felt as if she hadn't moved forward, and to that end she rang Lily, who she hadn't heard from all week.

'I might have another job for you,' Tiss began when Lily picked up on the third ring.

'Oh, oh, what's happened now?' she laughed.

'Is there any way to find out who a company's shareholders are?'

'Strange question, but yes, I believe there is. Why, what's going on?'

When Tiss explained everything about Anita Jazmin's art, Lily let out a long whistle. 'This just seems to get more and more complicated,' she correctly observed.

'I know, and I bet you haven't made any progress finding out who that stalker of mine is.'

'I'd love to tell you that I have, but you're right, he's as elusive as everything else is.'

'Damn.' Then Tiss remembered about her burglary and the fact that Lily didn't know anything about it.

'And this detective constable said that he might be able to help?' she asked after hearing her out.

'He did, but I'm not entirely sure how long it will take him to find out as I imagine it's not a priority.'

'But yet again it's just something odd to add to the ever-increasing list of oddities, isn't it?' Tiss couldn't disagree with her on that.

Following that call, Tiss rang Anita. She was determined to ask her about Fred Marshall and how she'd come to be involved with him.

'Are you still in love with my painting?' Anita asked as soon as they'd greeted one another and Tiss thanked her for sending it via a courier. She'd received it mid-week in the evening, and it was now hanging pride of place in her living room. It looked perfect, complementing and finishing the room off nicely.

'I am and you know I am!' Tiss laughed. 'I'm in love with all of your work. If only I could afford it all. And, actually, your painting is something I wanted to ask you about.'

'Oh?'

'Yes. I was somewhere the other day and saw paintings which were similar to the ones that were commissioned for your exhibition.'

'Where did you see them?'

'In a nightclub called *Lux* in the middle of town.'

There was silence for a while as Anita thought. 'Ah, yes. Oh, that was a few months back now. They were commissioned by the same person. I thought you weren't enamoured with my black and reds!'

'I'm not,' Tiss said jokily, 'but I thought they looked the same style.'

'I know. They're not really me, but the guy paid a pretty penny for me to do them for him.'

'Really?'

'Yes. Megabucks, as our American cousins say.'

'Wow. And who is he exactly, a businessman, an art connoisseur, or just a man with a lot of money to spare?'

Anita giggled on the other end of the phone. 'All of the above I don't doubt. I don't really know very much about him, if I'm being truthful. Yes, I did try to look him up, but it didn't bring back many results. The one thing I did know, however, that he was a shareholder in the club you've just mentioned because he told me. But beyond that, the guy seems to be something of a recluse. Why are you asking?'

'It's because I met his brother just shortly before I met him. He came in to the practice and I was the one he was booked in with. It just seems a little orchestrated, that's all.'

'Well, he did say he wanted to meet you. Maybe his brother told him about you.'

'He did. I met Frank again recently and he said that he'd mentioned me to Fred. He's an admirer of my parents, apparently. I can't imagine why he'd want to me meet me, though.'

'There you are then. He's a fan of theirs and most likely wanted a way to meet them via you.'

'But if he wanted to meet them then he could have simply asked them, either in writing or by calling them. I'm not sure if they would have liked to have a stranger approach them in that way, but the option was there if he really did want to do it.'

'Then I don't know what to say, Tiss. Why are you letting it get to you so much?'

'It's just … it's just so, I don't know, so *planned*, so *organised*.'

'But maybe it is all just coincidental and you're making too much of it.'

Tiss sighed. 'Maybe you're right,' she said backing down. She couldn't see this conversation going anywhere, so what was the point of continuing with it. Anita didn't seem to know any more about Fred Marshall any more than she did – any more than even the world seemed to – so she left it at that.

'Okay, thanks Anita,' she said in the end. 'Please let me know when your next exhibition is and I'll be down again for my next oil painting fix.' She kept it light, and Anita said that she would, and that was the end of it. But, of course, Tiss wasn't going to let it go, not in a million years. All this was not usual in her mind; it was contrived, she knew it, but to what end, that was the question.

***

The next step in the seemingly curious journey came along on Monday. As usual, Tiss and Denise went to their café across the street for lunch, but this time it didn't pass without incident. Denise was in front of Tiss and had ordered her coffee and sandwich and had gone off with mug in hand in search of a table, leaving her to order. After placing it, she picked up her mug and went to the area where you could put toppings on your drink. She preferred chocolate, vanilla and cinnamon on a cappuccino, her usual drink of choice, all piled together on top. She already had two topping on, but it was when she was reaching for the third topping that she felt a hand brush against hers.

'Oh, I'm sorry,' a man's voice clearly said to her, making her look up at him. And in that second all the blood must have drained from her face. Looking at her and smiling was the man from the club who had spoken to them all those weeks ago, and the person who had appeared in her photos staring at her at Anita's exhibition. She looked at him, not quite knowing what to do, but as she was staring he continued to talk to her.

'I don't know if you remember me,' he began, 'but we spoke a few weeks back in *Lux*.'

'I believe that you tried to pick me up,' she retorted with the hint of a smile, finally gaining her composure and feeling that she had to play along with it. 'And did I also happen to see you at Anita Jazmin's art exhibition the weekend before last?'
He laughed, and she had to admit to herself almost reluctantly that he had a nice smile, 'Yes, you might have done. I saw you were taking photographs. So do you know the artist personally or were you there in a professional capacity, as a journalist or photographer?'

'Yes to the first, Anita and I are friends. While I'm not a professional journalist or photographer, the latter is a hobby of mine. Anita asked me to take some photos of the exhibition for her website.'

'Ah, I see. I was there with my uncle who lives in the neighbouring village. He said he wanted to go, so I said that I'd take him.'

'Oh, are you interested in art then, or in Anita's work in particular?'

'Me, not so much, but I have to say it's growing on me after seeing some of her work. Didn't expect to see you there, though.'

'It's been planned for quite some time. I always go to her exhibitions, and I always buy one of her paintings when I go.'

'Did you buy one that day?'

'Yes, I did.'

'It wasn't one of those red and black ones, was it?'

'Why?' Tiss laughed at the face he pulled while saying it; it was clear he wasn't much of a fan of the style. 'Didn't you like them?'

'I think you already know the answer to that,' he chuckled. 'No, but I preferred the work she had on display towards the rear of the hall.'

'Me too,' she agreed. 'That's more her usual style, but I gather she only did the other ones on commission.'

Then something seemed to click in him. 'I knew I'd seen something like it before,' he began. 'Hanging on the walls of *Lux*.'

Tiss nodded. 'I gather they were commissioned by the same person; one of the club's shareholders.'

'Is that so. They seem to fit the club somehow.'

'Yes, they do.' At that point Denise waving her hand in the distance caught her eye. Tiss realised that she'd been standing with the man for quite some time. 'Ah, there's my friend trying to get my attention,' she laughed. 'We're here on our lunch break, so not much time, I'm afraid.'

'My apologies,' he said in return. 'I'm just here for a takeout, but, please, take my card,' he added, producing a business card from his wallet and handing it to her. The act prompting Tiss to give him one of hers in return.

'Tom,' he said, holding out his hand for her to take.

'Tiss,' she replied.

'And if I wanted to call you and ask you out for another cappuccino,' he said with a smile and looking at the contents of her mug.

'Well, you have my number now,' she returned the smile.

'And you have mine. So you wouldn't mind if I give you a call?'

'Not at all.'

When he left she walked over to where Denise was giving her questioning looks.

'Who was that?' she asked as a waitress brought both their toasted sandwiches over to them. They both thanked her before Tiss continued.

'Believe it or not,' she said, 'he's the person whose identity I've been trying to find out.'

Denise gave her a puzzled look as Tiss hadn't discussed it at all with her.

'Let's just say he keeps popping up and I had no idea who he was.'

'And who is he?'

Tiss looked at the card he'd handed her. 'Tom Davenport ...' but it was the following information that stopped her in her tracks. '... solicitor.'

'What? Is another company trying to headhunt you or something?'

'I don't know, but he works for Dennison and James.'

'Oh, I've heard nothing but good things about them. Weren't they second in that list of best solicitors in that newspaper article?'

'I don't know,' Tiss admitted, not having seen past the fact that their company had come first.

'But what did he want, did he say?'

'He says he wants to take me out for a coffee sometime.'

'And are you going to go?'

'If he rings I'll think about it.'

CHAPTER NINE

Tiss didn't have long to wait to see if Tom Davenport would get back in touch with her again as he did so the very next day. She was sitting in her office with a client when she heard a message come through to her phone. Tiss naturally waited until she'd seen the client to open it up and read it fully.

Enjoyed meeting you yesterday ... officially! Would it be too soon for me to ask you out? If you'd like to go for that coffee with me, we could meet after work tomorrow if that's okay with you? I hope you say yes. Tom.

She smiled to herself without realising it as she read the message. It had been a very long time since anybody had asked her out on a date. As soon as she'd got home the previous evening she'd rung Anita and asked her if she knew him.

'Tom Davenport you say. The only Davenport I know around here is Dennis Davenport. He could be related to him, I guess. Why?'

'He said he was visiting your exhibition with his uncle who lived in the village, so I was curious.'

When Tiss went on to tell her she couldn't contain her excitement.

'Well, that'll make a change for you. Got to say, Tiss, it's been a long time coming!'

'And why is that?' Tiss laughed at her friend's comment.

'You're a great human being that's why, so I'd like to see you happy – and dating somebody for a change instead of stuck at home in the evening.'

'It's not like that; I am happy. I go out with my friends every Friday evening and we have a great time together.'

'Yeah, girlfriends, though,' Anita reminded her, not that she needed it. 'Not the kind of happy pleasure I was thinking about!'

'When it comes to men I'm just picky, that's all!'

***

The next day Tiss was sitting having her lunch in the staff room when Denise rang her on her mobile.

'Hey, what's up?' she asked on answering it.

'You have a visitor downstairs in reception.'

Tiss looked at her watch. She still had thirty minutes left of her lunch break and Denise knew that. 'I'm not free until 1,' she said to her.

'I know,' came the reply, 'but it's not a client, it's DC Woodhouse. He wants to have a word with you.'

'Oh, okay,' she replied, closing the reading app on her tablet and slipping it into her bag. 'Tell him that I'll be right there. I'll take him up to my office.'

'Thanks, I will.'

Tiss didn't have time to think further about it. She slung her bag over her shoulder and picked up her half-drunk cup of coffee to take with her, giving Lionel and Claudia a quick farewell.

'You've still got thirty minutes,' Lionel said looking at his watch.

'I know, but there's a police officer here to see me about the break-in.'

'Ah, I see. Well, good luck.'

'Thanks.'

As she walked from the break room on the ground floor to the reception area, Tiss saw DC Woodhouse sitting on his own and looking at something in a notebook. He looked up when he saw her and stood up to greet her, slipping his book back into his jacket pocket.

'We can go up to my room.' Tiss indicated that he follow her, thanking Denise as she passed by the desk. When they arrived at her office she took her seat and offered him the one across from her.

'I was going to call you later,' she said before he had a chance to speak.

'Oh? About?'

'Well, I've found out something about the person who I though was following me.'

'You have?'

'Yes. And it seems he was following me for a reason because he wanted to ask me out. I feel a little bit foolish about it all, actually.'

'And do you have a name for him?

'Yes, it's Tom Davenport.'

'Ah,' was all the detective said, followed by, 'Interesting.'

'Interesting?' Tiss repeated.

'Yes. I haven't been able to find anything out about him.' He laughed gently. 'It appears that you have outdone me in my job.'

'Well,' Tiss echoed his laugh. 'I wouldn't have had he not literally brushed against me in a café.'

'Okay, so I can tick that one off my list. But, anyway, back to the reason I'm here. I've found out a little about the Regency Club.'

'You have?'

'Yes. The reason you and your PI friend couldn't find out anything about it is because that's not how it's listed in Companies House.'

'You looked into the club for me?' Tiss asked in surprise. 'I only thought you were going to look into the person who was following me?'

'I was at first, but then your story began to intrigue me. And when I'm intrigued, I like to investigate.'

'I see. And what did you find out?'

As he began to speak, Tiss sat forward in her chair, elbows on the desk in front of her, fingers knitted together, eager to hear what came next.

'The club is owned by a conglomerate in the city. From what I can find out they're all Masons, and that wasn't an easy thing to delve into. But that's who they are. Most of whom are directors or executives of some of our biggest companies.'

'But why are they all interested in that club; is it specifically a Masonic one?'

'Ah, now, that's where it all becomes a little bit hazy. Even though I found this out, that was *all* I could find out. Other than that, what they do there is so secretive even all my police resources couldn't find anything more about the place.'

'But isn't that the point of the Masons in the first place, the fact that it's secretive?'

'Yes,' he agreed with her, 'but there's secretive and then there's ultra secretive, and this one's rubbing me up the wrong way for some reason.'

'You know, my friend thinks it's some kind of secret government establishment,' Tiss laughed as she told him.

'Well, for all we know it could be. But I'll tell you what else I found out.'

Tiss was all ears.

'Over the past twenty years, eight women have gone missing in that area.'

'Well that's not strange,' she said ironically, then had an additional thought. 'Please don't also add that they disappeared at five-year intervals?'

He nodded.

'What?' was all she could come back with.

'Exactly. According to their friends and relatives, none of them had links to the club, or the street where the club is.'

Woodhouse brought out the notebook from his jacket pocket, the one he'd been looking at before Tiss arrived, and opened it to the page he wanted. He listed off the dates of the disappearances, and it was apparent to Tiss that they were vanishing at specific times of year – half around the third week of March, and the other around the same time in December.

'You do know that they're both significant times of the year, don't you? Tiss said after a moment's pause.

He looked at his book again then up at her, a puzzled expression on his face, so she went on to elaborate further.

'If what I'm hearing is correct, it sounds like the one in March is the Spring Equinox, and the date in December is the Winter Solstice.'

'I don't get it,' he admitted, still looking confused.

'My father was very interested in astronomy when I was growing up, and he had lots of charts in his office showing the times of the equinoxes and solstices.'

'And they are what, exactly?'

'Well, the spring, or vernal, equinoxes are usually around the twenty-first of March and the winter solstice in December is around the twenty-third. An equinox is the time when the sun is directly above the Equator making day and night equal lengths, usually in March and September. The solstices are in June and December, usually around the same date in the months as the equinoxes, and that's when the sun's path is the farthest north or south of the Equator.'

'I see. But what would be the significance of that?'

'Many cultures have rituals around those times.'

'Rituals?'

'Yes, in that they celebrate the changing of the seasons. But I remember my dad talking about such things and also about Pagan rituals when I asked him to explain it all, although I have to stress that he didn't believe in all that, just that he knew about them in relation to the whole astronomy interest.'

'So, what are we talking about here, sacrifices?'

'I don't know if that's true or not, or just something that's told in supernatural fiction stories.'

'But it's a possibility?' he asked.

'I guess anything is a possibility.'

***

When DC Woodhouse left, a multitude of thoughts swirled around Tiss' head. It was troubling to hear about the missing women, but even more so to hear about the time of year they'd vanished. Surely this couldn't be related to the club, but if it was, then how was it, and, more importantly, why? But there was one thing she knew for certain; she couldn't just let the whole thing go as she knew getting to the bottom of things had now become an obsession. Tiss was the kind of person who needed to know the answers to a question, especially the more unusual ones, and this was certainly that. With that in mind, she picked up her phone and rang Lily. When she answered, she filled her in on what DC Woodhouse had said to her.

'Try as I might I still can't find anything,' she admitted when Tiss finished. 'I've never had a case where I couldn't find one single thing about it, it's an anomaly. I know the police have better resources that I could ever have, but I do have an IT whizz kid who knows their way around a computer and has some pretty devious ways of getting information out of it. But even he couldn't find anything for me, and that's not normal. It's like, and I know how this is going to sound, but it seems like everything about them or the club has been blocked.'

'Nothing about this seems normal, Lily. Can people actually do that, block themselves and property from search engines?'

'I guess if there's a way then, yes, it can be done. Anything can be done these days if people have the skills to do it. I'm sure Jeff would be able to tell me more about that if you're interested.'

'Jeff?'

'Jeff Rawlings.'

'Yes then, why not find out. Could you ask him?' Tiss paused for a moment before adding. 'And what do you think about the missing women?'

'That is perhaps the most puzzling thing of all. It's the timing that bothers me; the precise time of year they went missing. And the fact that the club seems to be featured in it all.'

'Yes, that's what bothers me too.' It was true what Lily just said: it's not normal for nothing to show up. 'Okay, thanks Lily. Let me know what your friend Jeff says on the matter.'

'Will do. Speak later.'

CHAPTER TEN

Tiss had to admit that she was looking forward to her coffee date that evening with Tom Davenport. Despite everything, she also had to admit to herself that she found him quite attractive, and now that she knew he was not stalking her for a reason other than him wishing to take her out, she felt comfortable agreeing to go and meet him after work. Another comfort was the fact that the last time she and DC Woodhouse had spoken, he said he'd found nothing untoward on him, so that gave her some added relief. Besides, she felt she owed it to herself to relax for a night that wasn't Friday, and if that was with a person who was keen to spend some time with her, then so be it.

Of course it would happen on the one night when she'd arranged something. With all the increased number of people calling the practice for legal advice thanks to the newspaper article, her last client's appointment overran and took a little bit longer than expected. When they finally left at almost 5.15pm, Tiss hurriedly collected her things together and made her way across the street to the café, hoping that he'd still be there and hadn't concluded that she'd stood him up. When she pushed her way in through the door, she looked around and saw Tom tucked away in a corner near the back. Breathing a sigh of relief, she stared across in his direction hoping that he would look up and she could catch his eye. But it wasn't until she'd ordered her coffee and was heading his way that he finally saw her.

'Ah, I was beginning to get a bit worried,' he said, politely standing when she approached the table. Not many people seemed to do that nowadays. Tiss thought it to be very gallant of him albeit a bit old fashioned.

'I'm sorry,' she said, putting the coffee down and sliding onto the booth-style seat. 'A client held me up, and I didn't even have the time to text you before hurrying out.'

He laughed gently and it was like music to Tiss' ears. Did she actually like the man? 'Well, I was starting to think that perhaps I'd been a bit too forward with you.'

'No, no, we agreed to meet,' Tiss returned the laugh. 'If I thought you were being a bit too forward I would have told you.'

'Like you did that night in *Lux?*'

'Touché. Friday nights are when the girls and I usually meet up. We have a meal then we head off to a club. It's our special time together.'

'And no room for men then?'

'I'm the only singleton of the three of us. One friend is getting married this year to her long-time boyfriend, and the other has just started seeing someone. Wait, have you been stalking me since then?' Another laugh bubbled up from within her, taking her by surprise.

'Well, I wouldn't call it stalking per se, just concentrated intent!'

'Even to the point of following me to my friend's art exhibition in the country?' she joked.

'In my defence, I was there visiting my family, so it was more a case of being at the right place at the right time.'

'Did you know I was going?'

'No. That was all pure coincidence.'

Over the course of the next hour they both settled comfortably into one another, and when they'd finished their drinks and Tom suggested that they go for dinner, Tiss easily took him up on the offer.

***

Come the weekend, Tiss decided to pay her parents a visit, calling first to make sure that they'd be in and that it was okay for her to stay until Sunday evening. What she really wanted was to throw a few questions by them, questions she hoped they might have the answer to, or if they didn't, be able to give her some advice or point her in the right direction. Tiss knew this was getting to her far more than it should do, but she was never one to shy away from seeking out the truth. It was one of the reasons why she enjoyed being a solicitor so much. The truth always mattered, especially in her line of work, and her parents had always told her to challenge things she was wary of or uncomfortable with until she was 100% happy with them.

'Oh darling, it's so good to see you,' Tiss' mother, Sarah, said as she swept her into her arms on the doorstep of their home in the countryside. 'Come on in!'

Tiss rolled her suitcase through into the open-plan hallway of the spacious cottage. She looked around, half expecting her father to also be there to greet her. 'Where's dad?' she asked.

'He's just down in the village getting something; he shouldn't be long, or at least that's what he told me when he went out!' she laughed gently; it was a joyous sound that filled the space they were standing in. Tiss had missed that. She could have easily popped in to see them in their practice in town, but she'd been so busy of late since that recent article in the newspaper had produced an additional onslaught of clients. She could never understand why one article would attract people to the services of a solicitor. In her mind, you either needed one or you didn't; features in the press didn't usually make up a person's mind for them. But, as long as the big bosses were happy at Sanderson and Barnes, then everything was well in their little slice of the world. Truth was, John Sanderson and Jonathan Barnes were relishing in the fact they'd been voted first choice for anything legal, superseding their unofficial rival firm of Atkinson and Daniels, something they delighted in telling anybody who cared to listen to them.

'Leave your suitcase and bag in the hallway and your dad will take it up for you when he gets in. Come, let's go into the kitchen and sort out something for you to eat.'

'Mum, I ate before I came out,' Tiss informed her, causing her mother to look her up and down.

'Well, you look like you've lost some weight since we last saw you. Don't worry, we'll feed you well over the weekend.'

'I don't need feeding up,' Tiss laughed. 'I'm eating very well, thank you. And in case you've forgotten,

I am a grown woman, and a professional one at that!'

'A cup of tea or coffee then,' Sarah insisted, picking up the kettle and looking at her with a questioning head tilt and smile.

'Yes, *mother*,' she stressed the word, 'I would like a cup of tea.'

'So working in the middle of town with all the trendy cafés they have there now hasn't converted you to all those fancy high-priced cups of specialised coffees?'

'Yes, it has. But right now I would love to have a cup of tea.'

'Good girl!'

Tiss laughed at her mother's insistence that a good cup of tea was the staple of British life, and that the "fancy high-priced specialised coffees" were anything but. She doubted if she'd even had one in her life, but that was her parents for you: traditional to the core.

After making tea for both of them, Tiss' mother led them both into the large lounge at the rear of the house. Tiss had always loved the view from here, and sat down in the best seat in the room to appreciate it, a large and strategically placed curved sofa in a dark beige colour. In front of her, the full-width glass folding doors led out to a conservatory filled with tasteful rattan furniture, and beyond that a well-kept and maintained garden. From May to early September it was always a haven of colourful borders and planters, but even at this time of year, when all the blooms of summer had long since died, the space was filled with evergreen bushes and coniferous trees along the outermost edges. It was her dad's domain, always had been, as he was the gardener of the two of them. Her mother on the other hand was all about the interior of their shared home. She weaved her magic with the inside of the house, all the soft furnishings and colour schemes were her domain, and he took charge of the outside, perfecting the space with his talented green fingers. As with all other aspects of their life, it was and always would be a symbiotic partnership. In some ways Tiss longed for the kind of relationship they'd built up over the years, but she'd never met the person she felt she could spend the rest of her life with. Not yet at least, but she had to admit that her evening with Tom Davenport had been more than a little pleasant. Perhaps one day she would, but she would wait until the time was right and the right man came along rather than flinging herself headlong into it just for the sake of doing so. She could wait. Half-way through her drink, when she had allowed herself to relax after her journey, she heard the front door open.

'I'm home,' her father's voice echoed through the open space. 'Where are you both?'

'We're in the lounge,' her mother called back to him just as loudly. When he came through the door he was holding one of the biggest bouquets of flowers Tiss had ever seen.

'For you, my love,' he said, bending over and giving his wife a kiss before handing it to her. 'And a little something for you too, Tiss,' he said looking over in her direction. 'Hello, my beautiful daughter, it's great to see you!'

As he spoke, he put a hand into his pocket and brought out a small square box and handed it to her. 'Hope you like it,' he added almost sheepishly as he placed a kiss on the top of her head.

Tiss took it from him and opened it. As she removed the tissue paper beneath the lid she found a beautiful gold pendant necklace cushioned on a pad of velvet. She gasped as she saw what it was: scales of justice.

'Oh, dad, it's gorgeous!' she exclaimed as she brought it out of its box.

'I couldn't resist it, and it was looking at me begging me to buy it!' he admitted with a smile. 'After all, you are named after it.'

After putting it around her neck she got up to look at herself in it. The gold gleamed in the sunlight reflected from the mirror. 'I love it. Thank you.' She ran over and gave him a hug then added a quick peck on the cheek.

'Let me see,' her mother insisted and she walked over to see it more closely. 'Very appropriate,' she said, scrutinising it and turning it over in her hand. For the rest of the day they caught up and chatted about anything and everything, and when dinner came around, Tiss decided that the time had come to discuss the one thing she'd been wanting to talk to them about all day.

'So, there's something I was wanting to ask you,' she said as they started their meal. Both her parents put down their cutlery and looked across at her. 'I know you both have Masonic connections, and I was wondering if you'd heard anything about the Regency Club in the middle of town.'

Both looked blankly at one another, and then at Tiss.

'It's not one that I know about,' her dad replied. 'Are you sure it's Masonic?'

'Definitely. I saw the square and compass symbol etched into a brick by the door. I had my PI friend Lily check up on a few things after I'd seen a client, and the club keeps cropping up quite a bit. But, and this is the strange part, it doesn't even seem to exist.'

'What do you mean, it doesn't seem to exist?' her mother asked with a frown.

'Exactly that. Lily and her IT guy have searched and searched, and according to any records – well, that's the thing – there *aren't* any records to speak of. Not a single one.'

'But that's impossible, darling,' Sarah continued. 'There has to be something you can find on it, especially these days.'

'I know that, yet there you are, there's absolutely nothing.'

On hearing her, Paul Lawson excused himself as he left the table, bringing his phone out of his pocket and headed for his study in the adjoining room. After a few minutes he returned and sat down again. 'Well, it isn't anything to do with the Masons,' he said, looking directly at his daughter. 'At least, it's not registered with them.'

Tiss didn't know who he'd called, nor was she going to ask him. That was how far she kept herself away from her parents' involvement with the society. Not that she didn't approve, in some ways she did, but she knew it was a secret society, and she also knew that her parents wouldn't disclose anything to her that they didn't want her to know.

'You're certain? I mean, I saw the symbol.'

'Absolutely. I mean, it might have been at one time, but definitely not now.'

Tiss wisely left it at that, but she did stress that she thought that something was decidedly off with the whole situation. Her parents agreed with her.

The rest of the weekend was spent pleasantly enough, laid back and easy-going, and once she'd asked the question regarding the club, Tiss relaxed somewhat, deciding that this was her time with her family, away from work and all it's complicated plethora of unanswered questions. Work was 9am on a Monday morning up until 5pm on a Friday afternoon; the life/work balance should be kept separate if only for the sake of her own sanity, and Tiss was determined to stay sane throughout all this.

When she got home late Sunday evening, she decided that she might have to take a different approach to her burgeoning thoughts. To that end, she decided on Monday morning to ring Lily again and ask if her IT guy, Jeff, could find anything about the women's disappearances. If all eight had vanished around the location of the Regency Club, two every five years, she wondered if the two who had gone missing over the course of one year had anything in common. Perhaps they'd known one another, worked together, known the same person? She knew she could have easily contacted DC Woodhouse on the pretence of asking for an update on the break-in, and then carefully bring it into the conversation somehow. Although how she would have done that eluded her as she was merely a civilian without any right whatsoever to enquire into police confidential matters. Even so, the detective constable was the one who mentioned it to her in the first place, so he would know that it had caused her inquisitive nature to go into overdrive. But she'd wait to see if Lily could find anything out about the cases first. There was something decidedly off about the whole thing, and it was something she found that she couldn't let go of. And why was the number five bothering her so much?

CHAPTER
ELEVEN

'**Y**es, of course, I'll see what he can do,' Lily said to Tiss after she'd asked if she could get the information.

'If he's got too much on I'll understand,' Tiss replied hesitantly, not wishing to push her friend into doing too much personal work for her. 'And I'll pay him for it; I'm not expecting anything for nothing.'

'No, it's good. Plus, the whole business has me intrigued as well.'

'Okay, if you're sure.'

For the next few days Tiss put her head down and worked solidly, tackling the ever-increasing number of clients the firm had taken on – seriously, did people never need solicitors before that newspaper article? It helped take her mind off what she now referred to as "the case". The case in question being the mystery surrounding the Regency Club coupled with the addition of the eight missing women. She had to take a moment and remind herself about how all this started off: Miriam Marshall and her young friend, who, despite her husband's initial suspicions of an affair, had explained to Tiss that the mystery man was merely showing her a potential event venue. She wasn't entirely convinced if that was true or not. If it was, fair enough, but if it wasn't, then what was it *really* all about. Then again, when she and Lily had gone to the Regency, their ledger hadn't shown anyone to have entered the building around that time, so there was also that. Whatever the truth was, the club was shrouded in a cloak of mystery; a mystery she wanted to get to the bottom of and wouldn't rest until she did. It had become personal for her.

Just before the afternoon session began on Thursday, Tiss received and email from Lily. Or rather, it came directly from her IT guy, Jeff. It read: *Not sure if email is the way to do this, so can we possibly meet. If you name a time and place, I'll be there. Best wishes, Jeff Rawlings.*

Tiss responded immediately: *Is today too early? The Daily Grind is just across the street from my office, and I can be there shortly after 5. If that is too short notice for you, I can be there the same time tomorrow. Tiss Lawson.*

Jeff came back equally as quickly: *Today sounds good. See you then. J*

Tiss was intrigued. She'd half expected an email with an attachment if he'd found anything of interest out rather than ask to meet her. This made it all the more secretive somehow. What exactly had he found out, as he'd evidently found something of interest? And whatever it was, why had he thought it inappropriate to forward it on to her in an email.

Jeff Rawlings wasn't at all how Tiss had pictured him. For some reason she'd imagined an IT guy to be a young, bearded gentleman with thick, dark-framed glasses, a thick padded coat with a messenger bag slung over his shoulder. Tiss hadn't asked him what he looked like in the email, but instead for some strange reason, had assumed that they would both recognise one another through their shared efforts. She was looking at something on her phone when she sensed a presence next to her. As she looked up, the presence took the shape of a clean-shaven man around her own age who was impeccably dressed in a dark blue suit and colourful quirky tie. It looked like it had flamingos in flight scattered all over it. Tiss frowned up at him, but then he held out his hand and said, 'Tiss, I presume. Lily described you perfectly.'

Tiss was taken off guard, wondering just how her friend had described her to make her seemingly impossible to miss; it was something she would have to ask the next time they were in contact. She smiled warmly up at him and invited him to take the seat opposite. Despite him not being as she'd imagined, he did have the expected messenger bag slung over one shoulder, which he took off and placed down on the vacant seat next to him.

'Do you mind if I order a coffee first?' he asked, and Tiss shook her head. It appeared that whatever he had to tell her it wasn't going to be a quick visit to hand her the files and leave. Seems he was going to be there for a while, or at least for the length of time it would take to consume a cup of coffee.

When he returned, he took one sip of his drink then opened his bag. 'This is way too big for a simple email, which is why I asked if we could meet,' he explained, taking out a batch of manila folders and laying them down on the table in front of her. Tiss stared at them then back up to him.

'Seems you've been busy,' she said as she reached across and took the top one off the pile. The sticker on the front said *Lisa Foster* and it was dated *2005*. Opening it up she scanned the pages. Jeff's work on the subject was detailed and immaculate, and comprised of police reports and eye witness statements on and around the time she went missing. Tiss was just about to ask him how he'd been able to obtain police reports but then checked herself before actually saying it. It was probably for the best from a legal standpoint that she did not know. By all accounts Jeff Rawlings was an IT expert. Lily had referred to him as a whizz kid, but Tiss thought perhaps the term *hacker* might be a more appropriate term given what she was now looking at. She only hoped viewing this wouldn't get her into trouble.

Lisa Foster was twenty-seven when she went missing, and was last seen according to one of the witnesses on the street where the Regency Club was. She was a librarian who lived and worked in a village just out of town, and, according to her friends and relatives, it was unknown why she was seen around that vicinity, having no reason whatsoever to be there. As Tiss went through each of the eight files, a pattern began to emerge. Each and every one of them was last seen near the Regency Club; each of them were of a similar age; each of them was single; and each were employed. When she put the last file down on the table she looked over at Jeff. 'This is crazy,' she simply said.

'Yes, I know. And you know what's even stranger?'

Tiss couldn't imagine anything stranger than this, so was intrigued.

'They all look similar to one another.'

Tiss had only taken a fleeting glance at their photos as she was more interested in reading the details, so she looked again and instantly saw what he meant.

'You know, in some ways they also look a bit like you,' he added as he took another sip of his coffee, and the remark sent a cold chill down her spine.

***

Now that she had the information, Tiss didn't really know what to do with it. She had considered getting in touch with DC Woodhouse again to get his take on it all, but then decided not to as doing that might put herself in the awkward position of having to explain how she'd obtained the information in the first place. The last thing she wanted to do was to involve Lily or Jeff, not wishing to expose them as being complicit, especially not the latter, whom she now saw as being a somewhat powerful hacker.

Jeff left the files with her to do as she wished, and when she got home that evening she decided to look through them all in more detail. As she sat at her dining table with all eight of them spread out across it, she could see the pattern running throughout it again, and not just in the five-year interval between each disappearance. Jeff had been right in saying the missing women all looked similar, and she had to admit she could the similarity to herself as well, something which really bothered her. But aside from all that, it was the time of year that intrigued her the most. DC Woodhouse had already told her about it, but it was even more disturbing seeing it in black and white in front of her. The first disappearance was in March 2005 and the last in December 2020, which, if a pattern was truly following, another disappearance would occur in March 2025, which was a only a few weeks away. This was like something out of History's Greatest Mysteries, only even more bizarre than that. When DC Woodhouse had first mentioned the missing women and the dates, Tiss immediately saw the connection to the spring equinox and winter and solstice. But that was more like something out of a novel about the supernatural and black magic practices than fact. It was just too fantastical to be reality, surely. Yet the facts of the matter were all set out in front of her. Could fact and fiction be blending somehow?

As Tiss went deeper into each file, she read through the interviews with family members, friends and eye witnesses who were the last to see each of the women. All of the latter said the same: last seen around the area of the Regency Club, and in her mind that wasn't a coincidence. A multitude of possibilities claimed her thoughts, from human trafficking, murder and even the inevitable one, prostitution. All of the women were young and healthy, prime pickings for something like that. The next thing she did was to check their whereabouts in the days leading up to their disappearances. Nothing stood out. None of them had reportedly met any strangers; none had started up any new relationships; they didn't have mutual friends; none of them had seemed any different to normal. But for some inexplicable reason, inexplicable to family and friends at least, they all were seen on the street the club was in before they vanished. What had led them all there? That was indeed the question. She had to discuss it with someone, someone other than Lily who was already involved in the whole thing, and the only other people she felt she could trust enough were her friends Ruby and Claudia.

'This just doesn't make any sense,' Ruby said the following evening as she put one of the files back down on the table.

'I know, it's … well, I don't know what it is,' Tiss replied with a frown. 'This is why I wanted both your views on it all, to get your take on it.'

'And they're all now cold cases?'

'It looks like they are, at least according to these files I've been given. I can't see the five-year-old ones still being open and it looks like the police appear to be completely baffled by it all.'

'I'm not surprised,' Ruby added as she picked up another of the files.

Claudia was still looking at one of the other ones, the one from 2015, but then suddenly looked up at both of them, a confused look on her face.

'Have you seen this?' she asked as she put the file down and pointed to something in it. Both the girls got up to stand behind her to see what she was meaning. As they looked over her shoulder, they could see that Claudia was pointing to something in a photograph. It was a copy of an article in the local newspaper regarding one of the last two missing women. It was of the street where Regency was situated, and the front of the building could clearly be seen, but it was what her finger had settled on that caught their eye. A man was climbing up the steps to the door of the club and he had turned around just as the photograph had been taken.

'I not 100% certain, but I feel sure I've seen him in the office at some point over the past few weeks,' Claudia continued, eyes trained on the picture.

Tiss looked closer at the figure. He was younger, but it was clearly the person who she thought it was.

'Yes and no,' she replied. 'It's his brother that you've probably seen.' She had already noticed the similarity between the two men, but the face she was looking directly at now was unmistakably that of Frederick Marshall, Frank's brother.

Although Tiss had vowed to herself that she wouldn't get in touch with DC Woodhouse, she now felt that she may have to give this piece of information to him, although how she was going to explain why she had it was another matter. Lily hadn't turned up anything interesting about Frederick Marshall other than the fact he was a businessman with his own import and export company, and who was also something of an art connoisseur. Nothing out of the ordinary there, but it was his link to the Regency Club that now intrigued her.

***

As soon as the girls left, Tiss mulled everything over in her head. Part of her told her to leave it alone, walk away while she still could as it was really none of her business. But because it was intriguing and she was now in so deep, she found that she just couldn't. She needed to know everything, every last piece of information about the mysterious club and the women's disappearances, so she rang DC Woodhouse despite it being against her better judgement.

'How on earth did you get all this?' he asked in all seriousness after he'd arrived at the house and was sitting across from Tiss at the dining room table. 'Some of this information is from confidential police reports.' He looked up at her with questioning eyes, looking as if he would explode any second, and she felt herself heat up.

'It's perhaps best that you don't know,' she said to him somewhat meekly.

He let out a long, weary sigh before answering. 'Well, wherever and *whoever* you've got this information from is highly skilled, I'll say that for them. Technically, I should arrest both you and them for having this information. But ...' he trailed off.

'But?' Tiss asked, her heart in her mouth, fearing for both hers and Jeff's freedom.

'But, you have me intrigued by all this. In fact, I've been doing a little digging of my own.'

'You have?'

Woodhouse bent down and opened up the backpack he'd brought along with him. Tiss watched every movement he made with eager eyes. He pulled out a folder laid it on the table in front of her.

'It took a while, but I've been able to add some more to this bizarre case.' Tiss wondered just how much more bizarre it could get, her eyes wide as she eagerly waited to hear what he would tell her. He must have read her mind as he added, 'You'd be surprised. The club, for one thing.'

'What about it?' she asked excitedly. Neither she, Lily nor Jeff had been able to find any information about it, and in many ways it was as if it didn't exist. Had he been able to find something they couldn't? She could only hope.

'It's a bit of an enigma, if I'm being honest,' he admitted.

'In what way?' Tiss was eager to hear his take on it.

'There's very little about it on record, which makes me believe those people who either own it or have a vested interest in it don't want to make themselves known.'

Tiss sighed, 'Yes, I'd noticed.'

'But,' he stressed the word and continued, 'that's where my spell in the cybercrime section came in handy.'

She quickly looked up at him. 'You worked in cybercrime?' she asked in surprise.

'Very briefly. I joined the force after university and that's where I started out. It was very interesting.' The glint in his eye told her that he knew far more than he was currently letting on.

'Crime?' she asked. 'Is the club involved in crime in some way?'

'Not as such, not that I can see, but the department showed me some skills as to how to retrieve information nobody ever wanted anyone else to see.'

'I'm listening.'

Woodhouse then went on to explain what he'd managed to glean from the records, firstly letting her know that it was to only be between the two of them. 'If anyone gets an inkling of what I've done, then I think I'd be for the chop.'

'Oh, please, don't jeopardise your career for my sake,' Tiss insisted, genuinely concerned for his career. 'That's not something I would wish on anyone.'

'I'm not, but I have to say I've taken risky chances with this. You sparked my interest from day one, simply because of all the secrecy surrounding the place. Seems you can sniff out a mystery, Ms Lawson!'

'Blame my upbringing,' she laughed gently in return. 'My parents instilled the need in me to seek out justice – if you'll excuse the pun – and this one just reeked of mystery.'

'And I'll agree with you on that observation. Go on, open up,' he urged.

Tiss reached forward and opened up the file which was about the Regency Club. She skimmed through it, paying heed to the sections the detective constable had highlighted. Then one particular section caught her eye.

'It's owned by the Milton Group?' she asked, and he nodded. The Milton Group was well-known in the business world as it was a conglomerate of most of the biggest companies in the country, and it was more than fair to say that it was seen as business royalty. Not only were its members some of the biggest household names, but its patrons also included politicians and some members of the actual royal family. 'Why would a seemingly quiet little club be owned by the likes of them? she added with a frown.

'Beats me,' Woodhouse said, shaking his head. 'But I agree with you, and I'm thinking a tax dodge at best.'

'I don't get it.' Tiss was flabbergasted as it didn't make any sense. 'Why would they be interested in something like this? I know you've just said it's a possible tax dodge, but that doesn't seem to ring true somehow.'

'I know, and I agree with you.'

'Do you have the names of all those in the group?'

'Not yet. I'm trying to put something together, but it's proving to be a bit of a problem.'

'Oh? How?'

'I've been using a computer down in the filing centre to log in, but the last couple of days there's a warning coming up on it.'

'A warning?'

'Yes. It's only happened twice, but a little red triangle flashes across the screen with a "not allowed" message, and I've got to confess it's got me a bit concerned.'

'Then by all means don't look into it any further. The last thing you want to do is lose your job over it, or worst still end up getting yourself arrested.'

Woodhouse chuckled slightly, taking her by surprise. 'No, I'm not laughing because of that,' he assured her, after seeing her expression, 'because that's no laughing matter. It's just the police force is not supposed to have any areas that can't be researched, unless of course the files are sealed for whatever reason. But as far as I can see, the information about the group is not sealed, so I'm puzzled as to why a warning message would ever appear.'

'Some files can be sealed?' Tiss asked curiously.

'Yes. It depends upon their sensitivity. For example, some police officers could be working undercover, and the cases they're working on are temporarily sealed to shield their identities from anyone except their superior officers.'

'To shield their identities even from other officers?' Tiss found that hard to comprehend.

'You'd be surprised.'

'Oh!' She hadn't expected that response, but she knew that corruption could exist in the most unexpected places, but the last place anyone should expect it is in the police force.

'Even so, please go very carefully.'

'I shall,' he assured her. 'Perhaps your source might be able to find out something about Milton?'

Tiss couldn't believe he was asking her this, and it was now her turn to laugh. 'You're asking me to actually go ahead and do that after you just said that you should be arresting the both of us for what we did?'

'I think you'd do it any way,' he said with a smirk.

'You ass!' she laughed loudly and threw a bunched up piece of paper at him across the table.

CHAPTER
TWELVE

'Is everything okay with you, Tiss?' John Sanderson asked after he'd unexpectedly called her into his office one morning. It wasn't often that her boss specifically asked her to join him in his room on the top floor. The view from the full-width windows and the passing trail of an aircraft momentarily caught her attention before she directed her eyes back onto him again.

'Yes, of course. Why shouldn't it be?' she asked having no idea why he'd even asked her to come and see him in the first place. But she was worried by its suddenness. 'Is there a problem with something I've done?'

'No, no, nothing like that. It's just that a few people have been saying that you seem to be a bit off your game of late.'

'A few people? Like whom, and how off my game did they think I was?' She gave him one of her best frows, hurt and annoyed by the thought that any one of her colleagues could have gone to him behind her back. She knew them all quite well, and that wasn't like any of them.

'Tiss, you know as well as I do that I can't go into details. Let's just say that it's been noticed and they brought it to my attention.'

'Then let me assure you, Mr Sanderson-'

'John, please,' he interrupted her. 'We've known each other for over three years now; I'm sure we can be on first name terms here.'

'Only being respectful.'

'I know, and I respect that. But we're good, always have been.'

'Then I have no idea how or why anyone would think that. I come in on time, I'm never off, and I do the work; how can that be off?'

'It's just that you seem to have a lot on your mind, that's all. People were concerned.'

Tiss hadn't seen her boss for a couple of weeks, which wasn't in itself that unusual. Sanderson was often out of the office in meetings with solicitors of a similar standing from other companies, and their paths didn't usually cross during the working day, so she was perturbed by what he'd just said. And who exactly were these "people", she wondered to herself.

'If there's something wrong with my work, John, then I'd appreciate it if you'd just come out and say it.'

Sanderson quickly got out of his chair and came around to her side of the desk and sat on the edge of it. 'Okay, let me rephrase it. Is there something outside work that's occupying your mind at the moment?'

On hearing that, Tiss froze. She'd been very careful not to let her regular work overlap with her now extracurricular investigation into both the Regency Club and the missing women, which made her wonder about her email correspondence with Lily Singer. Had someone, someone from their IT providers perhaps, seen it and raised a red flag to her boss? Was him saying that people had approached him simply been a ploy? She had to move carefully here and think very quickly on her feet.

'Well, if you must know, I'm seeing someone. Although that's not having any kind of impact on my work that I know of.' Nice one, Tiss, she congratulated herself.

'You're seeing someone?' Sanderson beamed. Probably the same way the rest of the staff would have reacted to that piece of information as they all knew dating wasn't really something she was into.

'Yes. It's new, but it's hopeful,' Tiss found herself making it up as she went along. Although it was true that she was seeing Tom again that evening as a follow-up to their first date the previous week. Could that even be called a date, though, as it was simply a cup of coffee at the café across the road after work? Maybe it was a date after all.

'Well, I'm delighted for you. You know, I spoke to your father just the other day and he didn't mention it.'

'No, he wouldn't have as I haven't told my parents yet. Early days,' she ended with a nervous laugh, really not wanting to continue this conversation with him. But at least it had directed him away from anything else he had in mind.

'Okay then, Tiss, I just wanted to have a few words with you about it, but I can tell there's absolutely nothing to worry myself over.'

'No there isn't … *John*,' she added with a smile, longing to get out of there as soon as she could. She would have to text Lily on her mobile to let her know not to use her office email address in future as this was a bit concerning – innocent, perhaps, but concerning, nevertheless.

***

'So you think your office email has been hacked?' was the first thing Lily asked her when Tiss rang her on her mobile.

'I don't know,' she admitted, 'but I can't be sure. Ever since that morning Frank Marshall walked into my office things have been a bit strange. Everything was fine before he came into my life.'

'But hacking? Why on earth would anybody even want to do that to you?'

'Like I say, I don't know. But I really wouldn't mind Jeff taking a look at it.'

'My Jeff … like my hacker, Jeff … coming into your office and checking your IT stuff out?'

'Yes.'

Lily let out a long breath. 'Well, I can ask him. But if someone *is* monitoring your access to the internet surely they'll know if he goes in to have a bit of a poke about.'

'Maybe there's something he can do to cloak himself against that?'

'I don't really know. He might not be able to do anything Tiss, but if you really want him to take a look at it then I'll ask him for you.'

'I'd really appreciate that.'

Much to Lily's surprise and Tiss' delight, Jeff Rawlings very graciously agreed. So the next afternoon, under the pretence of being a potential new client, he knocked on Tiss' office door. She swiftly guided him inside, ensuring no one would notice his presence despite his visitor status. To validate this, she had added his name to her diary after he confirmed his availability, and she also requested that he register himself as an official visitor upon arrival by signing the book on the reception desk.

'Lily briefly explained, but spell it out for me again,' he asked, taking the offered seat in front of her computer.

'It's probably not in any way related, and perhaps I'm overthinking things here, but I'd just like you to make sure that nobody is reading my emails. That is, if it's possible to do such a thing?'

'Yeah, I can do that.'

'And, like, not leave a trail in case anyone *is* somehow getting into them.'

'Sure.'

'And while you're also here, there's something else I'd like to ask you.'

'Let's see what I can make of this first then ask away to your heart's content.'

For the next twenty minutes Tiss watched as Jeff tapped away at the keyboard, tutting to himself now and again. Even though she wanted to, she didn't wish to disturb him in any way by asking if there was a problem. She knew that if there was one then he'd certainly let her know. When he finally sat back and looked at her, she became nervous.

'No, there's nothing,' he confirmed, causing her to let out the breath she didn't realise she was holding in.

'You're certain?' she asked, more than a little bit relieved. 'I mean, how would you even know if anyone had?'

Jeff laughed gently. 'I'd know,' he assured her with a wink. But if you like I can download a few things onto a flash drive and check them out further?'

'Yes, that would probably be for the best.' Tiss sat back and let him do his thing for a few more minutes.

'Now, what else did you want to ask me?' he said after taking the flash drive out of the computer.

She told him about DC Woodhouse and what he'd managed to do for her.

'He's getting into the swing of things, isn't he?' he smiled at that.

'Seems so,' she replied. 'And I can't say I'm not grateful, but I'd hate it if he put his job in jeopardy for me.'

'It sounds as if it's intriguing him as much as it is us. So, the Milton Group? Yes, of course I've heard of them, but I've never given it much thought after that. What do you want me to do exactly?'

'I was hoping you might be able to find out a little bit more about it all, and the name of all of the people in the group; the big bosses, the head honchos, who they are and which specific companies they work for.'

'Quite a challenge, but nothing's impossible.'

Tiss paused for a while, biting her lip. 'Are you sure you're okay with this.'

'Yeah, sure, of course I am. Who knows what I'll dig up!'

'You know, this whole Regency Club business has just about taken up my life, that and the missing women over the years.'

'Yes, that's a very strange thing all round. I think you're onto something regarding the equinox and solstice, you know. It's very specific … too specific for it to be not related.'

'But the question is what?'

'Precisely. But let me assure you, if there's something to be found then I'll do my best to try to find it for you.'

'Thanks Jeff, I really appreciate all you're doing here.'

'No problem, Tiss. A pleasure as always.'

***

Tiss was determined not to think about it again until she heard something back from Jeff Rawlings, and was equally determined not to let it spoil her evening out with Tom Davenport. It was a rare thing for her to go out with a man rather than her two best friends, but she had to admit that she was taking to it better than expected, and even looking forward to it. To that end, she was going to make herself look and feel as good as she could, for herself if not for her date. *Her date* - that sounded such a strange thing after so long! But the big question was, what could she wear for this unexpected occasion? She stood in front of her open wardrobe doors and began to search for something appropriate. After taking out and trying on more things than she probably needed to, she finally decided to wear the first thing she'd originally picked out: a dress she'd recently bought, along with a colour-coordinated jacket, matching handbag and shoes. If she was going to go to a posh restaurant, then she was pulling out all the stops and look the part. It was for herself, she told herself. Yes, definitely for herself, despite knowing for a fact that she was also making herself look good in order to impress her companion.

Luigi's was one of those extremely popular restaurants where you couldn't just casually drop in on the spur of the moment and expect to get a table. You were required to pre-book, and Tom had rung up and reserved a table as soon as they'd agreed to meet up again. It appeared he was determined to make an impression with her right from the start. And impressed Tiss was when she walked into it. *The Olive Garden* was hers and her friends' meeting place and they loved the comfort and coziness of it, but *Luigi's* was luxury on another level. She wondered how he could afford to take her to a place like this, and it was then that she realised that she didn't know very much about him at all. She knew he was a solicitor like herself, but that was all she really knew.

The woman standing by the reservation desk at the door asked if she had a booking, to which she said that her companion had arranged it and gave his name. It was then that she spotted Tom sitting at the bar nursing a drink and pointed him out to the receptionist.

'Ah, yes, Mr Davenport is already here. Please feel free to join him and we'll have your table ready presently,' she said with a beaming smile. So far so good, Tiss thought. As she approached she could see that he, too, had taken care to present himself well for the evening. He was wearing a dark blue suit with matching waistcoat, a crisp white shirt, and a truly spectacular tie which sported a multitude of colours in an abstract pattern. It was unusual but eye-catching like Jeff Rawlings' flamingo one had been, and she had to admit she felt a tingle go through her seeing him all dressed up like this. She'd only ever seen him in casual attire, not in a more formal outfit like this, and it looked so good on him that she couldn't hide her appreciation of it no matter how she tried.

'Ah, you're here,' he said looking her up and down with a smile when she stood next to him at the bar. It seemed that she was having an effect upon him in the same way that he was on her. 'Would you like an apéritif?'

Tiss graciously accepted his offer and opted for an Aperol spritz, which was her favourite drink. She loved the bitterness combined with the sweetness and found it to be the perfect apéritif, one which she'd chosen time and time again. Once the bartender had prepared it and passed it to her, a waiter approached them letting them know that their table was now ready, and they followed as he then led them to a cosy secluded area near the back of the restaurant. It was less populated than the main area, but not so far away from another table as to be out of the loop. It was quite an intimate setting for what was essentially a first date. In short, Tiss was impressed. Over the meal, she found that she and Tom had quite a few shared interests.

'So how do you know Anita Jazmin?' he asked about her artist friend when the dessert arrived.

'Bit of a long story, really,' she began, eying her choice with interest. It had been described as a Strawberry Surprise, which intrigued her no end, but when it arrived it was nothing short of a work of art in its own right. 'She was a client initially,' Tiss continued, plunging her spoon into the feast in front of her, her tastebuds salivating at the mere sight of it. 'Then when we got talking we found out that we had quite a bit in common. I'd studied art at school, although over the years I've abandoned it somewhat. She sparked my interest again from a purely appreciative side. I used to love to go to art galleries when I was younger, and when our friendship developed, I started going to her exhibitions whenever she held them, and I always came away with something or other of hers.'

'What did you do – sketches, paintings, or another medium?'

'I did a bit of everything at school, but I was always interested in sketching more than anything else. I liked the quickness of it. Painting took far too long to do, meaning I'd pretty much lost interest in it half-way through,' she laughed softly, remembering all those unfinished pieces her teacher had told her off about.

'And do you still do it? *Can* you still do it, in fact? If that were me I'd probably lose the ability to do it if I left it so long.'

'Well it isn't all that long since I left school, you know,' she chided, 'but, yes, if I put my mind to it I can still do a sketch or two.'

'That's so interesting. I didn't do art, couldn't draw to save my life, but I do appreciate the beauty of it, and the talent, of course.'

'I guess you've either got it or you haven't, I suppose.'

After that little interlude, Tiss finished her dessert off, feeling that her waist had increased by at least a few inches. Then they both had a cup of freshly brewed coffee to finish off the evening.

Yes, thought Tiss as she turned her key in the door an hour or so later, *he's quite the gentleman*. And she was happy that they'd arranged to see one another again the following week.

CHAPTER
THIRTEEN

On Tuesday afternoon an email came flying into the mailbox on Tiss' phone. She couldn't open it straight away as she was with a client, but she could see that it had come from Jeff Rawling and that the subject line read URGENT in capital letters. It distracted her enough, though, but she managed to keep up her professionalism and continue to give as much attention to her client as she could under the circumstances. Only when they left did she scramble to open it and read it.

Hi Tiss, it read, *Just to let you know that I have managed to dig up some info for you. It wasn't easy, but please see the attachment. Hope you are well. Any queries please don't hesitate to get in touch with me.*

Tiss hurriedly clicked on the attached file, and it sprung to life on her screen. At first she couldn't make any sense out of it, but when she looked closer she could see a series of numbers beside a variety of dates over the past month. But what did it all mean? Then she scrolled down to the bottom and it all fell in place thanks to Jeff's addendum.

*I've now scrutinised all the data I downloaded on the flash drive from your work computer. Despite my initial check it now appears that you **were** hacked. The dates are when you were hacked together, with the IP source addresses. I'm trying to find their origins, but thought you'd like to see this straight away. Doesn't look like it's come from inside your company, unless your IT department has several IPs – which would be very unusual. Be careful, and I'll get back to you as soon as I can. Take care.*

PS don't use your work email or search engine for anything you wouldn't want other people to see.

She sat back in her seat, flabbergasted. So she *was* being hacked, and it looked like from various sources. It would be interesting to find out exactly where from, and by whom.

***

'You're being what?' Claudia exclaimed when Tiss rang her that evening. She just had to talk to somebody about it.

'Yes, I've just had it confirmed today.'

'What are you going to do about it; are you planning to inform Sanderson or Barnes?'

'No!' Tiss jumped in quickly, then there was silence on the other end of the phone for a few moments.

'Why not?' Claudia asked in a more serious tone.

Tiss let out the breath she was holding in. 'I … I just don't know who to trust any more,' she said shakily. 'I don't know who's doing this, and that's something that frightens me.'

'Well I'm pleased that you think you can trust me,' came the reply.

'Of course I can trust you!' Tiss said somewhat indignantly. 'You and Ruby both. I'd trust the two of you with my life.'

'And what about the other people you're close to?'

'Like whom?'

'Like the detective constable, or Tom, or Anita.'

'I wouldn't say I'm close to Woodhouse; he's just doing a little investigating for me. Anita's good, I know she is, so there's nothing to worry about there.'

'And Tom, what about him? He's new on the scene, so do you already feel comfortable with him?

'I don't know yet,' Tiss admitted. Yes, he did seem to be okay, but Claudia was right. He *was* new on the scene, and perhaps the timing of it could be seen as more than a little coincidental. She didn't know. But knowing what she knows now, *should* she be trusting him? 'That's something I'm going to have to play be ear, I think,' she replied after giving it some thought.

'Very wise.' Tiss could almost see her nodding as she said it. A short silence followed with neither of them speaking before Tiss added, 'Perhaps we could all meet up some time, with our respective partners.'

'You mean like the six of us going out together?'

'Yes, why not. And that way both you and Ruby can meet and get a reading on Tom. It might just ease my mind a bit after what you've just said.'

'Oh, I didn't mean-'

'No, I know,' Tiss reassured her. 'But I would like both your opinions on him.'

'Do you think it might get serious then?'

'I honestly don't know, but I would appreciate your take on him all the same.'

And so it was arranged. After texting Ruby, it was agreed that they'd forgo their usual Friday gathering in favour of going for a meal with their partners on the Saturday night instead.

For the next few days Tiss threw herself into her work, trying to ignore the nagging thoughts and doubts at the back of her mind, namely the fact that someone had deliberately spied on her through her work email account. Why would anyone even do that? Then, of course, she began to wonder if that spying had extended to her home as well. After all, her home had recently been broken into even though nothing had been taken. But what if something had been *put* there instead, something like camera surveillance. And while she was thinking that what if something had also been planted in her office to keep an eye and ears on her. To that end she rang Jeff Rawling while on a lunch break on Friday, waiting for Denise to arrive at *The Daily Grind.*

'Well I could come and do a sweep if you like, both at work and at your home,' he said in a matter of fact way like it was an everyday question he was being asked. 'And while I'm there I could take a look at your laptop and phone too.'

'And you have the equipment to do that; I was really only after advice?'

'I do.' *Of course you do*, Tiss thought. 'And transmission blockers if I were to find anything.'

'But if there is something there, wouldn't that alert whoever's put them there that I'm on to them?'

'Possibly, but that might actually work in our favour.'

'What do you mean?'

'Bring them out into the open. I could put a warning alert on your personal equipment in the event that someone might be trying to access them, and I can also install a camera in both your home and at work. And if anybody's either watching or listening while I do it we could just talk casually and say something on the lines of it being a motion sensor, something to do with your company's insurance. It might give them second thoughts about any equipment they've installed, and it might make them come and take it out. If that were to be the case, then we'd get a good look at whoever does that.'

'That's actually a good idea,' Tiss admitted, 'but now that's frightened me a bit. If somebody *has* installed a camera or a microphone, then they'll already know that I've spoken to you and my friends about all this; they'll have been listening.' Then she realised something else as well. 'Oh, and all the clients I've had in here would have been overheard.'

'Let's check it out first before you have a complete meltdown. If they have installed a microphone then it would have been to hear you and not them, but I do get your concerns about this what with client confidentiality and the like.'

'I don't think Lily has told me everything there is to know about you!' Tiss added with a slight laugh a few moments later.

'No, she probably hasn't, and I don't doubt there's a lot *she* doesn't know either! But suffice it to say that I know a bit more about things than what people assume of me.'

Tiss lifted an eyebrow at that remark, and it was as if Jeff could sense it without seeing it.

'Let's just say that I help a lot of people in various walks of life,' he added as confirmation.

'Now that sounds intriguing, but I'm not going to push you on it.'

He laughed. 'Perhaps that's for the best. If you like, I can come over to your office on Monday, and depending upon what I find I can then follow you home and check there too.'

'That sounds like a plan.'

***

She didn't know why, but Tiss was nervous about everyone getting together on Saturday evening. It wasn't like she didn't know everyone, apart from Claudia's new boyfriend that is, but it was the fact that she wanted her two friends' opinion on Tom that worried her the most. It was something she couldn't explain. And apart from everything else, she was now frightened to talk to anyone on the phone, to the extent that when anybody rang or if she needed to call someone she took the phone out into the back garden with her just to be safe. The sooner Jeff checked her house out and gave it the all-clear or not the better. Maybe that was what all the worry was about, because the idea that your house and office might be bugged wasn't conducive for any kind of calmness. But she would have to be patient and try to relax and enjoy her evening as best as she could. At least she wouldn't be at home when she was having any kind of conversation that might or might not be bugged.

Sadly, Claudia's new boyfriend had cried off at the last minute; something to do with his work and he had to travel to another city. It was a pity as Tiss was looking forward to finally meeting him. But despite that, they still intended to have a good time. There was really only one place where they'd be happy going out to for dinner. After ringing up beforehand and changing their usual Friday night reservation at *The Olive Garden* to the following day, when they arrived on the Saturday evening they found that their regular table at the restaurant had been set up to accommodate the extra two seatings. Tom was quickly introduced to the rest of the group, and was well-received by all of them. The two men gelled immediately, and Tiss could tell that Ruby and Claudia had also taken an instant liking to him. During dinner the talk was easy-going and casual, with each becoming more familiar with the new addition to the girls' circle. So no initial worries there for Tiss as he seemed to have been readily accepted by the group, and they by him. Thankful for that little piece of reassurance, she relaxed a bit more and settled down for a good night out.

Once dinner was over, they all naturally leaned towards spending the rest of the evening in *Lux*, and everyone agreed that was a good idea. By the time they got there, they'd all drunk just enough to take the edge off things and really let loose.

'I haven't felt this free in a long time!' Claudia chirped up at one point when the girls had taken a bathroom break together.

'I know,' Ruby instantly agreed as she washed her hands under the stream of running water.

'And I'm glad Tom is mixing in well with both of you and with Josh,' Tiss nodded, mainly to herself as she looked herself over in the mirror above the sinks.

'He seems really nice,' Ruby's reflection smiled over to her, 'and he's definitely smitten with you. So do you think this could be going somewhere?'

'I really don't know,' Tiss admitted, turning to face her, 'but I'm enjoying his company so far.'

When they got back to the table, they saw that Tom was missing.

'Where's Tom?' Tiss asked, only to be told that he said he'd seen someone he knew and went over to speak to them.

'Ah, which way did he go?' she asked, determined in her slightly warm and fuzzy way to go and find him. Maybe she had had a little more to drink than she realised, especially as people's bodies were starting to look a little hazy around the edges.

'Over there,' Josh vaguely indicated the area directly diagonal from where they were sitting. Ruby hit him playfully on the arm, saying that wasn't at all helpful. 'Well, I don't know,' he retorted, 'that's where he was heading when he left, but I guess he could be anywhere by now.'

Tiss laughed and started to make a move in that direction.

'Hey, where are you going?' Claudia shouted rather than spoke.

'To find him,' Tiss replied over her shoulder as she continued through the throng of people.

The funny thing was, she knew she was perhaps just that little bit more intoxicated than she'd intended to be thanks to the very satisfying meal they'd all had. By the time she'd crossed the dancefloor, having to struggle to weave her way through the undulating crowd, she wondered to herself with a chuckle why she hadn't just gone around it instead, but then she saw the person of her search. She was just about to put her hand up, shout and wave, when she suddenly stopped herself and backtracked slightly to merge with a group of people dancing directly behind her. She wasn't close enough to hear, but she could quite clearly see who Tom was talking to: Frank and Fred Marshall.

What the hell?

CHAPTER FOURTEEN

The sight of her new boyfriend with the Marshall brothers had immediately sobered Tiss up somewhat; it had the same effect as if someone had thrown a bucket of ice cold water over her. Still trying to stay out of sight, she made her way out of the group of people and to the clearer area that surrounded the dancefloor. She learned her lesson from the last time about trying to manoeuvre herself through the throng again. When she got back to the table, she looked at Ruby then Claudia, then indicated with her head that they join her away from Josh. Both looked at one another and frowned before rising to follow her. She led them to what seemed a semi-private area where she could have a conversation with them and be heard above the music.

'I've just seen Tom talking to Frank and Fred Marshal,' she said in almost hushed tones, fearful of anyone hearing her apart from the intended parties.

'That seems a bit odd. I mean, why would the two men be here in the first place, they're both in their fifties or something, aren't they?' Claudia said without thinking that what she said could be construed as being ageist.

'You know, I'm not entirely sure Fred Marshall doesn't have something to do with this club,' Tiss admitted, but giving her an odd look because of her comment. 'Well he was at Anita's art exhibition recently, and she said he was something of a connoisseur in the matter, and it's still bothering me that the art in here is very like what she produced at his request.'

'That seems like a very big coincidence,' Ruby added.

'I know, that's what I mean.'

'Look, why don't you just ask him about it when he comes back?' Claudia asked.

'Maybe I shall,' came the reply.

Tom had returned by the time they got back to the table.

'Where did you get to?' Tiss asked as she sat down next to him, fully expecting him not to mention who he'd been talking to.'

'To the men's room,' he supplied, adding, 'but then I met someone I knew. I don't know if you remember, but he was at Anita Jazmin's art exhibition a few weeks back, Fred Marshall.'

'Yes, I think I do,' Tiss blatantly lied, not wishing him to know that she was more than familiar with both him and Frank. She didn't dare look at her friends.

'Well, it seems he has connections with the club in that his brother is a shareholder or the like, and they were here for a meeting.'

'At this time of night?'

'I suppose if he's busy during the day then it's the only time he can manage.'

It seemed logical enough, and Tiss nodded despite herself. 'I guess,' she admitted, albeit begrudgingly.

'Anyway,' Tom clapped his hands together, looking around at the rest of the group, 'let's get back to the fun, shall we!'

Tiss couldn't tell if he was trying to avoid the subject or if he was genuinely keen to keep the party atmosphere going. She felt like she wanted to go and find the Marshalls just to see what they were up to, perhaps even getting close enough to hear what they were talking about, but knew in her mind that apart from being impractical, it was also bordering on fanatical. Jeff Rawlings and DC James Woodhouse were busy doing their thing and trying to gather together information for her; perhaps she should just sit back until they had something for her instead of brooding continuously over the matter.

For the rest of the evening Tiss let the matter go and concentrated on enjoying herself in the company of her friends and respective boyfriends. Oh, and the alcohol helped a bit, too.

***

Jeff Rawlings was booked into the 4.15pm slot on Monday afternoon. Tiss was careful with what she said to clients coming in to see her throughout the day, mindful that every word either she or they said could be being recorded by someone; it was something she found far harder to do than expected. She was now desperate to know whether her office was being bugged or not, and needed Jeff to assure her that it wasn't. If on the other hand it was, she would leave all the technical stuff needed to correct that to him. She was fairly certain he'd used the term debugging, whatever that was, if he did find anything. So, at 4.14pm she welcomed him into her office to start his assessment. As she began to speak he silenced her by putting a finger up to his lips. This stopped her instantly. He then took a piece of equipment out of his bag and scanned the room with it, taking in every nook and cranny. Once satisfied with the results, he laid it on her desk and removed yet another device from his bag, this time something that resembled an alarm clock. He turned a few dials and repeated his actions. Tiss looked on in awe and bewilderment as we walked around the room with it. After about five minutes he turned the equipment off and it joined its companion on her desk.

'Would you like the good news or the bad news?' he asked.

Tiss' eyes widened. 'The good, I guess,' wondering just what he'd found lurking around her office.

'Well, the good news is that I can't find anything obviously nasty in here.'

'And the bad?'

He gave her a cheeky smile. 'There isn't any bad. You're all clear.'

Tiss let out the long breath of anticipation she'd been holding in, relief pouring over her. 'Thank goodness!'

'So, do you still want me to follow you home and do the same thing there?' he asked as he started to put the devices back in his bag.

'Most definitely.'

As Tiss didn't have any more clients to see, she left for the evening with Jeff in tow. He'd parked his car in the multistorey where she usually parked hers, making it convenient for him to follow her. Although, as he seemed to be an expert in so many fields, she didn't doubt he would have any trouble doing something as simple and mundane as being able to find his way to her home. Once they were both at her house, he did his thing again with the instruments he was still very secretive about, and Tiss was thrilled to learn that her house, like her office, was clear. She felt like how the family in the film *Poltergeist* must have felt on hearing that their home had been cleansed.

'In that case, why don't you stay to dinner? It's the least I can do considering how you've eased my mind considerably, although I'm still puzzled why anyone would break in in the first place, especially as they didn't take anything, and, as we now know, didn't leave anything suspicious behind either.'

'We may never know the answer to that,' Jeff admitted, 'but, yes, I'd love to stay. While you're doing that I'll take a look at your phone and laptop.' Tiss gratefully handed him her phone from the table and went in search of her laptop, which she'd left on the bedside table in her bedroom the previous evening. By the time she'd returned back downstairs, Jeff had already confirmed that nothing malicious had been installed on her mobile. She watched with interest as he opened up her computer, and once she'd logged herself in, his nimble fingers set to work on bringing up screens she'd never seen before filled with figures and strange symbols. This continued for another five minutes before he turned it off and closed the lid.

'All clear,' he announced as he handed the device back to her and she took it with a smile, more than relieved to hear that her laptop had also passed his scrutiny.

'I really don't know how you do that,' she said, to which he replied that he had a very misplaced childhood, spending a vast amount of time playing with and designing video games.

As they ate, Tiss learned a bit more about Lily Singer's go-to guy for all things IT-related. And by IT-related she also meant all things hacker-related. Despite her thinking to the contrary, he wasn't just some guy who'd played computer games growing up and had found ways to hack into them to further his play, he'd graduated university with a master's degree in information technology and also a secondary degree in Political Science. So he was an intelligent man, and more than a bit of an enigma if she was being honest with herself.

'But why hacking?' Tiss asked as they finished the meal off with a cup of coffee in the more relaxed setting of the living room.

'I suppose the answer is, why not?' he replied as he cradled his mug. 'The vast majority of my work is legit; I mean even have a designated parking space in the company I work for! But as I've said, I also do outside contract work for companies, and some of their requests are highly confidential.'

'Meaning you do some unscrupulous work which involves hacking?' Tiss stated with a smile on her face.

'Should I not be saying this to a solicitor?' Jeff gave her a humorous glance, obviously waiting for her response.

'I think it's a bit late for that. If I'd had any doubts about it I wouldn't have asked Lily to get you to work on this in the first place.'

'And,' he continued, drawing the word out longer than it was, 'you could also act on my behalf if I *do* get myself into hot water.'

'Well, I'm not sure my boss would be happy about that,' she said with a laugh as she imagined John Sanderson's reaction to that piece of news.

'No, I suppose not.'

Conversation was easy between then, and after Jeff finally left, Tiss went to bed that night feeling a little bit more secure in the fact that nobody was bugging either her office or her home. She also had to admit to herself that Jeff was becoming … how could she even describe it … that he was growing on her … that their interconnectivity becoming more than expected? She didn't know, but one thing she did know was that the break-in was still bothering her.

CHAPTER
FIFTEEN

When Tiss entered the office on Tuesday morning it looked as if all hell had broken loose.

'What's going on?' she asked Denise on reception as her eyes took in the crates of boxes being taken from one part of the building to the other by complete strangers.

'Looks like we're having a bit of a reshuffle,' she said rolling her eyes skyward. 'Nobody really tells me anything.'

'A reshuffle of what?'

'Beats me,' Denise shrugged.

Just then Leonard walked quickly past clutching several folders to his chest and Tiss accosted him by the arm before he could go any further.

'What's going on?' she asked the flustered young man.

'Oh, management want to see some files from way back. They've had half of us in since 7am,' he said hurriedly, eager to get what he was holding to the person who had requested them.

'Is this some sort of accountancy thing?'

'I really don't know, Tiss. All I know is that there are a couple of guys in from head office, and their lackies are making some pretty unreasonable demands right now. Sorry, I've got to go.' And with that he rushed off to one of the side offices.

'What was all that about?' Tiss frowned. 'Are we scheduled for an audit or anything?'

'Again, not the right person to ask about such things. As ever, I'm kept in the dark about most things.'

'Well, if you hear anything will you let me know?'

'Of course. Listen, I know we usually go out for lunch on a Monday and a Friday, but I haven't brought anything in today and was wondering if you'd fancy something across the road?'

Tiss hadn't brought anything either as she'd forgotten, her mind on so many other things, so she readily agreed. Perhaps by then one or the other of them might have heard why the office had become so animated.

When she reached her office and opened up her computer, she found an email from John Sanderson in her inbox marked private and confidential. She quickly clicked on it and found that she and all the other solicitors had been invited to attend a meeting that afternoon at 4.15pm in his office. That didn't sound like good news at all. Was this something to do with what was going on downstairs, Tiss thought, because it seemed too much of a coincidence not to be. Was the firm being taken over? Was it going under? Both these thoughts crossed her mind as she read through it again. There was nothing to suggest either of those things were on the cards, but there was nothing to suggest that they weren't either. This was worrying. She picked up her phone and dialled Claudia's extension after first checking if she was with a client or not.

'Have you opened Sanderson's email?' she asked when her colleague answered the phone.

'I'm just reading it now,' Claudia said to her. 'What do you make of it?'

'I'm really not sure. As far as I can tell it can only be one of two things, and neither of those things seem to be good options.'

'You mean a sell or sink scenario?'

'Exactly that. What else could it be?'

'What do you make of all the commotion on the ground floor?' Tiss asked.

'I've no idea. We've had no warning of this, no heads-up, so perhaps it's something that's happened suddenly. The email was sent last night, so the bosses knew then what this was all about.'

'But they're keeping very quiet about it. How do they expect us to get through the day with this hanging over our heads?' Tiss felt so frustrated. Functioning under these circumstances was going to be nigh impossible. 'I'm going to go and see Sanderson. I don't have anyone coming in in the next hour, so I have time.'

'Do you think that's wise,' Claudia said with concern. 'He did specify a time to meet.'

'I'll take my chances,' Tiss replied. She'd been there far longer than Claudia had and was never one to hold back when she needed to get an answer to anything.

'Well then, please let me know if you discover anything.'

'I will.'

Tiss read the email again before seeking out her boss in an attempt to read between the lines. However, there was nothing to find. The email was worded plainly and it was to the point. There was a meeting at 4.15pm. End of story. But it was the hurried activity downstairs that had alerted her to something beyond that. Why would Sanderson call some members of staff in at 7am, and why were boxes of information being scrutinised in one of the downstairs offices? There was more to this simple "meeting" than met the eye.

She rapped on John Sanderson's door twice and waited for a response. When she heard him call "come in", she did just that. He smiled warmly when he saw her yet his eyes hid something quite different. Was it fear she saw there?

'Tiss, please sit down. And what can I do for you this fine Tuesday morning.'

Sitting as instructed, she looked him straight in the eye and asked what was happening with the firm.

'In what way?' he asked. She noticed his left eye twitch slightly, something she'd seen in the past when he wasn't comfortable with a question he'd been asked.

'Like the meeting this afternoon, and all the commotion currently taking place downstairs.'

'We're just doing a bit of a sort before the tax year ends, that's all.'

'I know, we do that every year, but I've never seen people rushing about like headless chickens before.'

He sat back in his chair and spread his arms out wide. 'What do you want me to say, Tiss?' he asked.

'I want you to say what's really happening.'

He sat and stared at her for a moment as if he was debating with himself as to what he should tell her. Finally he said, 'You'll hear with everybody else this afternoon.'

'Are we going under?' she asked him bluntly.

'What? No, whatever makes you think that?' He looked genuinely shocked by her somewhat forceful question.

'Well, it's either that or we're being taken over.'

Sanderson brought himself forward in the chair and rested his arms on the desk. 'Tiss, it's nothing like that I promise you. Please just wait until this afternoon's meeting and all will be revealed then.'

Tiss reluctantly nodded her head, wanting to push further but knowing her boss wouldn't tell her any more than what he'd just said. 'Okay,' she murmured as she started to rise from her seat.

'It isn't bad news, Tiss. I'll at least say that to you.'

She knew that was his way of appeasing her, so as she got up she gave him a weak smile and promptly left his office. For some reason she felt more anxious now than when she first went in.

Tiss had two clients in the morning and a further three in the afternoon, but when half-twelve rolled around she was glad of the break in the café across the road.

'So have you heard anything about what was going on this morning?' was the first thing Diane asked as they were leaving the office.

'No, not much,' Tiss replied, then went on to tell her what she knew.

'I didn't get an email,' Diane pouted when she heard about the afternoon meeting.

'It must just be for the solicitors then.'

'There was a lot of coming and going after you went up; stacks of boxes and files went through to the last office down the corridor.'

'Did you see one of our accountants in there, or someone you didn't know, like a stranger?'

'No. I think they must have come in earlier and stayed in there doing whatever it is they're up to.'

'Sanderson insists there's nothing to worry about,' Tiss explained, but even she found it difficult to believe it.

'What do *you* think's going on then?'

'I've no earthly idea. I asked if we were either being taken over or going under, but all Sanderson could say was that whatever was going on wasn't bad news.'

Diane let out a long sigh. 'I certainly hope we're not going under. I really love this job and all the people who work here.'

'Then I guess we'll just have to wait and see.'

At ten past four all the solicitors began to assemble in John Sanderson's office. There were five in total, and when they arrived additional chairs had been arranged for them in front of his desk. The man himself wasn't there, but he had made it known only minutes before that he would be in the meeting presently. Tiss began to feel very uncomfortable about the whole thing, especially when she noticed two more chairs positioned behind the desk next to his. About five minutes after everyone had got themselves seated and had quietly discussed it amongst themselves, Sanderson arrived, but he wasn't alone. Alarm bells started ringing in Tiss' head and, she didn't doubt, in the heads of the others as well. Following John Sanderson was Jonathan Barnes, and behind him a stranger. Sanderson sat in his usual seat with the two man sitting beside him.

'Right,' he began cheerfully, loudly chapping his hands together. Out of the corner of her eye, Tiss saw Claudia jump at that action. 'Thank you all for coming along, and I'd like to introduce you to Jonathan Carver.' The man nodded his head. 'Mr Carver is here to represent the Milton Group, who I'm sure you've all heard of.'

Muted murmurs filled the room. 'And I'm pleased to announce that Sanderson and Barnes will be joining the group as from the beginning of next month.' He ended on a happy note and smiled broadly at everyone. But of course nobody present knew exactly what that would entail, so Leonard being Leonard spoke up.

'Excuse me for saying this Mr Sanderson, but what will that mean for both the company and its employees?'

'Well,' he began, 'it means that we will now be part of the biggest conglomerate of companies in the country, and will be hoping to expand to other cities. It also means that we will be able to offer each employee shares in the company which, as I'm sure you will understand, is quite an attractive prospective.'

'But our jobs are all safe?' Claudia asked. Like Denise the receptionist, she'd only been with the company for a relatively short time and was worried about being made redundant in light of this unexpected news.

'Yes, yes, of course they are,' he trilled. 'And I think we're all going to be in a much better position financially from being under the umbrella of such a prestigious organisation and through expansion into other towns and cities. In short, it's good news for us all!'

Tiss could tell that everyone, herself included, was trying to take it all in. Then of course she now knew that the Milton Group, thanks to Jeff Rawlings' diligent research work, also owned the Regency Club. This was way too much of a coincidence now in her mind, and she could only wonder if that was the real reason Frank Marshall had visited the practice to see her that day – to check the company out as a possible purchase or amalgamation into the group. To say she was a little unhappy was more than an understatement.

The first thing Tiss did when she got home was ring Jeff Rawling. She needed more information on the Milton Group, and she needed it as soon as he could possibly give her it.

'Yes, I'd heard,' he said as soon as she told him about the firm's amalgamation with the group.

'You heard ... already?' she gasped as he said that.

'There's not much gets past me, Tiss. Surely you should know that by now!' he said with a mild chuckle.

'So it seems. I know you are already digging into the company, but can I ask you to try to find out all you can about them as soon as possible?'

'As in not the information openly visible to the public?'

'Yes, precisely that.'

'I'll see what I can do,' he assured her before they both mutually ended the call, with him promising to get back in touch as soon as he could.

After grabbing herself something to eat, Tiss decided to take a look again at the missing women files both he and DC Woodhouse had left for her. The reports had mainly concentrated on when they went missing, together with details of their addresses and next of kin along with witness statements, but there wasn't a great deal of information regarding where each of them had worked. She didn't know why, but Tiss thought that to be an important factor. She wondered if they had been abducted, had it been by someone who had worked with them and was known to them, or was there some larger thing at play here, something like supply and demand with them fitting a distinct type for human trafficking. That could easily explain their disappearances, and indeed their physical similar similarities to one another. But the time of year they were taken was also an interesting aspect, and the one part that intrigued her the most. In any case, it was worth looking into, and for that purpose she felt the need to contact the detective constable again. She dug out the card he'd left her with his contact details on it and dialled his mobile number.

'Hello Tiss,' his voice came over the phone after a few rings.

'Oh, you know it's me!' she exclaimed, not expecting him to immediately know who was calling.

'Yes, I programmed your number into my phone.'

'Oh.'

She heard him laugh. 'Sorry, that sounded a bit creepy, didn't it!'

'Just a little,' her easy laugh echoed his.

'No, I just wanted it reachable if I found anything else. What can I do for you?'

'I've had a bit of a funny day-'

He immediately jumped in before she could continue, sounding very concerned. 'Has something happened?'

'Something at work, but that's not why I'm calling. I came home and started to think about the files you and ... that you left.' Thankfully she stopped herself in time from mentioning Jeff Rawling's name. That would have been the worst thing she could have done, make a police officer aware of the hacker who was also helping her. Although, he had told her that he'd been doing a bit of extracurricular investigating on his own. But she continued. 'And I was wondering about where all the women who went missing over the year worked.'

'Was that not in the files?'

'Some of them yes, but not all of them. I thought I may have overlooked it when I first read through, but I can't find very much information at all in there.'

'Okay, I'll see what I can find out for you. I'll give you a call if and when I find out anything.'

So that was two people she was now waiting to hear from. It was going to be a suspenseful time all round, what with waiting for this and now having the upheaval at work.

***

The next few days at the office were chaotic. The amalgamation into the Milton Group had been announced in the press, and clients were

151

constantly ringing up to find out how that would affect them. Diane certainly had her work cut out passing them on to those who would best be able to provide them with satisfactory answers.

Somewhat expectedly, the people who had been working secretly with the files in the downstairs office were revealed to be from Milton's accountancy department, carrying out an audit of the firm's last five years' worth of accounts. Tiss thought they could have just as easily asked the company's own accountants for that information instead of bringing in the big guns, but maybe they did that with all the companies they amalgamated with just for the show of it. By Friday afternoon they'd thankfully packed up and moved on, so things could now get back to normal – or at least as normal as it could with an amalgamation looming over their heads. To celebrate Friday's arrival, and overcoming the added stress of the audit team, Tiss was looking forward to her regular night out with the girls more than usual. She hadn't seen Tom since the previous weekend due to his work, and for that reason had had to cancel their date, but had spoken to him on the phone during that time, and they'd planned a get-together for one evening the following week.

Before anybody knew it two weeks had passed, and the transition from a privately-run company to being part of a much larger organisation was getting closer. The decision had been made by the powers-that-be and nothing could be done to avoid it. From the solicitors' point of view, they were mere pawns in a game of chess and nothing had changed. They were carrying on as normal and trying not to think about it, but they knew that behind the scenes things were very different. There was a hubbub of activity in the accounts section, where contracts were being scrutinised from every which way before they needed to be finally signed by the two partners and forwarded on to the Milton Group who now had the controlling stake in the business. It was what many would describe as organised chaos. Others wouldn't be so polite.

Tiss received a call from DC James Woodhouse the day before the official amalgamation took place. She'd been attending a last-minute meeting in John Sanderson's office along with the other solicitors when it came through and had missed it due to her phone being on silent for the duration. When she returned to her office after the meeting, she saw that she'd missed a call and that there was a voicemail waiting for her. After listening to the message she immediately rang the detective constable.

'Sorry I couldn't answer, I was in a meeting,' she said as he answered the phone. 'Your voicemail sounded urgent.'

'It was, and thank you for getting back to me so quickly. I know it's taken a while to contact you again, but I've been digging and I've found some very interesting things out.'

'Oh, really?'

'Yes, but I can't discuss them over the phone. Are you free tonight?'

Of all the nights it had to be one where she'd arranged to meet Tom. 'I'm not, actually, but how about we meet at the café across the street? I finish at 3.30pm today if that's convenient to you that is? I'll be free in about an hour's time.'

'Yes, that's good for me. So, I'll see you there then?'

'Yes,' she confirmed.

Tiss sat in a quiet corner of the café near the back and cradled her cup of coffee; her eyes trained on the door for the detective's arrival. The sun was still shining despite it being a bitterly cold day, and its rays filtered through the windows and onto the tables, casting a warm golden hue over them. It looked cosy, and any other time she would have enjoyed the simple beauty of it all, but today her mind was more on what information he was bringing for her rather than the ambiance of her surroundings. As she was wondering what it could be, the gently tinkle of the bell over the door drew her attention back to it. DC Woodhouse strode in purposefully, looking around him as he did so. She raised a hand in the air to catch his attention, and he made his way directly over to her table without even stopping to order himself a drink.

'Hey,' he said, pulling out a chair and sitting down. Tiss returned his greeting and watched while he leaned over and pulled a manila folder out of the backpack he'd put down on the floor. 'This is what I've found,' he announced as he laid it in front of her. 'I'm going to grab a coffee while you're taking a look at it.' And with that he rose and walked back to the counter.

Tiss spent no time pulling the file closer to her to open up and read. She quickly glanced around her to make sure nobody was looking, but she needn't have worried as she and the police officer were now the only ones left in the café. She had no idea when it had emptied; she'd been so caught up in her own thoughts. Woodhouse returned presently with a frothy cappuccino in one hand and a slice of pie in the other and set them down on the table. Tiss had already skimmed through the file, picking out the information she'd been seeking. Unfortunately, it hadn't been all that helpful to her. She'd been hoping to see a link between all the missing women through the places they worked, but there wasn't anything obvious that stood out to connect them as far as their occupations were concerned as they were all distinctly different, ranging from housewife to administrator.

Tiss looked over at him with a heavy heart as he dug his fork into the pie and pushed a sliver into his mouth. 'I had hoped for something,' she admitted, feeling decidedly underwhelmed by it all.

'I gather you haven't read it all then,' Woodhouse mumbled through his mouthful of food.

Tiss frowned as she looked at him and he said, 'The last page.'

She quickly turned to it and read the information on it. As she read her eyes began to widen. She looked over at the detective then back to the page, before finally settling her gaze on him again. 'I don't believe it!' she spluttered, to which he could only smile and tilt his head.

CHAPTER
SEVENTEEN

Tiss was distracted all night, and although she didn't think it was affecting her evening, Tom eventually just came out with it and asked her what the matter was.

'Oh, just work,' she lied, finally realising that she hadn't been as stealthy with her thoughts as she'd hoped. 'I'm sorry, I've been a really awful companion tonight, haven't I?

'No, not at all, but I could tell you had something on your mind.'

'Yeah, something I should have left at the office if it's throwing a cloud over the evening.'

'Do you want to talk about it?' he asked in all sincerity, and Tiss was bowled over by it. They'd gone out for dinner at a restaurant he'd recommended, so she now felt guilty that he'd noticed her mind wasn't on it. But how could she concentrate after reading that piece of mind-blowing information in the file DC Woodhouse had presented her with. She hadn't even had time to contact Ruby and Claudia and inform them of it yet. She'd sat longer with Woodhouse than intended just talking about it, and as soon as she'd got home, she'd literally changed into her evening outfit before leaving the house again for her date.

'No, not really; business stuff, that's all.' Most of Tiss' answers to people not in the know all seemed to be lies these days, and it was something she was ashamed of. However, she couldn't reveal all that was on her mind to anyone other than those who already knew about it, and the least number of people who knew the better.

'Is it about the amalgamation?'

'Yes,' was all she could muster after being pushed on the matter. At that moment she resolved herself to put all thoughts of it out of her mind and concentrate on the evening itself and her companion rather than dwelling on something out of her control for the moment.

'You're bound to be overwhelmed by it,' Tom said, still in nurturing mode. 'I think I'd be anxious about the whole thing too if it was me in the same position.'

Tiss grabbed his hand and squeezed it. He was being so thoughtful and she was being horrendous and she knew it. 'Yes, it is a bit, and thank you for understanding. I promise from now on I'll push it to the back of my mind!'

'It's okay, but it's just that I don't like to see you fretting like this.'

For the rest of the evening Tiss was more mindful of her companion and relaxed enough to give in to the moment. There'd be plenty of time when she got home to contact her two friends and tell them what she'd found out.

At 9.30pm their shared Uber dropped her at the kerb beside her house before whisking Tom away to his. She hurriedly let herself in and shrugged her coat off before settling down in the living room and getting in touch with her two friends on a conference call.

'They were thinking it was a what?' Ruby asked after Tiss related the contents of the police file to them.

'They may not have found the bodies, but they were definitely being investigated as ritual abuse.'

'As in the supernatural you mean, devil worship and the like?' Claudia asked.

'Yes, exactly that.'

All three women were quiet for a while.

'And the Regency Club was also under investigation?' Ruby asked at last.

'Yes, as all of the women disappeared near to it, they and all the other properties on that street were questioned. There are some very detailed interviews with some of the establishments but, wait for this, none whatsoever from the Regency.'

'I find that very hard to believe,' Claudia huffed.

'As do I,' Tiss agreed.

'So what are you thinking?'

'Well I'm thinking that they're either involved in some way or ...' she trailed off.

'Or?' Ruby asked.

'Or, as the place does have connections to the Freemasons, then perhaps a fellow Mason in the police force took care of the statement.'

'You mean disposed of it?'

'Yes.'

'But this is ...' Ruby continued but then paused. 'I don't really know what it is,' she admitted feeling somewhat helpless.

'I know, it defies reason,' Tiss sympathised.

'But reeks of corruption, and something a little more sinister,' Claudia filled in the gap. 'Do you think you can trust DC Woodhouse, I mean completely trust him? I know he's an officer of the law, but if there's one bad apple in there deliberately removing information then there could also be others.'

Tiss was dumbstruck as it wasn't something she'd considered before. But perhaps Claudia had a point. What if all the information he was providing her with was false? Yes he was a police officer, but it was clear that each and every police officer wasn't squeaky clean, especially if vital information was being removed by certain members of the force for reasons best known to them or to those who they serve.

'I ... I think so, or at least I thought so before I heard that evidence could go deliberately missing.'

'Claudia has a point,' Ruby chipped in. 'This situation is so bizarre that we can't really know anything about anything or anyone at the moment.'

'But what he's given me supports what Jeff Rawlings has provided me with,' Tiss insisted. 'The man is independently contracted and does the work himself without having anyone else to answer to.'

'As far as you know,' Claudia added, throwing even more doubt on the detective. 'Are you even sure you can trust Rawlings?'

'Then if we can't trust anyone where would this mistrust end,' Tiss asked defensively. 'We can't not trust anyone, because if we go down that route we'll end up not even trusting ourselves.' Her statement left everyone quiet.

'So what do we do, and who do we believe?' Claudia continued.

'I trust Jeff implicitly. He's independent and completely admits to being a hacker, and he's gone out on a limb for me, so I can't see any reason why he'd want to pass on false information. I'll get him to check out this latest piece of information and see what he comes back with. After that we can take it from there,' Tiss said to both of her friends. 'Before having this conversation I'd have said that I totally trust DC Woodhouse, but you've thrown doubt even on that.'

'Fair enough,' Ruby commented. 'But be careful, Tiss. We really shouldn't be getting ourselves so engrossed in this, especially if there's any hint of corruption involved. Those kind of people can be very dangerous beings.'

And so the conversation ended. Tiss walked into the kitchen to make herself a drink and watch a bit of mindless television before heading off to bed, but she'd only just put the kettle on when she heard her phone ringing again in the living room. When she picked it up she saw that the call was from her artist friend, Anita.

'Hey, good to hear from you,' she began as she answered it.

'I'm sorry to call you so late,' Anita began, her voice a little shaky. 'but I was wondering if you were free tomorrow evening?'

'Yes, of course. Why, what's wrong?' Tiss sensed the tone in her voice and an urgency in that question.

'It's … I don't think I want to talk about it over the phone if you don't mind, but it's something I need to speak to you about quite urgently.'

'O-kay.' Now Tiss was concerned but she didn't push for an explanation. 'I'll be home by around 5.30 if you want to come over after that. I can make us a meal if you like.'

'That sounds good. Thank you, and I'll see you then.'

Tiss stood and looked at her phone, her friend having ended the call abruptly from her end. Thoughts were swirling around her head as to what could be wrong. *Everything's coming at once!* she said to herself.

***

Tiss was so curious as to why Anita wanted to speak to her, so she spent the next day at work thinking about the upcoming meeting that evening. When the time finally came around for her to leave for the day, she hurried to the car park in order to get home as soon as she could. Her colleague Leonard tried to have a word with her before she was out of the door, but she apologised saying that she had an appointment and brushed him off. 'Text me if it's important,' she called over her shoulder as she pushed her way through the door, but didn't hear his response as it closed behind her cutting him off.

True to her word, Anita arrived shortly after half-five as arranged. She looked distressed as Tiss ushered her into the living room and indicated that she sit down on the sofa.

'Would you like a drink?' she asked her friend. 'Because I've got to say you look like you could need one.'

'I wouldn't mind, if that's okay.'

Tiss retreated into the kitchen to open the bottle of sparkling wine she already had chilling in the refrigerator for them to have with their dinner.

Once she'd poured two glasses she returned and handed one to Anita.

'Thank you for agreeing to see me so quickly,' she said after talking a long drink from her glass.

'Anytime, you know that.'

There was a long pause before Anita said anything. It was as if she was trying to work something out in her head. 'You remember the night you came to my exhibition,' she finally said.

Tiss nodded and she continued. 'You remember the person you asked me about, the one who was in the photograph you showed me, and you said his name was Tom Davenport?'

'Yes. I said that he was there visiting an uncle that lived nearby.'

'That's right. Well, I saw him the other day, and wouldn't have thought anything of it but ...' she trailed off.

'But what?' Tiss aske with a frown, but added, 'I feel I should let you know that we are going out together.'

Anita looked horrified, as if it was the worst thing she could have been told. 'Then there's something I have to tell you.' Tiss felt a chill go through her, fearful of what would come next. 'I was in town yesterday at Fred Marshall's behest.'

'Why didn't you come and see me while you were here?' Tiss felt let down. She would have really loved to have seen her friend while she was in the area.

'The reason I didn't was because Marshall arranged everything for me right down to providing a car to collect me from home and take me back again. I would have loved to have come and see you, but I didn't have time to do it so I didn't even get in touch. I'm sorry. But what I'm wanting to tell you is this. I'd already done some paintings for him for the club *Lux*, and he asked if I'd be interested in doing some more work but for his brother Frank this time, for a club he has interests in. I thought it would be for another nightclub, but then he took me to somewhere called the Regency Club. It wasn't what I was expecting.'

Tiss went cold at the mention of its name. Anita didn't know about it, or the strange things that had happened around it, so just nodded her head and said that she'd heard of it. When Anita looked at her strangely she added that Frank had been a potential client of hers but without going into any detail. She didn't want anyone else involved in whatever was going on there – if indeed there was anything going on. Everything was just circumstantial at this point, but the fact that the place kept cropping up was disturbing.

'But here's the thing. I saw Tom there with Fred's brother.'

Tiss' mind went back to the time in *Lux* when she'd seen Tom with both the Marshalls. 'Well, Tom *did* say that he'd met Fred at your exhibition.'

'Does Tom have connections to the club? I don't know him as I only know the family name and its connections to the area. Didn't you say his uncle lives there near me?

'Not that I know of. But like I say Fred was at your exhibition, so it's possible that they met there and have a mutual friend or something; perhaps Tom's uncle knows him or his brother.'

'I guess, but I really don't know. Anyway, they all showed me around and said they would like a few paintings for several areas of the club, but they wanted them similar to what I'd produced for *Lux*. I thought that was odd as the club had a very traditional, and some would also say old-fashioned, feel to it.'

Tiss nodded again; any words she tried to say were stuck in her throat before she could say them.

'However, that's not the strangest thing. While we were walking around I heard Frank ask Tom about you.'

That caught Tiss' attention and her head snapped round sharp to look at her friend. 'He asked about me?'

'I assumed it was you, and later on I was almost certain I heard your name mentioned.

'What did he ask?'

'He asked how it was going, and he said that everything was going to plan.'

'Going to plan?'

'Yes, that's what he said.'

Tiss felt sick. Was she just a pawn in whatever was going on here? She thought things were going well with Tom, perhaps a little too well considering the short time they'd known one another, but now it was being implied that it could all be false and was some kind of an arrangement between him and the Marshalls. She realised that she could just be imagining all this, but it was yet another ridiculous coincidence that was bugging her so much.

Seeing Tiss' face Anita added, 'But I could be wrong.'

'There's a lot going on here that you don't know about,' Tiss said to her, causing her friend to look at her with a frown.

'What do you mean?'

'I don't want to drag you into all this, but there's something very off with that club.' Anita was about to speak but she was cut off. 'Please don't ask me about it as the fewer people know the better.'

'But I've agreed to do some art work for them now.' She sounded distraught, which wasn't what Tiss wanted to hear.

'Don't let that affect your business. A commission is a commission.'

'Is there anything underhanded going on, because I don't want to get mixed up with anything like that.'

'No, nothing underhanded, just some odd happenings around that area over the years.'

'Such as?'

'Please believe me when I say that it has nothing to do with anything illegal.'

'Then what is it?' Anita asked determinedly.

'I suppose it's just that it seems that the place has been in the wrong place at the wrong time.' Tiss instantly knew that she'd probably said more than she'd intended, and the look her friend was giving her seemed to substantiate that. *Shit!* she thought.

'I don't understand,' came the response. Of course she didn't, which is why, against her better judgement, Tiss was now going to have to bring her into this mess that was currently her life.

Anita listened attentively as Tiss went through everything she knew about the Regency Club and the Marshalls. Her face fluctuated between shock and astonishment to doubt and disbelief, but by the end of it, she knew as much as Tiss and her friends did. It was something Tiss didn't want to involve her in, but her friend had all but insisted on knowing. Tiss sat back in her seat and waited for the reaction. Anita's mouth opened and closed a few times, as if she wanted to say something but couldn't find the exact words to express it. In the end she too sat back.

'Do you think I could have another glass of wine?' she asked, looking at the glass on the table beside her and realising that she'd finished it off without even knowing it. Tiss took both their glasses into the kitchen to replenish them. When she came back she asked exactly what it was that Fred Marshall had commissioned her to do.

'Oh ... something a little similar to what I'd done for *Lux*.'

'In a place like that? I mean, it's very traditional from what I've seen of it. I would have thought it would have preferred something like a Stubbs than anything modern.'

'It wasn't specifically for the main areas. Marshall said they had a more private area where it was more liberal than the rest of the premises, and that's where they wanted the paintings for.'

'I know *Lux* is quite the liberal place and your paintings were appropriate for there, but I would have thought a gentleman's club to be straight-laced and buttoned down by comparison.'

'Yes, having seen inside both I'd have to agree with you.'

'And did he tell you what his connection to the club is?'

'*Lux* or the Regency?

'Both, I suppose.'

'He said that his brother had shares in both. Well, I already knew that about the nightclub because of the past commission, but it wasn't until yesterday that he confirmed his brother's connection to the Regency as well.'

'This is getting more and more complicated,' Tiss mused as she took another large swig of her wine. But then she had an idea. It wasn't one she thought she should be considering, but under the circumstances felt that it was a viable option. Anita could see she was mulling something over in her head and asked her what it was.

'I was just thinking,' Tiss began, hesitant yet still wanting to ask. 'Are you going back to the Regency any time soon?'

'I think he said he'd like me to go there to do some sketches so that he can see what I could come up with. Why, what are you thinking?'

'Well, I know it's a little risky, but I'd like you to take note of things that you see and hear.'

'What kind of things?'

'Anything, really. For example, has he shown you the areas where your paintings would hang?'

'No,' Anita admitted, 'he just took me through the ground floor rooms and then into one of the private rooms at the back.'

'There are private rooms too?'

'Yes, or more like an office, really. It seems there are offices once you clear through all the public areas.'

'I've been up to the manager's office, but that was on the first floor.'

'I didn't go up there. Maybe the downstairs ones are where the members have meetings? I really don't know.'

'Yes, that seems credible,' Tiss admitted. 'And are all the rooms you saw decorated like the rest of the building, like it was last done at the turn of the 20th century?'

Anita laughed at that description. 'That's probably the best way to describe it, but the office I was in was like any other office – modern, with a desk, printer and filing cabinets. You know, the usual.'

'So does he want modern ones for the offices then?'

'Perhaps, but I don't know. Maybe when I go back he'll show me where they're for.'

Tiss and Anita didn't talk any more about it over dinner, just sharing what had been happening with them in general. But all the while at the back of Tiss' mind was what her friend had said about Tom. She needed to ask him what he had to do with the Regency Club, but she couldn't for the life of her think of how to bring it into a conversation.

CHAPTER
EIGHTEEN

When DC Woodhouse contacted Tiss the next day she could barely take in what he was telling her. A woman had gone missing, and had last been seen near the Regency Club ... again. Then she realised the date. After all that had been going on, what with her having been given the missing persons files from both the detective constable and Jeff Rawlings, and the firm amalgamating with a much bigger company, she'd been distracted and had almost forgotten that the first day of spring was fast approaching. The spring equinox was only a few weeks away; this was no coincidence and just had to be related.

'Who is it?' she'd asked shakily, almost afraid to ask.

'A girl who worked in a restaurant down the street from the club. She left work a couple of nights ago and hasn't been seen since. She fits the profile

JUSTICE

of the other missing women: same age range and
overall appearance.'

'Why are you only finding this out now?'

'The police have to wait a certain length of time
before a person can officially be regarding as
having gone missing.'

Tiss knew the drill, of course she did, but with
the history of missing women, somebody should
have picked up on the time of year they'd all
disappeared. But then again, only someone in the
cold case squad would be aware of them, even the
ones from five years ago. From what she'd already
read in the files, there hadn't seemed to have been
much of an investigation after the fact, and the
overall consensus was that the women had simply
left the area of their own volition despite their
disappearances being overseen at one point by the
ritualistic crimes unit. No bodies had ever been
found, so if they had been murdered in a ritualistic
way then it stood to reason that it couldn't be
proven one way or the other. Somebody had joined
up the dots and put the equinox and solstice as a
factor, enough to call in a special unit to attempt to
handle it, but it had in its own right seemed to have
vanished just as quickly as the women had. Tiss felt
that something decidedly fishy was going on here.
After thanking him for letting her know, she rang
Jeff Rawlings.

'Yes, I've just heard,' he said when she told him
the news.

'How on earth have you heard so quickly?'

He laughed gently. 'I have my sources,' was all he
said in reply, and she could imagine him tapping a
finger against his nose as he said it.

'Of course you do,' Tiss acknowledged. She
should have known by now that would be the case;

why was she even shocked any more. 'You're better than a breaking news report, you know that?'

He laughed again.

'I'd like to know a little bit more about the missing woman, if you can dig anything up, that is.'

'I'll see what I can do.' That seemed to be Jeff's go-to sentence, and Tiss was more than grateful for it. She didn't doubt for one moment that he wouldn't. If there was one thing she'd come to expect from Jeff it was his efficiency to easy find information that other less industrious people would have trouble with. There was a time not so long ago when she would have been, but in this respect she was no longer bothered by the morality, or lack of, of hacking, especially as it seemed there was so much being withheld from the public on a daily basis. She couldn't believe she was even thinking this, what with her background in the legal profession and all, but it seemed to her that sometimes it becomes necessary.

***

Jeff Rawlings contacted her quite unexpectedly the very next day. The body of the missing woman had been found.

Tiss' mind was in a turmoil. This was the first woman who had gone missing around the times the others had who had turned up dead, the others had never been seen or heard from again. This was new. But then there was always the possibility that her disappearance might have had nothing to do with the other ones.

'Where was she found?' she asked, to which Jeff replied that she'd been discovered late last night down by the river.

'The police reports are saying that it looked like she'd been dead for a day or two and that it hadn't just happened last night.'

'One day I'm going to ask you to show me how you do what you do,' Tiss said without missing a beat.

'Not to have me arrested I hope.' Despite his serious tone, Tiss knew it wasn't a serious question.

'No.' She managed to lift her voice up a bit on hearing that. She was genuinely curious as to how Jeff could seemingly find out almost anything he wanted online. Although she was admittedly pretty hopeless at all things relating to how computers work from a programming point of view, she was still interested and intrigued by it. She knew what she knew to get her through her working day, and the sum total of that was logging on and filling in forms, nothing as remotely intricate as finding out things which were supposed to be 100% secure. Anything other than what she knew was alien to her, and she sometimes wished that it wasn't. So, yes, she *was* curious.

'I'm on a half-day today so I'll drop a folder off at your office. Is your receptionist the safest person to hand it to?'

'Yes, Diane and I are friends. Wait, are you suggesting that I should be wary of my fellow solicitors?'

There was a moment of silence on the line before he replied. 'I'm still a little bothered about your hacking incident.'

'You mean somebody could have simply come into my office and twiddled about a bit and done it that way?'

'I don't think "twiddled about" is an accurate term,' he chided her gently for her description, 'but, yes, it's more than possible that somebody could have physically done it and routed it off to an external source.'

Tiss sat back in her chair and let out a loud exhale. Her mind was working overtime. If that had indeed been the case, then who could it have been? She knew everyone, at least she *thought* she knew everyone, and considered them all to be her friends to varying degrees. But this … this was something she'd never in her life contemplated. Could one of her so-called friends had been spying on her on somebody else's behalf?

'I'm finding that very difficult to comprehend,' she admitted.

'I know it's hard, but in my line of work I've discovered that anything, and I mean absolutely anything, is possible, and usually from the most unlikely source or sources.'

'In other words, trust no one.'

'That's my general philosophy, yes.'

'Then I feel honoured that you're trusting me.'

'Well, you're different, Tiss. I *know* you are trustworthy.'

'Thank you,' she smiled into the phone even though he wouldn't be able to see it. 'But how is it even possible to know that about another person? You seem to have an uncanny knack of being able to do it.'

'Ah, it takes time. As well as being able to root out information, I've come over the years to know if a person is being genuine or not, or just cleverly covering up something they don't want others to know.'

'You'd do well as a solicitor, you know that?' Tiss laughed, imagining him being invaluable in a case.

'Or a police officer,' she added. 'So, you're like a human lie detector then?'

'I guess you could say that,' he said proudly.

'Then I'm glad you're on my side.'

***

True to his word, Jeff dropped a large brown envelope off for Diane shortly after lunch. As soon as she had it, the receptionist immediately took it up for Tiss as she'd been forewarned that he would be coming in with something for her. Although she was a friend, albeit not a close one, she'd already involved enough people in this case as it was, and informing an extra one of what she was doing wasn't necessary or advisable. Diane didn't need to know anything about this, and it was probably best not to. Tiss thanked her for it the envelope, then opened it up with her paperknife after she left.

As ever, Jeff had been thorough, and even though the information had just come in, he'd managed to accumulate a great deal for her, presumably from the police and the coroner's office. She wasn't going to ask or even think about its origins. Tracy Dimmock was twenty-seven, and was found on the banks of the river by a dog walker late the previous evening. The coroner's report had concluded that death had been caused by drowning, but on closer examination the water was found to be from a household source rather than from the river. So she'd been killed elsewhere and moved to the spot probably to just get rid of the body. At first Tiss couldn't see how this could possibly be related to the other eight missing women, but as she turned the page she found herself looking at the photo of Tracy and she knew instantly that it was. Tracy, like the other missing women, was dark-haired and had more than a passing resemblance to both them and also to Tiss. The thought sent a chill down her spine when she realised that that could have easily been a photo of herself she was looking at. Was that why Woodhouse was keeping so close, to act as some kind of protection shield for her? If that was the case then she needed to know and, perhaps more importantly, she needed to know why. Exactly what did he know that he wasn't telling her?

That night Tiss did something she didn't ordinarily do; she turned on the local news, something she normally avoid at any cost. As expected, the death of Tracy Dimmock was all over it, but she knew she wouldn't glean anything from it other than what she already knew from Jeff's report. However, she was very surprised to learn that the police already had a suspect in custody. She was also concerned that DC Woodhouse hadn't been in touch again to let her know about it, but then, perhaps he was just busy with the case and all. She quietly chastised herself for her thoughts, about expecting to be first to hear about anything that came up regarding the case. She knew she didn't have a right to assume that.

Tracy Dimmock had worked as a waitress in a restaurant on the same street as the Regency Club. When questioned, her family and friends had all described her as a lovely girl who had been excitedly planning for her wedding with her fiancé Paul in a few months' time. When she didn't return to the home she shared with him that night, he'd approached the police but had been advised to wait for the obligatory twenty-four hours before officially reporting it. Naturally, he had been beside himself, and when she'd been found dead, everyone was shocked beyond belief at what had happened. Her family had also criticised the current police legislation regarding the waiting time to report people going missing, something Tiss had long since agreed with. Granted, some people could and did disappear of their own volition for whatever reason, but when a person's relatives knew categorically that a sudden disappearance wasn't in their behaviour, then they should be listened to and believed by the police and an investigation started immediately. Feeling despondent, Tiss turned the television off. She'd seen all she wanted to. She knew more than ever that she had to get to the bottom of this before anybody else had been reported missing or dead.

CHAPTER
NINETEEN

'Is Dad home?' Tiss asked as she held the phone to her ear. She'd debated whether or not to call, but had eventually relented.

'No he's out at the moment, dear. Is there anything wrong?' Sarah Lawson, Tiss' mother asked, her voice full of concern. 'Is there anything I can help you with?'

The last thing Tiss wanted was to discuss the Regency Club with them again, but found it to be a necessity bearing in mind the latest news of another woman's death in the area. However, as a man, it was her father she needed to speak to the most.

'No Mum, it's him I wanted to speak to. Sorry,' she laughed gently, 'that sounds so rude said out loud.'

'No, no, Tiss, it's not rude at all. But you know if there's anything you want to talk to us about, then we're both here for you. You know that, right?'

'I know, Mum, it's just about what we were talking about when I last came down to see you.'

'That Masonic club that isn't a real one, the Regency Club wasn't it?'

Tiss was surprised she'd remembered, but it seems that she had. 'Yes,' she replied.

'It's still bothering you somehow, isn't it? We did see it on the news the other night about that poor girl's death; do you think it has something to do with the club?'

'I really don't know,' Tiss admitted, although in her heart of hearts she knew that was exactly what she thought.

'And do you think that this has something to do with the Masons, or the society purporting to be them?'

Tiss could hear concern in her voice; concern, most likely, as she herself was part of the women's side of things. 'Again, I really don't know; it's just that I wanted Dad's take on something, that's all.'

'Okay,' Sarah Lawson sounded a bit happier at that response. 'Shall I ask him to give you a call when he comes in then?'

'That would be good. Thanks Mum.'

'And how's it going with that new boyfriend of yours?'

Tiss stiffened. The simple question struck her like a bolt out of the blue. She'd never mentioned Tom to either of them, so how did she know that she was seeing somebody? 'How did you know about that?' she asked, almost frightened to hear the answer.

'Oh!' Tiss mother declared, perhaps realising something that she perhaps shouldn't have been privy to. 'Someone your dad met the other day, someone who knows who you are, said they'd seen you with a boy in a restaurant they were in.'

Yet again another coincidence, one in the many others in this case. The fact that someone they knew had seen her and Tom together, then had gone back to her parents and reported the fact to them, left her feeling cold and, if she admitted it, somewhat suspicious. It seemed so impossible.

'Early days, Mum,' was all Tiss admitted to. 'I was going to tell you, but I don't know how it's going to play out yet, so I thought I'd wait and see.'

'Quite wise,' Sarah said, and Tiss noticed that the tone in her voice had changed. It made her curious. 'Anyway, look, I've got to go out soon, so I'll tell your dad that you called and let him to know that you're waiting to hear from him. Don't be a stranger now.'

'I won't. Speak soon,' and with that the call ended. Tiss didn't quite know what to make of it. It make her wonder if she should ask her father what she wanted to ask him, or perhaps not bother.

***

After ended the call, Tiss' head was spinning, so she rang Jeff Rawlings.

'Hello?' Jeff asked cautiously.

'Can you come around?' she asked with a degree of urgency in her voice.

'Yes, what's the matter?'

'I just need someone I can rely on to talk too,' came the reply.

'On my way.'

Tiss looked at her phone, seeing that he had disconnected, and put it down on the dining table. She pulled out a chair and sat down on it, her elbows on the table and her head resting in her hands. This had got out of control, and she knew it.

It took Jeff around thirty minutes to get to her, and when he rang her doorbell, she invited him in and into the living room.

'What's happening,' he asked as he sat where she indicated.

'I think I'm going completely mad,' she said.

'Okay. In what way?'

'I don't even think I can trust my parents now,' she admitted, causing him to furrow his brows.

'Why, what's happened?'

Tiss went on to explain the fact that both her parents were Freemasons, and she'd wanted to speak to her father further regarding the Regency Club, but then was disturbed by the fact that someone had seen her out with Tom.

'You're seeing someone?' was the unexpected question Jeff asked after hearing her out.

'Well, I've only seen him a couple of times. Why?'

'No, nothing. I didn't know you were with someone.'

'I'm not, not really. I just agreed to go to dinner with him.' For some reason, and one she didn't have an answer for, she left out the fact that she'd introduced him to her friends.

'It could be just coincidence that a friend of your parents saw you out and about.'

'I know, but with all the other weird coincidences that have been going on, it bothered me somewhat.'

'And what is it that you wanted me to do?'

Tiss sat back in the chair and looked at him. 'It's going to sound strange.'

'Believe me, I've probably heard stranger,' he laughed.

'I'd like you to visit the Regency Club.'

Jeff stared at her, which she had to admit made her feel a bit uncomfortable.

'Well, say something,' she said meekly.

'Okay,' he said at last.

'Okay?' she asked in surprise. She'd at least expected an argument, or a logical reason why her suggestion was such a bad idea. What she hadn't expected was for him to agree to do it.

'Yes. It seems like a good idea.'

'And would you be able to pull it off. I mean, could you easily pass as someone who potentially wanted to join the Freemasons?'

'I'll let you into a little secret,' he said as he leaned forward in his seat. 'The company where I officially work has been trying to get me to join them for years, but I've always told them that it's not something I'm interested in. I know for a fact that I could easily get an introduction if I wanted one.'

'And you're willing to do that ... for me?'

'Like I say, I think the reason behind it is sound. If I'm being truthful, you've got me hooked on this thing as much as you are, and I'd welcome the chance to take a look around the place.'

Tiss just sat open-mouthed hearing him out. She'd never in a million years believed that he would agree to it, and had envisaged a long drawn out conversation of her trying to persuade him.

'You know, I've always fancied myself as a bit of a detective,' he admitted with a smile. 'Now I might just get a chance to live out my childhood fantasy!'

'I certainly didn't have that as a childhood fantasy, but it seems to have turned out that way!' Tiss laughed, albeit somewhat nervously. 'I always knew where I was going to end up.'

'But was your choice of career based on what you wanted, or what your parents' heritage was, or what was expected of you as their offspring?'

Tiss frowned at that question. 'You know, Jeff, nobody has ever asked me that. Like I say, there was never any doubt in my mind about what my future would hold. However, if I had to do it all again, I might not be so certain.'

'And why is that?'

'This whole case. I think it's opened my eyes to a world I really didn't know existed. My life, as relatively short as it's been, has been centred on representing truth and honesty. But then this whole business has opened my eyes somewhat to the fact that people can be less than honest – very dishonest, in fact. For starters, the police force. Why had the Regency Club not been questioned about the disappearances when every other business in the street they are on has? Had someone on the inside wiped that information from existence, as it's certainly starting to look like that. And why is there very little about them available publicly? You've only found out what you can about them through your expert skills.'

'My expert skills, eh?' Jeff smiled before continuing. 'But, yes, I know what you mean. And that's one of the reasons why I'll gladly do this to satisfy my own curiosity as well as yours.'

'Well, I'd be extremely grateful if you could do this. I think I'd be forever in your debt.'

'There's no need for that; no debt required. I'm happy to do it for you, and I only hope I can give you some answers to all this.'

CHAPTER
TWENTY

Tiss' father got back to her later that night,
and she asked him to tell her all that he could
about the spring equinox and winter solstice
and any rituals surrounding them. He'd been
slightly amazed that she remembered that from all
those years ago, but if he was curious as to why she
was asking, then he didn't ask. She learned a lot
from him, and he even sent her a few links to
websites of interest. It was during her search that
she discovered why the number five had stuck in
her head when she'd heard about the span of years
between the women going missing. In hindsight,
how could she not have remembered? The five-
pointed star, or pentagram, traditionally
represents the five elements: earth, air, fire, water,
and spirit, but today is seen as having a close
connection to the supernatural, and specifically as
a defence against witches, evil spirits, and demons.
Sometimes the inverted figure of the pentagram,

with two points facing upward and one facing down, is associated with negative or black magic and devil worship. So this is why the ritualistic team got involved, she thought. Did they believed the women going missing had something to do with black magic, or had they actually found something to substantiate it? She didn't know, and Woodhouse hadn't said, but Tiss had to admit that even the thought terrified her. She'd seen horror films of that genre, and it wasn't something she wanted to get herself, or her friends, mixed up with. It never seemed to end well for anyone that did.

Tiss spent most of the next few days thinking about the plan she'd set in motion with Jeff, wondering if he'd managed to pretend to relent to the requests and get himself invited to join the Freemasons. The temptation to ring him was overwhelming, but he'd said that he would be in touch as soon as he had news for her. The waiting, however, was intolerable, so she threw herself into the job, seeing the throng of new clients the amalgamation had attracted in addition to the ones they'd already acquired from the publicity a while earlier. All in all the business was thriving. Then there was the upcoming spring equinox on her mind and what that meant in relation to everything. The dreaded date was fast approaching; would another woman go missing before then, or would another one turn up dead like Tracy Dimmock, assuming, that is, that her death was in any way related to the mystery surrounding the club.

She was deep in thought when there was a sudden knock on the door. 'Yes?' she called out and watched as the door opened to reveal Diane standing there.

'Can I come in?' the receptionist asked sheepishly, in a manner so unlike her normal bubbly self.

'Yes, of course. There's no need to stand on ceremony,' Tiss said with a chuckle, but Diane's face didn't show any sign of humour. In fact, she looked troubled.

'I've just heard something that I think you should hear,' Diane said as she gently closed the door behind her and approached Tiss' desk.

'Oh?'

Diane sat down and began to fidget nervously with her hands, and Tiss wondered what she could have heard that had distressed her so much. Her whole manner wasn't like the woman she knew.

'I was taking a signed for letter along to Mr Barnes' office, and was just about to knock when I overheard something he was saying. I knew I shouldn't have listened, but ...' she trailed off temporarily as if having in internal battle with herself. 'Anyway, as I could only hear his voice I assumed he was on the phone to somebody. But he was talking about you, Tiss.'

'About me? What was he saying?'

'Well, it's so strange, but I knew that I had to come and tell you. He said that, and I quote, "things are going well with Ms Lawson".'

Tiss shuffled in her seat, assessing the information. 'But that could just mean that he's happy with my progress professionally, don't you think?'

'Yes, I agree. But it was what he said next that troubled me the most.'

Tiss felt a shiver go through her, a primal fear that what she was about to hear would not be pleasant. 'Go on,' she instructed her friend.

'He said that it's getting close to the time and that he and whoever he was speaking to should move things forward.'

It wasn't as expected and, again, Barnes could be referring to her work. She began to open her mouth to speak, but Diane cut in again. 'He said that you were the key to everything in the future, the key to their success.'

Tiss sat back in her chair. Whereas what had come before could easily have been taken as something to do with work, the actual phrasing of that latest piece of information was suspect. 'I'm the key to what?' she muttered, almost to herself, but Diane picked up on it.

'I don't know, but I didn't like the sound of it. It sounded conspiratorial if you ask me.' She then rose from her seat. 'I just had to tell you. I'd better be getting back; people will be wondering where I am.'

'Yes ... thank you, Diane,' Tiss said, watching her friend as she walked to the door and left the room. When she'd gone, she mulled over what had been said. It would have all sounded normal in her opinion had it not been for the last thing: the key to their success. What on earth did that even mean? Making a grab for her mobile phone, she dialled Jeff. Apart from Ruby and Claudia, he was the only one she really trusted in all this.

'Hello?' came the questioning response. 'Is everything okay, Tiss?' a concerned Jeff asked her.

'I don't know,' she said to him. She heard movement down the line, the sound of voices then a door opening and closing, as if Jeff was moving to somewhere he couldn't be heard as he spoke to her. She waited, feeling frantic, and drained of all her normal composure, but when he asked her to explain what herself she managed to tell him what was bothering her.

'Well, I mean it could all be nothing, but I agree in that it sounds odd,' he finally said. There was only his voice now, no other sounds around him. Wherever he was it was safe for him to talk … and private.

'I think that's putting it mildly.'

'And you think that it's directly connected to what we're looking into?'

'If not then I don't know what is. Barnes referred to me as the key to everything in the future, to their success; I can't see that as being anything to do with my work.'

'Then I really don't know what to make of it.' The line fell silent for a while, and Tiss heard a ventilation fan start up somewhere. It was the only noise she could hear. Finally, Jeff said he'd try something, but was adamant not to tell her what that was.

'It's illegal, isn't it?' she asked.

'Don't ask,' came the reply. 'But, just to let you know, I've put a few feelers out to the people who invited me to join the Masons. One of them has just come back to me this morning, and we're going out for a drink to discuss it this evening. You won't believe where we're going for the drink.'

'Not the Regency Club!'

'Not quite, but it's across the street from it.'

'That's great. But listen, are you sure you're okay with doing this?'

'I am. To be honest, I've always been a bit curious about what goes on with the Masons. This will feed two things with one stone.'

'That's kill two birds with one stone!' Tiss corrected, allowing a small laugh to issue forth from her.

'Yeah, something like that,' he laughed. Talking to Jeff was so easy. In all the time that she'd known Lily, she now wondered why she'd never met him before. For one thing, she told herself, she'd never found herself in this precarious position before, that's why. In any case, she was glad of his involvement now.

The next morning, just after she'd got into work, he texted her two words: I'm in.

***

Despite his innermost sense of bravado, Jeff Rawlings admittedly felt anxious as he and his colleague Dave headed to the bar the latter had recommended to him. Was it coincidence that it just happened to be near the club? He thought not. There was nothing at all to feel anxious about, he reminded himself. All he was doing was taking him up on an offer he'd made some time ago and hear him out on the matter– even though he wasn't really taking him up on anything, and it was all for this bizarre case he was working on with Tiss. And it was bizarre, he admitted that to himself. What he'd planned to do at some point was say that he'd heard good things about the Regency Club in the hope that he'd be invited to go and see it before deciding whether or not he'd join the Masons. But he still had that churning sensation in the pit of his stomach, nevertheless. He was good at stealth computer work, always had been, doing things behind the scenes without having to even speak to anyone most of the time, so actually being out there in person was something entirely different for him, and he had to admit that it scared him somewhat.

'You know I've been waiting a long time for you to agree to this,' Dave said as they sat down at a table in a secluded corner of the pub.

'I haven't agreed to it yet,' Jeff smiled, 'only to get some more information about it all.' He took a drink from his pint and rubbed the froth from his upper lip with the back of his hand as he set the glass down on the table.

'But I can tell you're keen,' came the reply, along with a broad smile.

'Well, yes, admittedly I am.' Jeff decided to play along with it as best as he could. When he and Lily Singer became acquainted a few years back, he'd never envisage the day would come when he would become involved in a bit of private detecting himself. His association with her was always to be in the background, as a tech backup for any information he could glean which was relevant to any of her cases. It was different on the front line, and he wondered how she did it every day of her life. He knew that some of his work could be classed as deception, well, the vast majority of it, but doing it face-to-face was an entirely different matter. It was frightening.

As the evening wore on, Jeff learned more about the Freemasons than he thought he knew. Despite his belief that it was steeped in religious ceremony and a means by which to forward oneself, he found that it was quite the opposite. He learned about the benevolent aspect of the society, which made it amongst the biggest charitable donors in the UK. He also learned of the camaraderie amongst the members, rather like social media connections than business ones, and Dave stressed that it was frowned upon to use any connection to other members for personal gain. This surprised him as he believed along with many other people who didn't fully understand how it operated that personal gain was the intent of joining. After hearing him out, Jeff made his colleague aware that he was now more inclined to accept the offer of acceptance than he had been before. He managed to discreetly mention the Regency in that he'd heard that it could be a Masonic lodge. Dave had responded just the way he'd hoped, although he did say that it wasn't a lodge in the normal sense of the word, which intrigued him even more, but he didn't push for an explanation. When Dave then invited him along on the Friday evening to see what he thought about it, he agreed without hesitation. Dave said that he would meet him outside at 8pm and take him in as his guest and show him around. He couldn't believe his luck, so first thing the next day he texted Tiss to tell her that he was in.

'That's great,' she'd texted back, asking if she could call him instead of continuing with text messages. He said that she could.

'Tell me all about it then,' she said from the safety of her own office. She'd been sure to check if anyone was waiting on one of the seats outside before ringing him. She knew that even if her door was closed, somebody sitting across from her office door would still be able to hear her, and it was not a conversation she wanted anyone to hear – especially with Barnes' rather odd comments to whoever on the phone about her.

Jeff went through all the details, eventually asking what it was she wanted him to specifically take in at the club.

'When my friend Anita was there she told me that there were rooms at the back of the building, just beyond the main body of the club. I'm just wondering what they actually are. Fred Marshall told her that they were meeting rooms for anyone wanting a more private meeting space.'

Jeff laughed at that point.

'What?' she asked, curious as to why he'd thought that to be amusing.

'You know what that sounds like, don't you?'

'No,' she admitted.

'It sounds like a place where a couple of the patrons might like a little one on one time with each another.'

The penny finally dropped. 'Oh,' was all Tiss could say, admitting to herself that that was the last thing she'd could have ever envisaged.

'Well it is a club for gentlemen,' he continued with a slightly humorous note in his voice.

'But what about Miriam Marshall going in with a young companion that time? I know her husband said she was there enquiring about a place where she could hold a meeting, or something like that. Do you think it's possible then that the club is being used as a brothel on the side?'

'Who knows what people get up to these days. I'm not sure anything would surprise me if it's the case.'

'Interesting,' was all she could find to say.

'I'll take in all I can when I'm there on Friday. Do you want me to call or text when I'm done?'

'Friday night I'm out with my friends, and I'm not sure what time I'll get back home as we always go on to a club after we've eaten. Perhaps we could meet up on Saturday if you have anything interesting to tell me?'

'That seems like a good idea. Actually, there's a new restaurant just opened that I hear is good, so maybe we could meet up there?'

'Sure, why not.'

'So, I'll let you know sometime on Friday if I have news or not and we can take it from there?'

'Yes, that sounds good.'

CHAPTER
TWENTY-ONE

Despite the fraudulent nature of the situation, Jeff Rawlings decided to dress to impress. He figured that if he scrubbed up nicely it would look like he was being undeniably sincere in his desire to become a member of the fraternal organisation. So he chose a smart charcoal suit, the one that he normally saved for important business meetings, a close-fitting light grey shirt, and topped the whole look off with a silver patterned tie. He decided to give the matching waistcoat a miss; he wasn't going to a wedding after all. As he looked at himself in the full length mirror in his bedroom, he smiled to himself. He looked good, even if he thought so himself, but that was the whole intention. He wanted to create a positive impression of someone who had gone out of his way to look presentable for something those he would be meeting considered to be important. First impressions, and all that.

He caught an Uber to the club, and alighted from it at exactly five minutes to eight. Early enough not to show over-eagerness, yet prompt enough to show keenness. The street was situated in an historic part of town, and he'd only taken a tertiary look at it when over the street at the bar with his friend from work. The textured walls, asymmetrical shapes, and decorative trims of the buildings clearly revealed their architectural origins to be from the Victorian era, a period in history known for its eclectic and ornate style. As the car drew away, heading off to pick up its next customer, Jeff looked up at the building's façade. For some reason it stood out from the rest, as if it exuded an aura of historical significance apart from its neighbours, giving the impression of existing in a kind of time bubble which preserved it for posterity. It aligned perfectly with Tiss' description of it, and he couldn't wait to see the inside.

'Impressive, isn't it?' Dave's voice as he descended the steps of the building to welcome him brought Jeff out of his reverie.

'Just a bit,' he enthused, finding it easy to slip into his role at this point. He *was* impressed, and it looked as if his face couldn't hide that fact.

'If you're impressed just standing here, wait until you get inside,' he laughed, gesturing for him to follow him into the building.

As Jeff ascended the stone steps he could feel his pulse quicken. He was about to do it; he was about to embark on his first physical interaction in the world of deception, which was much more concerning than sitting behind the security of a computer monitor to access hidden information. Here he was out in the open, laid bare and having to exist on his wits alone. Yet, as much as it was terrifying, it was also intoxicating, and he secretly thanked Tiss for giving him this exclusive opportunity.

Once through the heavy oak doors, Jeff found himself catapulted headlong into another world. Just as Tiss had described it, the dark green velvet curtains and the loud patterned wallpapered walls reeked of a past life, a life the Freemasons were evidently stuck in. He found it hard to see how such a society was relevant today, apart from it being a way to further oneself both career-wise and financially despite what Dave had told him of its supposed benevolence.

'I have a guest with me today, George,' Dave proudly announced to the elderly uniformed gentleman behind the mahogany desk.

'That's good to hear, sir,' came the reply as the man indicated the sign-in book on top of the desk. Heeding his notion, Dave picked up the pen that was resting in the crease of the book and wrote something in it. Jeff couldn't see what it was, but assumed it was both their names and the time of their arrival.

'Right then,' Dave clapped his hands together after laying the pen down again. 'Let's get you a drink and then I'll give you the guided tour.' Jeff was on high alert, ready to take in every last thing he saw ready to report back to Tiss.

Jeff followed Dave through a set of double doors off from the main reception area. This led, not unsurprisingly, to another Victorian-inspired room more fitting with the images of gentlemen's clubs he'd ever seen on television. The rich mahogany of the reception desk followed through into this room by way of a series of panels along the lower half of the walls. Another vivid wallpaper, similar to the one he'd already seen but with a mixture of greens and reds, graced the upper walls. The aroma of wood, leather and fine whisky reached his nostrils; it was an intoxicating and heady smell, and very masculine. No floral fragrances in the establishment. A few club members sat in leather chairs or sofas as he passed by them, heads turning to look at him as he followed Dave to the well-stocked bar.

'What can I get you?' Dave asked to which Jeff replied that he'd have a whisky on the rocks.

'Make that two, John, and put it on my tab.'
The bartender nodded and proceeded to make both men their requested drinks.

'Well, what do you think of the place so far?' Dave asked with a beaming smile. He was trying his hardest to recruit him by the look of it, and Jeff wondered if introductions earned the introducer a commission. Either that or some other form of reward might be doled out for bringing new blood to the fraternity.

'Yes, I like what I'm seeing,' Jeff nodded enthusiastically, thinking he'd like it much more if he could come away with something, anything, to offer Tiss.

'Good, good. Right then, follow me,' he said as he picked up both glasses the bartender put in front of them and handed one to Jeff.

Jeff followed along as he was led through a variety of rooms, including a games room, a dining room, and a library. The building was far bigger inside than it appeared from the street, and he was still only on the ground floor. Tiss had said that the first floor was office space, at least the section she'd been taken to, but if it echoed the size of this then it was enormous up there, and he was sure there was another floor above that according to what he'd seen of the building from the outside. Anything could be going on in here, legal or illegal, and nobody would be the wiser.

After a while they'd come full circle, and Jeff found himself back in the room where the bar was. The interested eyes of before gave him a tertiary glance again before continuing with what they'd been doing beforehand.

'You're lucky in that we have a couple of the shareholders in here today, and I know that they'd be happy to meet a prospective new member. Are you up to meeting them?' Dave asked hopefully, his face aglow with hope once again. Yes, Jeff thought, this man was definitely on some kind of compensation.

'Sure, why not.' He followed Dave to a section separate from the main club. The modern decor of magnolia walls and preformed MDF doors were in stark contrast to the rest of the club's Victorian theme. Jeff instinctively knew this was where Tiss' friend Anita had been taken to discuss business. They walked down a corridor until Dave stopped at a door and knocked.

'Come in,' came the reply, and Jeff indicated Dave should enter the room first before him. Upon entering it became clear that he'd been expected, as the two men sitting behind a desk rose from their seats to greet him. 'Thanks Dave, we can take it from here,' the elder of the two men said to Jeff's companion, and after nodding, he left with a quick "see you later" to Jeff before leaving, closing the door behind him.

'Good evening Mr Rawlings,' the man said with a friendly tone. 'My name is Frederick Marshall and this is Tom Davenport, we're both on the board of directors and fully affiliated club members ourselves.' Jeff managed to conceal what he was thinking as he shook the offered hands of both men. 'Please take a seat.' He sat down on the chair which had been set out for him, his mind reeling about what this meant for Tiss. Across from him sat the person she'd been seeing for the past few weeks, and here he now was at the heart of the Regency Club and whatever else might be happening in the place. He wasn't sure how she was going to take it. Although he *did* know how she was going to take it – she wasn't going to take it well.

'Nice to meet you,' he managed to say in the calmest way he could manage.

'So, you're thinking about joining us then,' Marshall continued and Jeff nodded his head in response. 'And exactly why would you like to do that?'

Jeff, to his credit, had remembered a great deal from all the times somebody had tried to recruit him, and there had been a few over the years. At the time, though, he'd politely refused and put it to the back of his mind, but now found himself having to draw on his memory of everything that had taken place to provide him with a satisfactory answer, or at least one that would appease them. He also drew upon what Dave had told him the previous day and responded as best as he could, which must have been the correct reply judging by the smiles he got from the two men. After a further ten minutes or so of him being carefully scrutinised, Fred Marshall gave his final deliberation.

'Well, Mr Rawlings, it's been a pleasure meeting you. We will, of course, have to meet with the other members of the board to put forward your application, but I can tell you now that we will be recommending you for membership.'

Jeff let out a breath he didn't even know he was holding in. Part of him was thrilled, yet another part of him was horrified. The last thing he ever wanted to do was become a member of the Freemasons for job furtherment or profit as that was something he could do on his own terms using his own talent. Yet here he was, for the sake of a case, finding himself being accepted into it. As the two men rose to their feet, Jeff did the same and once again shook their proffered hands.

'Oh,' Marshall added as they were walking him to the door, 'we'll have to get you in a couple more times before then, but we'll try to get everything completed so that you can join us for our annual general meeting on the 23rd of March. We usually hold them twice a year, in the spring and in the winter.'

'We think you'll enjoy it,' Tom Davenport added with a smirk. 'I wasn't with them for the last one, but I've been told that the members really get to let their hair down on those dates.'

'Let your hair down?' Jeff tried to act casually even though he fully realised that the implications of the spring and winter meant.

Fred Marshall laughed. 'We're a male-only club apart from those two nights. We usually hire in some female company for the evenings, if you get my drift!'

'Ah, I see,' Jeff nodded, forcing a smile. But then, a thought came to him, something he would have to put past Tiss and see what her reaction to it would be.

Once back in the corridor, he saw Dave standing at an open doorway chatting with someone inside.

Seeing Jeff leave the office, he said something to the person on the other side of it and made a move towards him.

'I'll leave you in the capable hands of Mr Dixon then, and we'll see you soon I expect,' Marshall ended with before retreating back into the office.

Jeff stayed longer than expected, and had a couple more drinks with Dave before heading home, his mind working overtime. It was now far too late to contact Tiss; he'd contact her first thing, even though he wanted to do so right at that very moment.

CHAPTER
TWENTY-TWO

'They said what?' Tiss almost shouted down the phone. She'd opened up and read Jeff's text message as soon as she got into the office, and had to call him straight back.

'I knew you'd say that,' he replied as he held his phone away from his ear, 'which led me on to doing a bit more research when I got back home. What Fred Marshall said implied that the club hired … how can I put this … ladies of the night-'

'That's very prudish of you, Jeff,' Tiss laughed despite the seriousness of the situation.

'Well, call me old-fashioned. But that led me on to look at the files of the missing women again. I know a guy who knows a guy, and I'm going to ask him if he recognises their names.'

'And who exactly is this *guy*?' she asked.

'Someone who knows a bit about the town's underbelly. In other words, he knows the names of quite a few women who would fit into that category – depending, of course, if the two things are linked.'

'And he knows them how; personally or by association?'

'In his case, I think a bit of both. But what I'm trying to say here is, in light of what Marshall told me, I think it's fair to say that they hire in women on these two AGM nights at the club.'

'But you're not suggesting that the missing women were all hookers, are you?'

'That I don't know. Escorts are not necessarily all hookers – to use your choice of the word. I do know from some people I've spoken to that they sometime hire someone to accompany them to events, for the sole purpose of being their "date" for the night. No sex involved, just payment for a service that's all.'

'Ah, I see. But we could be way off the mark here.'

'In what way?' he asked, as the idea seemed the only logical explanation to him, and logic was something thought he knew so well.

'It's just an assumption after all, but I *do* think if they accept you – and it looks as if they will – it will be good to have access to the club and everything that's going on in there.'

'You mean you want me to snoop?'

'I kind of thought that was the idea,' Tiss came back with. 'But safely, of course. The last thing I want you to do is get yourself so embroiled in this that you get caught.'

'But at least I'll have a good solicitor if I do.'

There was a moment's pause on the line before Tiss began laughing. Not that the situation was funny, but rather what Jeff said offered a respite from the seriousness of what they were discussing.

'What have I said?' he asked, oblivious, but she continued laughing. He thought it best to allow her that before he told her the next piece of information as he didn't think she would enjoy it. 'There is one other thing I think I should tell you,' he continued when her laughter died down some.

'There's more?' she asked in all seriousness, no hint of either sarcasm or fun.

Jeff didn't quite know how to tell her, but tell her he knew he must. 'It's just … the two men I saw, well, you are familiar with them both.'

'Who are they?'

'Fred Marshall and …' he hesitated slightly before continuing. 'And … Tom Davenport.'

'Tiss, are you still there,' Jeff said into what was now a dead line. She'd hung up.

***

It wasn't until lunch time that Tiss rang him back. He was in a meeting, but he excused himself in order to answer it.

'I'm so sorry, Jeff. I didn't mean to-' she began but he cut her off.

'Hey, hey, stop that. It was a shock, I realise that, and I held off telling you until the moment came that I couldn't. Listen, I think my joining was a mere formality, as Marshall said that he intended to get me initiated and into the society before the 23rd. Hopefully, by then I'll be able to gather some information about what's going on, and Tom's involvement in it all.'

'But didn't Marshall say they were both on the board of directors, so he must be involved in it somehow. If you're going to be doing what I think you'll be doing, like hack into their computer system, I can only hope that you'll be careful. I'd hate to think I'd initiated all this and left you vulnerable and exposed.

'I will; I always am, you know me.'

'But this is dangerous, Jeff. Like *really* dangerous.'

'Tiss, you've no idea about half the things I've been hired to do. I'll be careful, like I always am.

'But if these people are murderers … what about then?'

'Well, I'll just have to find out if they are first, and that means having to go undercover.'

'But you'll end up being a Mason, and I know for a fact that's not something you want.'

'Tiss, I don't mind in the slightest if it means we'll get to the truth and manage to stop whatever's happening there. Besides, I've discovered that it's not quite the establishment I falsely believed it to be.'

'So you're okay with it?'

'To a point.'

The line went quiet for a while before Tiss asked about what he'd said - that she had no idea about half the things he'd done.

Jeff laughed. 'One day, Tiss Lawlor. One day I'll tell you, but not today.'

'That bad, huh?'

'Well …' he drawled, 'you know.'

***

Tiss began to feel that she was living two lives: the life of a solicitor, and the life of a private investigator. And the worst of it was she didn't know which of the two she currently preferred. There were now only two weeks until the 23rd of March; two weeks for another woman to go missing and end up who knows where, dead more than likely. It was almost more than she could bear.

Jeff knew he had to go through two more "trials", vaguely comparing himself to Hercules at one point, and an initiation ceremony before his acceptance and admittance to the club and the AGM, and Tiss was admittedly very worried for him. She'd been the one to suggest he go through with the process in the first place just to appease her curiosity about the club. Had she asked too much of him, she wondered. He'd happily agreed to it, but was still worried that he'd simply done as she'd asked. So with that in mind she decided to ring her private investigator friend.

'Yes, he's told me all about it,' Lily confirmed after Tiss had explained the situation.

'I'm worried about him,' Tiss admitted.

'You know he is a big boy,' the PI chuckled.

'I know, but I'm worried I've put him in a precarious situation.'

'I'm sure he's been in far worse.'

Tiss knew Lily was probably right, but it still didn't stop her from having second thoughts about his involvement in it all. She felt guilty for asking him to get mixed up in this in the first place. 'I wish Frank Marshall had never come into my office that day,' she sighed.

'Do you want to meet up for lunch?' Lily asked after a pause.

'I can't today, but if you're free after work I could do with a really strong drink!'

'I can do that,' came the enthusiastic reply.

Tiss could barely get through the day. All the events of the past few weeks kept overwhelming her thoughts, and she felt sure that her professionalism was slipping along with it. She had to ask one or two of her clients to repeat what they'd said to her, barely taking their plights and woes in as they talked to her about their problems. In truth, she felt as though she shouldn't be in work at all today with all this going on in her head. She only hoped none of her colleagues noticed her distraction and reported it to Sanderson. By the time 5pm came around she was done in, and so looking forward to meeting up with Lily.

'What's really worrying you about all this?' Lily asked as they sat down in a quiet spot at a bar where she'd recommended they meet.

'That it's dangerous,' Tiss replied succinctly.

'Life can be dangerous every day of the week.'

'You know what I mean.' Tiss downed half the contents of her wine glass in one go, causing Lily to raise an enquiring eyebrow at her.

'Wow, this is really causing you some problems, isn't it?'

'Isn't this bothering you though? You've known Jeff far longer than I have, so do you think he'll be okay doing this?'

'To a degree, but only a small one. You know, Tiss, Jeff and I have been involved in some pretty hair raising situations over the years, some even more difficult than this one, and we've managed to scrape through all right. You may just see him as a computer hacker, but he's as much as an investigator as I am, probably better, in fact.'

'I don't just think of him as a computer hacker, not now at least. I'll admit that I did at first, but my conception of him has changed the more I've come to know him.'

'He likes you, you know,' Lily said quietly as she sipped at her glass of wine, taking her time with it rather than chugging it as Tiss had done. She glanced across at her friend, waiting for her reaction to what she'd said.

'And I like him,' Tiss replied matter-of-factly as she looked intently at her now half-empty glass, wondering how it was far less than Lily's.

Lily knew she hadn't heard her properly. 'No, I mean that he really likes you, as in he's very fond of you. Why do you think he's so invested in this?'

Tiss looked across at her friend, eyes wide at the connotation. Did Jeff really think of her in that way? If he did then she'd never picked up on anything that would define it to her. Yes, she had to admit that she liked him, but she'd been so caught up in the whole sorry mess she'd got herself entangled in that perhaps she'd overlooked that blatantly obvious piece of information – obvious to anybody else but her, that was.

'I ... what?'

'He likes you Tiss, in that he'd like to go out with you. I can't say it any plainer than that.'

'He ... what? He actually told you that?'

'Well he really didn't need to as I could see it all for myself, but, yes, he actually told me that.'

Tiss sat back in her seat, her mind working overtime. Firstly she'd discovered that her would-be boyfriend, Tom Davenport, was somehow mixed up in this convoluted case, and now that her partner-in-crime, Jeff Rawlings, was somehow secretly holding a candle for her. This was not how she'd expected her day to go. She let out a laugh, which surprised her companion.

'What's wrong?' Lily asked frowning. She hadn't expected that kind of reaction. An argument or a claim that it couldn't possibly be true. The last thing she'd expected was a full-on belly laugh.

'Oh, Lily,' Tiss wiped her eyes, avoiding her mascara as best as she could. 'I've spent years, and I mean years, without the companionship of a man, and now here I am with two of them competing for my attention. This is the old you wait hours for a bus and then three come along all at the same time kind of thing. How have I become so attractive to the opposite sex all of a sudden!'

'Come on, Tiss, you're an attractive woman. I've often wondered why you're still single. Men should be lining up to want to date you.'

'Ha! My parents would tell you that I'm a workaholic. It's true, I am, but it's also true that I've never found who many would refer to as "the one". Nobody's ever come close to fitting that bill for me, so I guess I'm far too particular in that respect.'

'You're selling yourself short, you know that, right?'

'Am I?

'Yes, you are. You're a catch, girl, and the sooner you realise that the better. And when you do, you have somebody ready and waiting to step up.'

'Oh, come on,' Tiss tsked. 'Really?'

'Tiss, he's even willing to join the Freemasons for you in order to find some resolution to your case. Like I said, Jeff is keen, and he's waiting for the green light.'

Tiss was so thrown that she could barely remember why she'd agreed to come out for a drink in the first place. Ah, yes, Frank Marshall; the source of everything that was going wrong in her life right now. She wanted somebody to sound off with about him, but here she was discussing Jeff's little crush on her. Her life was normally a straight line from A to B with everything in its place, and she enjoyed it, until, that is, Frank Marshall walked into her life that morning and had turned it all upside down.

'So,' Lily said bringing Tiss out of her internal ramblings, 'the only thing now is to let Jeff do his thing at the club and see what kind of information he can glean from them before the 23rd.'

'And if he doesn't?'

'Then I don't doubt there'll be another missing woman by then.'

CHAPTER
TWENTY-THREE

All Tiss could do now was sit and wait, but apart from the Marshall brothers and the Regency Club, she now had something else to think about: Jeff Rawlings. She was also troubled by what her friend Anita had told her regarding Tom Davenport, to the extent that she'd told him she couldn't meet him for their prearranged date that week, citing extra work related to the amalgamation of the company into the Milton Group as the cause. Further than that, she had no idea what to say to him until Jeff could provide any more information. In truth, it had changed her opinion of him, of course it had. Things were starting to turn over nicely, and she admitted to herself that she'd started to like him *that* way rather than them just meeting up for a meal or a drink as friends. And she was worried about what had been said, that things were "going well" with her. What on earth had that meant? Had their relationship been planned from the start for nefarious reasons unknown to her at this point? It didn't bode well for Tiss, so she'd keep her distance from him until such a time as it did, or he was proved to be using her for an ulterior motive.

Work was hectic. Apart from the increased workload the business had picked up of late, each solicitor had been asked to write a thesis of no less than two thousand words describing what their work entailed prior to the amalgamation. Tiss felt like she was back in university again.

'And they now want us to write two thousand words to justify our existence!' Tiss exclaimed as she sat next to Diane in *The Daily Grind* across the street at lunch time. She looked at the sandwich in front of her in disgust, as if it had personally affronted her.

'They've asked me as well,' Diane admitted, 'albeit only a thousand words. Seems we are all having to justify ourselves. It must be the Milton Group's doing rather than Sanderson and Barnes and they already know what we do and how we do it.'

'Yes, probably,' Tiss was still staring her cheese and tomato concoction down as she mumbled her response. She was furious; furious at having to do it in the first place, and furious about Tom Davenport's connection to the Regency Club. In fact she was furious about almost anything at the moment, but there was also anxiety mixed in with the fury. She was worried about Jeff Rawlings and the depth to which he was getting himself mixed up with the Freemasons even though it was at her request. But then she was reminded of the words her father had spoken to her a few months back. He's been adamant that the club was nothing to do with the Masons, and if anybody would know then he would being one himself. He'd even gone as far as calling somebody up on the telephone to confirm it for her. But how? How did members of the society not know the location of another Lodge? And then it hit her. Although she'd seen the symbol etched on a brick outside the main entrance to the building, which must have been there for as long as the building was, that didn't necessarily mean that it *was* a Lodge, at least not an official one. So, what was it then, a pseudo one? She had to ring Jeff and tell him after her lunch break. Suddenly the sandwich in front of her didn't look all that bad.

'Makes sense, I suppose,' Jeff said pensively on the other end of the line.

'So it could all be a fake then?'

'I mean, it could just be a bunch of rich public school businessmen forming their own little Masonic-like club; there's nothing to say there can't be breakaway groups I guess.'

'But didn't they say they were the Masons?' Tiss continued.

'Well, yes, they did, at least that's what they're calling themselves. But if they want to have a little members-only group that they want to refer to as "Masonic" without it actually being so, then that's their prerogative I suppose.'

'But isn't that bringing anyone in under false pretences?'

'Essentially, yes. I know what you're saying, and I get it, and I don't like it either. I don't like any of what seems to be going on in there, but if there's a chance of getting into the place so that I can delve a bit deeper into it, then I say we give it a go and take it.'

'We? It's you who's in the firing line here. You're the one who's having to do all this, not me, and I'm concerned for your welfare. It's dangerous; *they're* potentially dangerous.'

'I'm touched that you're concerned, but we've set the wheels in motion now and I know neither of us want to give up and let it go.'

Tiss remained silent. What he said was true as she couldn't give this up now if she tried.

'Tiss?'

'Yes, I hear you, and you're right. But please be careful.'

'I will be. I've just heard that they'd like me to go in on Friday for the second part of the induction.'

'And what's that? Will it make a difference now that you suspect that they're not officially part of the fraternity?'

'Yes and no to the difference thing as I'm going to play it by ear. They want me to meet with the board of directors and be questioned by them.'

'Questioned? As in ...?'

'Just an extension of the questions Marshall and Davenport asked me, but more official rather than the informal chat we had. The final hurdle, as it were, to be accepted. Now that we've had this discussion I feel a little better about the fact that it might not being official as I was never happy about secret societies and the like. If it wasn't for the fact that it would likely set alarm bells off, I'd come out and ask them straight if it's legit or not, but I want to get in and snoop around a bit and see what's what.'

'You'll let me know how it goes afterwards?'

'Of course.'

'And do be careful.'

'Always.'

***

How Tiss got through the week she'll never know, but Friday came around before she knew it.

'Are you okay?' Ruby asked her with concern as they sat around their table at *The Olive Garden*. 'You've been a bit off since we met.'

'Am I?' Tiss didn't realised she'd seemed that down to everyone, but there was a lot on her mind, like how Jeff was doing at his meeting with the board of directors. 'As Claudia will tell you,' she nodded her head in her coworker's direction, 'things are quite hectic at work what with trying to get everything in order for the first of the month when the amalgamation takes place.'

'Yes, that's right,' Claudia chimed in. 'And as for that thesis we have to do, well, what a carry on. Felt like I was back in school again, and I certainly don't want to remember that.'

'What thesis?' Ruby asked, her eyes flitting from one to the other. Of course, she didn't know anything about it.

'We had to write a two thousand word thesis to justify our positions,' Tiss almost spat out, such was her disgust. 'Well, maybe not to justify our positions per se, but we had to write down our job titles and what our daily duties were.'

'How can you even stretch that out to cover two thousand words?' Ruby shrugged her shoulders. 'You're both solicitors and you meet with clients; isn't that enough to explain your duties to anyone. Anyone with half a mind knows what solicitors do.'

'It's for the Milton Group,' Claudia explained to her. 'Seems they don't know what we do, or at least they want us to explain it to them in a set number of words.'

'Wow! And have you both completed them?'

'Yes,' Tiss and Claudia said as one. 'Although,' continued Tiss, 'it was quite a struggle, but I just listed everything I did on a typical day, and then added flourish to fill it out. Pretty pointless, really.'

'So, how's it going with Tom,' Ruby asked after a few moments, 'you haven't mentioned him in a while.'

Tiss felt reluctant to say anything, but had to under the circumstances. 'We're … ah … we're having a bit of a break right now.'

'Why?'

'It's all the work we're having to do before the amalgamation and-'

'But I'm not giving my boyfriend a miss because of it,' Claudia interjected. All eyes turned to her as she was never this abrupt about anything. 'I know we're new, but he keeps me grounded half the time, and it's nice to have somebody to talk to about what's going on at work and in the outside world. I certainly wouldn't put him on the back burner because of work, so I'm surprised you're doing this, Tiss. Really surprised.'

Tiss felt trapped. She thought she'd given a plausible explanation for her not seeing Tom, but hadn't expected Claudia to take offence by it or sound off like this.

'Ah, well, it's … it's a little bit more complicated than that, but I didn't want to talk about it.'

'So not just because of work then?' Claudia continued.

'No, not exactly.'

'Okay, I see. Sorry,' she sat back against her seat again, her features softening. 'I just assumed, and I know that's not something any of us should do. I really should have let you finish instead of just leaping in like that.'

Tiss put a hand on her arm. 'No, I should have explained the situation better, starting off with the fact we were having a break. It's just that I didn't want to say too much about it that's all; I hope you'll understand.'

'Yes, of course. Are you planning to get back together again, after all this work business has settled down?'

'I really don't know at this point. I guess only time will tell.'

'Shame. I really liked him. Josh did too,' Ruby added her views on the matter.

When things had calmed down a little bit, Tiss ordered another drink to calm her nerves. Not because of what had just transpired between her and her friends, but because she knew that right at that very moment where Jeff Rawlings was and what he was doing.

CHAPTER
TWENTY-FOUR

The door in front of him opened. 'Come on in, Jeff,' Frank Marshall said as he stood in the doorway and greeted him with a broad smile on his face. He'd been asked to sit and wait on a chair across the way from an ornate wooden door on the first floor of the Regency Club. He made a mental note that this was most likely where Tiss said she'd been taken to meet with the club's manager that time; its decorative theme had continued up from downstairs. He'd consulted his watch when he'd first sat down there, and quickly once again just before Marshall had made his appearance. Ten minutes by his calculation. Ten long gruelling minutes of wondering when somebody would come to get him and start the questioning. He liked to think that he wasn't bothered by it, but he was. Apart from anything else, Jeff was very much a loner in his work. Yes, he had his job at the company he officially worked for, but he worked on his own there out of private room and not in one of the company's open planned cubicles. His work was considered far too delicate and discreet for someone else to see and get an inkling of what he was working on for them. Likewise his work for Lily was mainly home-based, where his spare room had been taken up by a row of computers and any implements he required to carry out his sideline business, like the bug and hacking checkers he'd already shown to Tiss. Apart from Lily, she was the only person he had ever shown those kind of things to. In the ten minutes he'd sat waiting he'd thought about all he was going to say to them, pondering over whether or not to ask them if they were a legitimate part of the official Freemason fraternity. He'd hummed and hawed about it with himself, only to reach an initial stalemate, but then wondered if being open about it might give him an advantage and show that he'd done his homework. He was just about to tell himself that perhaps that was the best way to go when Marshall appeared in the doorway to usher him in.

As he entered he saw a long desk in front of him with six men already seated behind it. Marshall closed the door firmly behind him and made a move to resume his place with the others, the vacant central seat which implied he was the most senior person in the room and would be conducting the interview. Or should that be interrogation, he wondered.

'Please take a seat, Jeff,' Marshall waved a hand to the chair as he rounded the table, and Jeff obediently sat down on it. 'First of all, welcome. We're all so please that you decided to join us.

Before we start, are there any questions that you'd like to ask us?'

Now was his chance. Should he speak up or, as he and Tiss had agreed upon, just play along with whatever they were saying to him. In a snap decision he decided on the former option.

'Just the one question,' he began, his eyes set on Marshall and ignoring the nerves that were threatening to overcome him. He hadn't felt this anxious for a very long time, not since the very first job he applied for after leaving university. 'I've been doing a bit of research, and the club here doesn't appear to be on any of the registered lists of Lodges, so I was wondering if you could clarify that?'

Jeff thought that the mood in the room suddenly changed. Had he said the wrong thing; had he said the right thing? He couldn't tell. After what seemed like an eternity, Marshall spoke.

'Well, I can see you've done your homework.' His comment seemed to lighten things again, and Jeff caught one or two members of the panel with a slight smile on their faces. 'But then again, you would have, wouldn't you?'

Jeff frowned, wondering what that meant. Did they know about the extracurricular work he did, both independently and for his company? And if so, then how?

As if reading his thoughts, Marshall replied. 'We do tend to vet all our applicants thoroughly before inviting them. Many don't get past the first stage, but we were very keen on getting you with your expert computing skills.'

So they knew, Jeff thought. Did they also know what he was doing there, which was essentially spying on them?

'A man in your line of work is an asset to anyone or any organisation,' Marshall continued, and a shiver passed over Jeff's body. This was the first time he'd ever felt afraid whilst conducting his business, as he couldn't tell if what Marshall was saying was threatening or congratulatory as the man's face was a stony exterior.

'Thank you, I guess,' Jeff said feeling he should at least say something. Perhaps it was too much, or inadequate, he really couldn't tell.

Marshall continued. 'In answer to your question, Jeff. The Regency Club was indeed an official Lodge when it was first built. I believe you would have seen the logo on the brick at the front of the building.'

Jeff nodded. He hadn't, but Tiss had.

'However, today, even though we still refer to ourselves as members of the Masonic Temple, we are no longer affiliated to it. But we do still hold dear their principles and their methods of selection of men we would like to join us. Our own branch of the Masons, if you like. We are a benevolent and charitable group, as per the original intent, and we care for our community and its members therein. We see ourselves as separate yet still part of it. We may not be Masons in the true meaning of the word as you know it, but we uphold its ideas and ideals. If knowing this you no longer wish to join us, then it's our loss, but it's understandable. So, bearing that in mind, do you still wish to continue with your application?'

All eyes were on Jeff as he took this all in. It was as he'd suspected after hearing Tiss say that the club wasn't recognised as being an official Lodge, so he shouldn't be surprised. What he was surprised at was their willingness to lay it all out on the table for him. If something underhand *was* going on, then they wouldn't have been so willing to do so.

'No,' he said at long last, 'I'd be okay with that.'

'Splendid!' Marshall clapped his hands together, and a low mumble from the others filled the room as they spoke amongst one another. It seems that he'd said the right thing after all. 'Shall we proceed then?' he asked, looking at Jeff then at the other members.

***

At the same time Jeff was sitting in the room with the seven-man panel, Tiss was sitting with her two friends, still worried sick about him. But for the sake of her friends and their evening out, she successfully hid it under a cool and calm exterior. Inside, however, her mind was in a turmoil. How she managed to keep calm for the entire evening was beyond her, honing in on her long-forgotten acting skills she'd taken for additional credits while at university. Whatever she was doing seemed to have worked though, because after her initial unsettledness earlier in the evening, she was now covering her thoughts successfully. To that end, she probably had more to drink in *Lux* than she'd intended to have, resulting in her being a little bit tipsy and flirty. Her two friends saw it as her simply letting her hair down after an especially difficult week, but she knew otherwise: she was trying to delay the inevitable, hearing what had taken place at the Regency Club. By the time she returned home later that night, she had one almighty headache. All she could think about was thank goodness the next day was a Saturday.

The next morning loud music woke her up from a dreamless sleep. After a few moments it finally clicked that she was listening to the sound of her phone telling her she had an incoming call. She sat up in bed and reached across to her bedside table, inadvertently sending it flying across the room as she caught the edge of it. Cursing under her breath, she flung the duvet aside and hurried over to retrieve it, missing the call only by a second. It was from Jeff. She tried to ring back but the call had gone to voicemail and he was still on the line to her. When able, she rang him back without listening to it.

'I was just leaving you a message,' he began as he answered her call.

'I flung my phone across the room by mistake,' she announced, which caused him to utter a gentle laugh and made her also laugh in response. 'I had a bit of a bad night,' she admitted.

'I, on the other hand, did not.' Tiss could hear the pride in his voice as he said it.

'How did it go?'

'Better than expected; better than I'd hoped, especially as they seem to know far more about me than I know about them.'

'Meaning?'

'I got the impression that they'd done their homework on me, implying they knew all about my skills with the keyboard.'

'From that friend of your at your place of work, Dave?'

'I wouldn't really call him a friend as he's more of an acquaintance, but he's the only person I can think of,' Jeff admitted, 'so I'm not really surprised. What *did* surprise me was the extent of what he seems to know. I thought that only the top people knew exactly why they'd hired me, but that doesn't appear to be the case. Maybe it's common knowledge that I can peek inside another company without them even realising it, I don't know, but I certainly wasn't aware of it. It kind of defies the idea of the stealth nature of my work.'

'But they didn't question the morality of that?' Tiss asked with concern.

'I think the only people who wouldn't question that are people with a morality level on par with it.'

'Good point. So are you in, or do you have another stage to go yet? I believed you said there were going to be three.'

'There *were* going to be three, that's right, but they said last night that it wouldn't be necessary, and they've already accepted me into their group. And, by the way, you were right about it not being an official Freemason fraternity, it's just their own private boys' club rather than anything else.'

'Ah, I see.'

'Which means, I'll now have access to the club and access to any information I can glean from it.'

'But as they now know about your skills, won't they be keeping a check on you to make sure you're not going to be doing that?'

'Even if they are, I have ways and means that will make sure they're not even aware of it.'

Tiss laughed. 'Oh, I bet you have. So what's the plan?'

'Do you really want to know?' He asked humorously.

'I think I'm now as liable in all this as you are, so, yes, I really want to know!'

'I'm planning on bugging their computer system for starters.'

'Good idea. And they won't be aware?' she asked with concern.

'I'm good at what I do, Tiss.'

'Yes, I know you are.'

Their conversation continued on a bit more before ending the call. Tiss needed to get herself pulled together after her night of over drinking, desperately needing something to quench her alcohol-fuelled thirst. Breakfast first, she thought to herself, donning her dressing gown and heading down to the kitchen to make herself some breakfast. As she was descending the stairs her head started to pulse with the movement and threatened the return of last night's headache, so before making something to eat and drink she downed two Paracetamol with a glass of chilled water from the fridge. She didn't have a great deal planned for the weekend now that she'd let Tom loose. She still hadn't given him a better reason than the workload, and knew that she should have just ended it completely with him, having no idea why she hadn't. Was she still hoping that he was one of the good guys? Perhaps. But then she mocked herself. The one man who has shown any interest in her in the past few years and it turns out he might have had an ulterior motive to do so. Jeff, however, was unexpected and Lily telling her that he was romantically interested in her had taken her by surprise. Yes, she had to admit, he was attractive, judging by her reaction when she met him in the café that first time and he wore a business suit. She'd admittedly always liked a man in a suit. But she'd been far too engrossed in what she referred to as "the case" to even notice him any further than that and as someone she could perhaps go out with. Now that the thought was in her head though, she had to admit that it wasn't an unpleasant one.

After breakfast, in an attempt to distract herself from this and everything else on her mind, she took herself off to the town to do a bit of shopping. Now that spring was just around the corner, she thought that a few new additions to her wardrobe might be in order just to perk herself up a bit. The last couple of months had admittedly been the worst of her life, brought upon by Frank Marshall and his visit to see her just after the Christmas break. Her entire life had been turned upside down after that day, still was, and she wondered if she'd ever get back on track again as she missed the simplicity of her former existence: her work, her friends, and her family; they were all the stabilising influences she needed. She had to find some kind of an escape. Whilst out she considered ringing her parents to ask if she could spend the evening and the next day with them, but just as she was deliberating, she received a phone call from Jeff.

'Just wondering what you're doing today?' was the first thing he asked.

'Oh. Um … well I'm out shopping at the moment. Why?'

'Do you fancy meeting up for lunch. I think I need to formulate a plan as to what I should look for once I'm officially in with the pseudo Masons. You know, I'm so tempted to call them the maisonettes.' The last part was said with a slight laugh, which Tiss could tell was more a nervous one than anything else. 'And, wondering about the legality of it all.'

Tiss was the one to laugh at that. 'Oh now you're worried about the legalities!' she chuckled. 'I did say that I would be your go-to solicitor if you needed one!'

'Ah, but are you up for all the shenanigans?'

'Think I'll have to be,' she said with humour. After a brief pause she said that she'd be happy to meet him for lunch, asking him to choose where he'd like to go and she'd join him there.

'So, what's the next step in your undercover operation?' Tiss asked as they sat in a cosy little place she'd never been to before tucked down an unimposing street. It was small, the walls painted in rich mediterranean colours, but without being overwhelmingly so or giving the feeling that they were closing in on you. Rich dark brown wooden tables with a lit candle in an old wine bottle added to the welcoming ambiance of the place, the flame wafting gently by her breath as she spoke. Tiss imagined that if anyone came here in the evening it would still look the same. Perhaps that was the idea, to create a space that was out of time constraints. She thought that if the ideal atmosphere of a restaurant could be captured and sealed somewhere for posterity, this would be the prime example of it. Why hadn't she known about it before?

'Once I can come and go freely I'll be able to gain access to their computer systems, and then we'll *really* know what's going on in there.' Jeff interrupted her thoughts about the place.

'But you'll be careful?' she asked with concern. If anything happened to him just because she'd asked if he could help, then she'd never forgive herself.

'Yes, don't worry, I will be,' he replied confidently, yet it still didn't waylay her qualms.

The two fell silent after that, and Tiss was determined to quickly change the subject. 'This place is lovely,' she said after a few moments of looking at looking around her. 'Do you come here a lot?'

'I found it quite by chance,' he sighed, obviously entranced by the place as much as she was. 'Followed somebody in here when I was on a surveillance job for Lily when she was stuck with something else one day a year or so back. It seems I keep coming back to it for some reason.'

'I can understand why,' she admitted. 'It's enchanting.'

'Yes,' he laughed, 'that's the right word for it. It looks exactly the same in the evening too.'

'That was going through my mind just now, because of where it's situated down this lane, when you're in here you can't tell if it's breakfast time or approaching midnight, and that's all kinds of wonderful.'

'Yes, delightful, isn't it?'

A young waitress approached their table and asked if they were ready to order. 'Oh, I haven't quite had a chance-' Tiss began, but Jeff immediately came to her assistance.

'If you don't mind me suggesting something,' he offered, and Tiss looked up at him from the menu she'd barely had time to read.

'No I don't mind,' she replied, 'but I have to tell you that I'm vegetarian.'

'Yes, I already know; Lily told me about your dietary choices.'

'She did?'

Tiss swore she saw Jeff's cheeks colour slightly at his admission, but perhaps it was just the glow from the candlelight. But, then again, maybe it wasn't. She went with his suggestion, pasta with a delicious creamy artichoke and mushroom sauce, followed by a slice of the restaurant's speciality, salted caramel cheesecake. This was one of the nicest lunches she'd had in a long time. Eventually though, the conversation turned to what was expected of Jeff's involvement with the faux Masons.

'Well,' he began with a sigh, 'as they've officially welcomed me into their fold, I don't need to attend any more of their initiation ceremonies.'

'Tell me they weren't going to be anything like having you blindfolded and having to raise one trouser leg up to your knee?' Tiss asked with a smile.

'No,' he laughed, 'when they admitted that they weren't officially Freemasons, only an offshoot of, I did ask about that. They laughed when I told them how relieved that made me.'

'So you're in then?'

'Yes, I'm in. I have to go in Monday evening and be officially included in everything, like being on the list of members so that I can sail right through reception by showing a card.'

'You'll be card-carrying?'

'Looks like. After that, what with the twenty-third fast approaching and all, I'll spend some time in there to see what I can find out. If anyone gets suspicious I'll just say that my curiosity got the better of me.'

'But you will be careful, won't you?'

'You don't have to keep asking that, but yes, of course, don't you worry.'

'It's getting so close to the spring equinox,' Tiss muttered. 'I'm dreading it. The thought of someone going missing again is almost too much to bear.'

'Well, if they do have anything to do with it I'll try my damnedest to find something out before then. You will be representing me in court if anything goes wrong, won't you?' It was said lightly, with a twinkle in his eyes, yet Tiss hoped that it wouldn't come to that.

'If I need to,' was all she replied, but in her mind she was wondering who would be representing her if she was also arrested for her part in this.

CHAPTER
TWENTY-FIVE

Following lunch Tiss decided she'd go and see her parents after all, if they were free to have her and had no other plans for the weekend. So once she was back at her car she gave them a quick ring to ask.

'Oh sweetheart, of course you can come. We know you're busy, so we're always happy when you pay us a visit. Anything on your mind, or is it purely a family visit?' her mother asked. After the last time she called on them the question wasn't entirely unexpected.

'You're busy too, Mum, you and Dad,' Tiss replied, 'but it's a bit of both, I guess. Is it okay if I come over and stay the night?'

'You know you don't even have to ask. What time shall we expect you?'

'I'm out in town at the moment, so I'll set off as soon as I get home and pack a few things to tide me over. Probably around five or six. Is that a good time for you both?'

'Perfect. Just in time for dinner.'

'Okay then, I'll go. See you both soon.'

Even if Tiss was concerned about the upcoming spring equinox, she was more than happy that the nights were now starting to get much lighter, meaning that she arrived at her parents' house at five-thirty with the sun still high in the sky. Quite a change from her last visit. Even though it was a reasonably warm day, she hoped that they still had a roaring fire going in the hearth in the living room like they had the last time.

She was barely out of the car when she heard the front door opening, and looking over she saw her mother standing in the doorway with a welcoming smile on her face.

'Do you need any help?' Sarah Lawson called out as Tiss rounded the car to get her suitcase out of the boot.

'No, it's all in hand,' Tiss called back as she dragged it out and onto the ground, wheeling it along the gravel towards her mother.

'Come in darling,' Mrs Lawson held the door wide for her daughter to enter, where she was met by her equally enthusiastic father who had just entered the hallway from the kitchen.

'Just in time for dinner,' he said with a laugh as he walked over to her and enveloped her in his arms. 'Leave your case here and I'll take it up for you later. Unless you want to freshen up of course.'

'No, it's okay, I'm fine. Just looking forward to spending some time with you. Whatever you've been cooking in there smells divine,' Tiss laughed as she scented the air. From what she could tell it involved spices and smelled vaguely Eastern.

'Your favourite. Or at least it was while you were still living with us,' he said proudly.

'You didn't have to do that just for me,' Tiss said as she realised what they were having to eat. Every Friday night, come rain or shine, her parents would jointly make a vegetable curry which far exceeded anything she'd ever tasted from either an Indian restaurant or takeaway. She'd missed it on the occasions that she hadn't been able to come and see them on a Friday evening, although if she'd asked she felt sure they would have made it on any other night she was with them, just like they had done now. But it had been years now since she'd had it, and she wondered if they'd kept up the tradition regardless of her being there or not. She'd have to ask them later.

After the wonderful meal, which was every bit as delicious as she remembered it to be, Tiss brough up the subject of the Regency Club again. Although she knew that they didn't really like discussing matters concerning their joint membership of the Masons, she felt it necessary to tell them that he'd discovered it wasn't an official Lodge.

'Well that's very strange,' he father said while they were all sitting in the living room with their after dinner coffees. 'It sounds more of an in-house thing than anything else, but why would they even do that, announcing it as such, and, perhaps more importantly, how did you find out?'

Although somewhat loathe to involve them even further in this mess, she felt obliged to talk to them about her more in-depth unofficial investigation into the club.

'You need to be very careful there,' her mother said in a serious tone, 'and this friend of yours if he's getting himself involved in it.'

'How do you mean?'

'To me, anyone masquerading as a Freemason establishment instantly raises a red flag, and if this man is doing undercover work for you, what will happen to him if he's found out?'

'He's very good at what he does, Mum, but yes, I have to admit that I am a little concerned about him being admitted into their circle even though we now know it's not even a proper one. I know I asked him if he'd do it-'

'You asked him to get involved in it?' her dad asked incredulously, in a tone she wasn't normally used to.

'Um, yes,' Tiss admitted somewhat sheepishly.

'What on earth were you thinking?'

'I-'

'Sweetheart,' her mum began, 'you're a solicitor, surely you know you just can't get yourself involved in something like this without repercussions?'

'But there's something very strange going on in that place and I-'

'Well just tell everything you know to the police, Tiss.'

'I have done,' Tiss retorted, 'and I'm working with a detective constable on this too.'

Letting out a long sigh, Paul Lawson sat back heavily in his chair. Tiss felt like a small child again under both his and her mother's scrutiny. She knew in the back of her mind that she shouldn't have mentioned it to them the last time she stayed over, but these were her parents, and they were both Masons, so who would be better equipped to advise her on this matter? After a short while his features relaxed. 'If the police are now involved then that's a bit of a different matter, but I still don't understand why there's also a private investigator involved with this as well.'

After what had just been said she decided not to disclose to them that Jeff wasn't actually a private investigator but actually a very skilled computer hacker, so she said that he was doing it as a favour for her.

'Then he must be a pretty good friend,' Sarah Lawson said.

'I think he could be,' was all she said in reply, thinking to herself that she was growing fonder of him by the minute.

***

Tiss was startled awake the following morning to the sound of her phone making a strange noise. It took her a while to realise that she'd put her phone on silent overnight and the noise was actually someone ringing her. Pulling a hand out from beneath the duvet, she picked it up from the bedside table to see who it was. Ruby's face and name gave her an instant answer.

'Hello,' she said a little croakily as she hit the green accept button.

'Tiss, so sorry. Did I wake you?'

'No, it's okay,' she said as she sat up. 'I needed to get up anyway. What's the matter?'

'It could be nothing, but I can't seem to get a reply from Claudia.'

'What do you mean?'

'Just that. I've tried ringing her but it keeps ringing out. I know for a fact that she wasn't going anywhere today.'

'Yes, she said as much on Friday as I recall.'

'I was wondering, as you're closer to her, could you go around and see if she'd okay?'

'Oh, Ruby, I'm sorry but I'm not home; I'm at my parents' house. I decided to pop down yesterday afternoon on a whim and I'm still here.'

'Oh, right. Look it's okay then. I'll get Josh to run me over there. I have to admit that I'm a bit worried, even though I can't quite explain why.'

'Then yes, do go over. Will you keep me in the loop?'

'Sure. Look, I'd better go, but I'll text you when I find out what's going on, okay?'

'Of course.'

When the call ended Tiss stared at the blank screen. She was sure nothing was wrong and maybe, like herself, her phone was on silent and she couldn't hear it, but it still didn't keep her from worrying. Ruby was worried, and it wasn't like her to react as she had done, so she was also worried too. She knew that if her friend set off now as she said she was going to, then it would take around ten to fifteen minutes to get to Claudia's house, so in the meantime she set about getting up and getting herself dressed. Still anxiously awaiting a call back, she went downstairs to have breakfast with her parents.

'You okay?' her mum asked as she sat at the table with the Sunday paper spread out on it in front of her. 'You're frowning, and that's not like you.'

'Yes, well I'm not sure. I just had a call from a friend of mine saying that she can't get in touch with our mutual friend.'

'And is that unusual?' Sarah Lawson continued, biting the corner off the slice of toast she was holding.

'Perhaps not if her phone is on silent. Ruby rang me and mine was on silent but the sound it was giving off still woke me up. She thought I was at home and wondered if I'd go over and check on her as I'm the closest.'

'Well, I hope everything is all right with her.'

'So do I, Mum.'

After Tiss finished breakfast and had still not heard from Ruby, she decided to take up her father's offer of showing her around the garden. For as long as she could remember it was always his non-work pet project. He told her that he was planning to add a pond to the landscape and wanted her opinion on whereabouts to put it. However, she suspected that he didn't really require her input as her knowledge of gardening was minimal, and had been asked by her mother to keep her occupied whilst she waited to hear back from her friend.

'And I was also thinking about getting some fish to go in it,' he began, but was interrupted by the sound of Tiss' phone going off in her pocket.

'I have to get this Dad,' she apologised and pulling it out she retreated further down the garden.

'Any news?' she blurted out as soon as she answered it. There was a disturbing silence for a moment. 'Ruby … are you there?'

'Now I don't want to get yourself worried,' she began, which instantly worried her. 'But I've had to call the police.'

Tiss went cold, and it wasn't anything to do with the chill breeze that was blowing outside in the garden.

'I kept trying the phone all the while Josh was driving and still no answer. There was no answer either when I tried the door, but Josh managed to get over the side gate and look through one of the windows at the back of the house. He said there was no evidence of either the door or the windows being broken in order for someone to get in.'

'Oh, God!' Tiss gasped, enough to make her father look up from what he was doing in front of her and frown.

'And that's why I rang the police. We're still here waiting for them to arrive.'

'I should come back.'

'And do what exactly? We're here, and there's nothing you can do that we're not doing now.'

'Where do you think she is then if she's not in there?'

'We don't know that she's not in there though, do we?'

Ruby's words chilled her even more than the cold outside air did when she realised what was being implied by that.

'You don't think ...'

'I don't know.' A pause. 'I just don't know, that's why we're waiting for the police.'

'Then let me know, will you?' Tiss asked weakly, ending the call before going into full panic mode. She was afraid, and her friend was afraid, but she wasn't going to let her hear her panic as that would serve no purpose whatsoever; she'd already be feeling that way herself.

Tiss started when a hand touched her on the shoulder. 'What is it?' the sound of her father's voice right next to her drew her out of her burgeoning thoughts. For one brief moment she'd actually forgotten all about him and where she was; lost in a place where she felt completely helpless and hopeless.

'It's ... it's my friend,' she stammered. 'I think she might have gone missing.'

'What?' Taking a firm hold of Tiss' hand, he led her back indoors. 'Sarah!' he yelled as soon as they entered the house, and she came running in from wherever she'd been.

'What is it?' she asked, her eyes wide in shock as her husband wasn't someone who normally raised his voice for anything.

'Get Tiss a drink, will you. Something strong,' he asserted as he directed his daughter to sit on the nearest chair. Tiss flopped down into it; shock having taken over her. She vaguely heard her parents discussing what to give her before a glass with a couple of fingers of dark liquid was thrust into her hand.'

'Here, drink this,' her father instructed and she obeyed without question, the alcoholic burn catching her throat as she swallowed all of it down in one go. He waited until the initial effects had worn off before continuing to question her, sitting alongside her mother on the sofa opposite. When the alcohol had taken the edge off, Tiss told both of them what Ruby's phone call had entailed. They listened attentively, concerned by both her friend's apparent disappearance and the timing of it as she made them aware of the finer details of the missing women over the years.

'And you're thinking, what, that Claudia may have been taken for that reason?' Sarah Lawson asked, maintaining, like her husband, the calm exterior both barristers were renowned for. Although appearing so, Tiss doubted that they were as sedate as they looked and were just putting up a front to help her through her current anxiety regarding her friend and colleague.

'That was the first thing that entered my mind, yes,' she admitted sadly.

'But it could all be so very innocent; she was away from the house and her phone had died. Don't you think that's a possible scenario?'

'Yes, of course it is,' Tiss said rather abruptly after hearing her mother go all solicitor-mode with her response, 'and I'm not on the stand, Mum. I'm concerned, and Ruby is concerned, so there's due cause.' Even though she'd verbally criticised her mother for slipping into the words of her profession, she had, in fact, used it herself to reply. Thankfully, the moment of tension was broken by the sound of her phone ringing. Taking it out of her pocket, she looked down at it to see the call was from DC Woodhouse. 'I need to take this,' she said as she rose from the chair and made her way out to the hallway for a bit more privacy.

'Hello, Tiss,' he began when she acknowledged him. 'I thought I'd let you know that I'm currently on my way to your colleague Claudia Romano's house.'

'My other friend is already there,' she replied, her heart beating furiously in her chest as she spoke. 'She said she was going to call the police as she couldn't get a response. This is such a coincidence though; how did you manage to get assigned to it?' Tiss had already discussed who she could and could not trust with Jeff, and she'd reluctantly admitted that she wasn't sure any more about either him or Tom Davenport. It didn't help the matter that it seemed he'd been assigned so quickly to the matter.

'I've been working closely with another officer who deals with cold cases, and we've been worried that something like this might happen this month with it being the fifth anniversary of the last missing women.'

'So you think that this might be related?' she asked fearfully.

'I hope not, Tiss, but I wanted to get in there straight away, more so that I recognised the name as being your co-worker and your friend.'

'Thank you for that.'

'Okay, so I'm nearly there; I'll update you after I've assessed the situation.'

'Thanks.'

Although it was comforting to know that he was attending, Tiss was still worried beyond words. What if the worst had happened and Claudia had been taken? What if she was lying lifeless on the floor of her home? What if? What if? The questions were all swirling around in her head to the point of making her dizzy and feeling nauseous. When she made her way slowly back to the living room, her parents' faces looked as distressed as hers must have.

'What's happening?' her father asked as she sat down once again opposite him.

'That was the police officer I've been in contact with, and he's going over to Claudia's house now. All I can do is wait until either he or Ruby calls me back to say what's going on.'

CHAPTER
TWENTY-SIX

When DC Woodhouse drew up at the home of Claudia Romano, he saw a man and a woman standing by the gate waiting for him. Or at least he knew that they weren't specifically waiting for him, but rather for an officer of the law to attend – which also happened to be himself. He hadn't met either of Tiss' friends before, but he instinctively knew that the woman was Ruby Duran, and the man with his arm protectively strewn around her waist must be her fiancé, Josh Scott. He slowed his car down and came to a stop at the same time as a police car with two uniformed occupants rounded the corner and parked up behind him. He waited until they'd both alighted the vehicle before getting out himself.

'Ms Duran?' he called over to the pair who were standing on the pavement and eying him anxiously. Ruby nodded as Josh released his hold on her. 'I know your friend Tiss Lawson,' he said as he approached them, 'and I've just spoken to her on the way over here. What do we know so far?' As Ruby explained how she couldn't get an answer, either via the telephone or by knocking on the door, Woodhouse nodded over to the officers and one of them went to the boot of his car and brought out a breaching tool, a long, thick tube-like device with two attached circular handles to hold on to. It was strong and effective, and Woodhouse had seen it used many a time.

'What are you going to do?' Ruby asked, even though she realised what the next step would be.

'If there's no answer then it seems that the only other option in that case is to break in.' But before going straight to the front door and forcing their way in, Woodhouse directed one of the officers to go around to the back to see if he could gain entry that way.

'I climbed over the fence,' Josh offered, pointing to where he'd managed to get over, and as Woodhouse nodded, the officer sprinted off to where he'd indicated, 'but I couldn't see anything,' he added as clarification. The other officer was instructed to go up to the front door to wait for further instructions. It seemed to take forever, but when the officer returned from around the back and shook his head, Woodhouse then nodded to the other man waiting by the front door to force entry. He pulled back the heavy tool and slammed it forcefully at the door. There was a crunching sound as the door lock cracked beneath it, causing the door to swing open.

'Wait here,' the DC instructed the two civilians as he could see they were about to set off as well. 'We don't know what's in there and it's safer if you stay outside.' He was also thinking about the extra fingerprints they'd leave if they got inside. Ruby and Josh could only stand and nervously watch and wait.

The inside of the house was cold, as if no one had been in it for quite some time. While the two uniformed officers checked out the ground floor, Woodhouse took two steps at once as he clambered up to the first floor to check it out. Everything looked in order in that the bed was neatly made and there didn't look like there'd been a struggle with things being strewn around the place. The same had applied to the downstairs he'd briefly seen. But he did get a sense that something was off. It was early on a Sunday morning, and he knew from experience that Sunday mornings weren't usually so organised; in fact, the whole appearance of the place looked like it had been staged.

Descending the stairs again he asked the two men if there was anything that caught their attention, to which they said that it had not; everything looked normal, the fact that it had being what actually raised Woodhouse's suspicion. 'Go outside and ask the couple if they'd trying ringing the occupier's number, would you?' he said to one of them, directing the other to go upstairs and listen for anything that resembled a telephone ringing. Woodhouse watched from the doorway as Ruby put her phone up to her ear before going from room to room, but there was still no sound to be heard. Wherever Claudia Romano had gone it seemed that she had her phone with her, and that, he thought, was the way to try to find her. He walked out of the house and up to Ruby.

'You can turn it off now,' he said as he approached her.

'Anything?' Ruby asked anxiously.

'Nothing at all. Her phone's not in there which must mean that she has it on her. Do you happen to know who her phone provider is?' After giving him that information along with her number, he walked over to his car and got in, picking up the communication system installed on the dashboard. After receiving a prompt response he asked the person on the other end of the phone if they could connect his work mobile to Claudia's mobile phone provider. Within minutes he was speaking to a manager and instructed him to get in touch with his detective sergeant at the station to confirm his identity, providing him with his warrant card number. The manager did this and Woodhouse stayed on the line whilst he was on another.

'And what can I help you with Detective Constable,' the manager who identified himself as Brian asked.

'I need you to turn on the GPS on a phone number I'm about to give you. The person is missing in suspicious circumstances.'

'Okay, and what is their number?' After giving him it Woodhouse heard the man tapping away on his keyboard. 'It's turn on and currently stationary,' he replied after a while. 'I can send you the coordinates to your phone, or the actual address, whichever you'd prefer?'

'Either or,' the detective replied, and as quickly as he said it he received a text message. He put his phone on speaker while he looked at it: an address about six miles away popped up as a pinpoint on a map. 'That's great, thank you,' Woodhouse said quickly, adding his appreciation from both him and the police force for providing the information so promptly and efficiently. He ended the call and exited the car again. Even though it wasn't necessary, he felt he couldn't just leave Ruby and

Josh standing there without any explanation of what he'd learned. They were friends of Tiss', after all, and he couldn't just ignore them as they had been the ones to notify the police of their concern for Claudia in the first place. It was lucky that he was working with the person from the cold case unit as both he and the section had been on high alert to any news of women going missing in the area bearing in mind the time of year, hence his being able to attend the scene so quickly. After speaking briefly to Ruby and Josh and telling them what was happening, he urged them to return home as there was nothing more they could do at that moment. To his great relief, they agreed.

Woodhouse drove to the location Claudia's phone provider had given him in about fifteen minutes. The directions brought him to a cul-de-sac in the quieter part of the village, but he drove further on to make sure that neither his nor the marked police car could be seen on the road from any of the houses. The last thing he wanted was to draw attention to their arrival. He'd already formulated a plan during his drive over: he'd knock on each door in turn and say he was campaigning for a local political party. As it was March and the local elections were at the beginning of May, his presence wouldn't be seen as entirely far-fetched. He instructed the two officers to remain in the car until needed, then walked casually back to the crescent-shaped layout of eight houses and took his phone out of his pocket and set it ready to ring Claudia's number. Woodhouse methodically went from door to door, giving an impressive political speech even if he said so himself, but despite hitting the call button to connect to Claudia's phone, no sound of one ringing could be heard from any of the open front doors. The phone was in this crescent, he knew it as the facts pointed to it, but finding it was proving just as difficult as it was at finding her. When there was still no show by the time he reached the final door, he decided that the best thing to then do was to go around the back of the houses in the off chance that the phone had been thrown away in one of the waste bins. He knew, of course, that the phone could have been on silent, and if that was the case then the only other option would be to get a warrant to search each of the properties in turn; that it itself would take at least a few hours to get sanctioned, and at worst a few days regardless of the fact that Claudia's phone had been pinpointed to this spot. It would mean extra officers would have to be deployed. Fortunately, each of the houses' bins were next to the gates at the rear of the property. Woodhouse also breathed a sigh of relief that the fences themselves were of the six foot variety, and thereby sheltering him somewhat from being seen by whoever was inside. However, as he walked around the full length of the crescent with his phone in his hand and the line open to Claudia's, no corresponding ring tone could be heard. He lowered his head in despair. Ending the call he rang his cold case contact at the station, hoping that he may be able to have some kind of leverage to hasten a warrant being issued. *Stay there and I'll see what I can do*, sounded hopeful, so he did, going back to the two uniformed officers and making them aware of the plan.

Two long hours later, while draining the dregs of his takeaway cup of coffee one of the uniformed officers had brought him, Woodhouse's prayers were answered. Notification came through that a warrant had been issued and sent to him as an attachment to an email. He hurried out of the car to the one parked up behind him and instructed one of the men to stand on watch at the entrance to the cul-de-sac and the other to watch the rear while he knocked on each door. By the time he got through all eight not one person had objected to the search, but neither Claudia nor her phone had turned up despite everything pointing to the fact that it was right in the area where he now was. His initial thinking that the phone was on silent now seemed to be likely, and apart from the warrant allowing him to search the properties in-depth, doing so to include lofts was nigh impossible. As the search didn't reveal any traces of either Claudia or her phone, the only other thing he could do was search the area surrounding the cul-de-sac, like the bushes and bases of trees. However, the area surrounding the back of the houses was massive; the development backed onto a small woodland, making searching every part of it impossible. The one thing he did know, though, was that even though her phone may be here, she most definitely wasn't. Defeated, he pulled his phone out of his pocket and rang the station and his contact there. He didn't know what else to do.

CHAPTER
TWENTY-SEVEN

'Please sit down, Tiss,' her mother pleaded to her as she paced up and down in the living room. 'You'll wear yourself out. I know you're wearing me out just watching you, and goodness knows what you're doing to the carpet.'

'I can't,' her daughter admitted, not even realising that she was. As she spoke she glanced hopefully at the phone in her hand. It had been hours since Ruby had initially contacted her and DC Woodhouse had also let her know that he'd attended the scene without finding Claudia at home.

'Your mother's right,' her dad added. 'Try to relax a bit.' Relax? How on earth was she expected to relax under the circumstances? Her friend and colleague was missing; they weren't helping her anxiety one bit by trying to placate her. She was just about to say something when she remembered that she hadn't even rung Jeff yet. How had she even forgotten about him? Okay, so she was distracted, but if anyone could help from another angle, then it was him. She headed out into the hallway again, not wanting to involve them in what she was about to say.

'Hey, what's up?' Jeff asked cheerily. Of course, he wouldn't know anything about what had happened.

'I'm surprised I know something before you do,' Tiss replied without any trace of humour in her voice.

'What's happened?' His voice instantly changing its tone on hearing that reply.

'Claudia is missing.'

'Missing?'

Tiss felt like she was going to snap she was so tense, but she kept on going, bringing Jeff up to speed on the events of the morning.

'Like I said the yesterday,' Jeff responded, 'I have to go into the club tomorrow evening to finalise everything and I can snoop around a bit to see if I can pick up on anything.'

'Do you think they might have her, for whatever they want to do on the solstice?'

Jeff sighed. 'Tiss, don't go there, don't even think that.'

'But it's all I can think of at the moment; the idea never leaves my head! DC Woodhouse is on the case and he hasn't got back to me yet, so he obviously hasn't found her. If they haven't taken her, then where is she?'

'I don't know. Are you at home right now, because I could come over if you like.'

'No, I'm at my parents for the weekend.'

'Good. At least you're with someone and not alone.'

'I might as well be,' she retorted. 'I can't cope with this, Jeff. Claudia is out there somewhere, missing, and goodness knows what else; what am I going to do?' Tiss could feel herself tail spinning.

'Hey, hey, calm down. The police are doing all that they can, and I like I say I can get into the club tomorrow and find out all *I* can. If they're holding her then I can find out all about it.'

'Tiss, darling, are you okay?' Her mother's voice sounded fraught and tense as she appeared through the doorway to seek out her daughter.

'Jeff, I've got to go,' Tiss said into her phone, 'but please keep in touch, yes?'

'Of course I will.'

'I'm okay, Mum,' Tiss forced an unwilling smile on her face to appease her.

'Well, you don't sound it. Come on, come back into the living room. I'll get you a cup of coffee.'

Tiss smiled at that despite the high level of tension running through her. Whenever things went wrong her mother's response was to offer either a cup of tea or coffee, like it was the solution to make everything right with the world again. Tiss loved her sense of hope in what either of those beverages would give someone. In any case it seemed to work as she felt herself slowly calming down again whilst drinking it. There was nothing she could do now but wait, and she knew it: wait for DC Woodhouse to get back to her, and wait for Jeff to go into the club the next day and work his magic on the keyboard of whatever computer he could find to get into. She feared for him, but not as much as she feared for the wellbeing of her friend, Claudia.

***

The call came at 2pm. When it rang Tiss picked it up from the coffee table in front of her and stared at the screen: James Woodhouse.

'Aren't you going to answer it?' her mother asked incredulously. She'd sat with her daughter since the earlier incident, seemingly unable to leave her side for a second. If she needed to go off anywhere her father replaced her, whether that was by accident or design, Tiss didn't know, but suspected the latter to be the case. She looked up at her mother then back to her phone again before hitting the answer button.

'Hello?' she asked sheepishly, bracing herself for whatever came next.

'Hi Tiss, it's me,' Woodhouse hurriedly said. 'Just to let you know that I still haven't found your friend.' Tiss' stomach sank on hearing that piece of information.

'O-kay.'

'Are you all right?' It was asked with genuine concern.

'No, not really,' she admitted. How could she be all right, her friend was missing at the exact same time another woman was due to go missing again if the five-year cycle was to repeat itself, and there was no reason to assume that it wouldn't. It didn't help that, apart from herself, Claudia's overall appearance was like that of the eight who had already disappeared from the face of the earth without trace. She was horrified that Claudia was missing, but was equally horrified that it could have easily been herself.

'We'll keep at it, Tiss,' he said softly. 'As I said before, I'm working with a cold case unit, and they've just told me that we have enough to get a warrant to search the Regency Club.'

That caught her attention. 'Really?' she asked in reply. 'They've said that?'

'Yes, and they're getting a warrant as we speak. They told me as it was recorded that all the missing women were last seen near the club, then that is enough reason to search it.'

'Oh, thank goodness!' she declared. At least that was something. However, she didn't dare mention Jeff's involvement to him. The last thing she wanted was for him to get in trouble because of it, even though they'd often joked about her defending him in court if he did. 'And will that be today?'

'Yes it should be, and I'll be going along with them.'

Good, she thought, that way they won't inadvertently bump into Jeff. She made a mental note to call him again after this conversation ended. In many ways she felt stuck between the pair of them, but at least both were trying their best with the case and with trying to find her missing friend while she was helplessly sitting around twiddling her thumbs.

Despite everything that was happening, Tiss wasn't as tense after speaking to Jeff again. He assured her once again that he would be careful and discreet, but his sole purpose the following evening would be to find out where Claudia was if the Regency Club had anything to do with her disappearance, if she hadn't already turned up before then that is. She had faith in him and knew that he would do that, but even with his irrefutable technical skills, would he be able to successfully find her? She had to believe that between him and DC Woodhouse they'd be successful as the alternative was unbearable. After speaking to Jeff she rang Ruby, bringing her up to speed with what

Woodhouse had told her. It wasn't an easy conversation to have.

For the rest of the day before she travelled home Tiss' parents tried their utmost to help her, but even they could tell from the start that it was a lost cause. They knew exactly how they'd feel under the same circumstances, so didn't even try to gloss it over for her. But they were there to support her, her mother even offering to travel back home with her and stay the night just to be there with her until both had to go into work the next morning. Tiss, however, refused, thinking that if things got bad she could go and stay with Ruby, or have her come over and stay with her. As a last resort she could even ask Jeff to come over. But why a last resort? Lily had already told her that he was very fond of her, to the extent that she thought he was going to ask her out, and she had to admit that feelings were beginning to blossom for him too other than friendship or a working relationship. But that wasn't the time to be thinking like that; Claudia was missing, and it wasn't an appropriate time in her mind to be thinking about starting a new relationship. Maybe after they'd found her. After all her deliberating, though, a glass of whisky before bed did the trick as it settled her nerves and sent her off into a deep and dreamless sleep until her alarm went off the following morning.

CHAPTER
TWENTY-EIGHT

Tiss awoke again to the sound of her phone ringing; a glance at the bedside clock told her that it was only 6am. Making a grab for it, she saw that DC Woodhouse's name was on the screen. A handful of messages from him while she'd slept also greeted her, but she'd have to check them later. She scrambled to sit up straight in the bed as she pressed the green answer button.

'Tiss are you all right?' he said. It sounded like he was out of breath. 'I've been trying to get in touch with you for hours.'

'It's only six o'clock,' she replied, voice still thick with sleep, but then realised the significance of the call and perked up a bit. 'Why, what's happened?'

'I wish I had something to tell you, but-'

'You've been contacting me to tell you that you have nothing to tell me?' she asked incredulously. He knew how anxious she'd been, knew exactly the kind of state she was in, yet he still persisted in trying to get in touch her?

'I just wanted to know if you were okay, and I got a bit worried when I couldn't get you.'

'I'm fine – well as fine as I can be under the circumstances. Did you go to the club yesterday?'

'Yes, we took a team of people in there to check everywhere.'

'And?' She could hear him give out a long sigh, so knew exactly what was coming next.

'Absolutely nothing. We've managed to get a list of the club's members and they're being checked out for alibis as we speak.'

At least that was something, Tiss thought, although they still hadn't found any trace of Claudia or any notion of where she was. And she had work to go to in a few hours. Thanking Woodhouse for letting her know and also apologising for her sharpness, Tiss decided to get up. Ordinarily, if she woke up near morning she'd try to get in a bit more sleep, but it seemed pointless even trying to do so today. So she got up and had a long, leisurely breakfast and tried to calm herself before even attempting to go into work to see the clients she had lined up on her calendar for today.

When she got to work, the place was a hive of activity, much like the time she went in to find members of the Milton Group scrutinising their accounts before the announced merger. This time, however, rather than accountants there were numerous members of the police force, both uniformed and plain clothed milling around. Diane looked in complete and utter shock as she sat behind the reception desk, gazing hopelessly at Tiss as she approached the desk.

'This is about Claudia,' Tiss stated rather than asked, and Diane nodded.

'I just can't believe it,' came the reply. 'And they're interviewing everybody too.'

Good, thought Tiss, at least they were doing something about it. Then she saw DC Woodhouse out of the corner of her eye, disappearing into an office with Lionel in tow.

'They've been here since before I got in,' Diane continued, not noticing Tiss' distraction, 'so I assume they rang either Sanderson or Barnes to gain entry.'

'Probably,' Tiss mumbled. She thought back to Woodhouse's telephone call; perhaps he was already on his way to the office at that point, yet he still didn't tell her what was about to take place. It made sense in a way, she determined, not telling any of the employees that a group of police officers would be awaiting them on their arrival. To her that seemed to imply that they thought someone at the firm could be responsible – but perhaps that was just her legal instincts coming to the fore, or just the fact that it was the natural progression taking place in the investigation. She was becoming way too suspicious these days for her own good; she'd never been like this before. Gone was the time when she would come into work, do her job, then go home again, only to repeat for the rest of the working week until the weekend came around. This had been her pattern until the beginning of the new year. There was too much now happening all at once, and she still believed that Frank Marshall was the cause of it all. The day he walked into her office was the day everything started to go wrong. The remainder of the morning was much the same, with police officers interviewing everybody before taking Claudia's hard drive away with them for their cybercrime unit to take a look at – that fact made known to her by Woodhouse. To her knowledge, Claudia hadn't had any threats, and she was sure her friend would have reported that to the authorities if she had. Clients coming in were stunned at first, quite rightly so, wondering, Tiss assumed, what kind of establishment they were coming to for legal advice when a swarm of police officers were hovering around the place. She had to explain to every single one of them who had an appointment with her, and upon hearing what had happened each were horrified to hear the reason why they were there. Every time she had to explain it Tiss felt as though she was about to be sick. Claudia had now been missing for over twenty-four hours that they knew of, perhaps even more, with no sign of finding her whereabouts. Woodhouse hadn't explained why he hadn't found her phone when he went off in search of it, but it was evident that he hadn't.

When lunch time came around Tiss couldn't even go out with Denise as was their wont on a Monday, choosing instead to stay in her room to call Ruby to see how she was doing. She discovered that her friend had chosen to take the day off work, as had Josh in order to stay with her; perhaps she should have done the same judging by her lack of concentration over the past few hours. Tiss was just about to go in search of DC Woodhouse when there was a knock on the door. Expecting the police officer, she was momentarily shocked to see Lionel standing there with a pack of sandwiches and a takeaway coffee in his hands.

'Denise said you weren't feeling like lunch today,' he said as she invited him in. He put the things down on her desk and frowned at her. 'You need to eat something, even if you're not feeling like it.'

'I know,' she admitted, flopping down into her chair. Lionel took the seat opposite. 'It's just … I'm so worried, Li.' She tried to keep her reserve but ended up with tears pooling in her eyes instead. His act of kindness had overwhelmed her.

'Hey, hey,' he said as he got up and rounded the desk to place both hands on her shoulders and massage the tense muscles he found there. 'You're way too tense.'

She relaxed into his soothing fingers as the tears now flowed freely. 'I just don't know what to do if anything's happened to her; I can't imagine what she must be going through right now.'

'Don't let yourself think that,' he urged as his fingers dug deeper.

'But I can't help it; I'm terrified for her.' Of course, Lionel didn't know what she knew about the missing women and the cycle of their disappearances, and to him it looked more like a kidnap than anything else.'

'I'm sure somebody must have checked with her boyfriend, right?'

'I assume so, why?'

'Isn't a partner the first person the police look to?'

'True, so I have to assume that they have.' Tiss didn't know why, but that question had made her feel even more uncomfortable. She'd have to ask Woodhouse about it.

CHAPTER
TWENTY-NINE

Claudia lay flat on her back in bed staring up at the ceiling after deciding to have an early night, which was unusual for her especially for a Saturday evening. She felt oddly tired and a little dizzy, both sensations unusual in themselves, and she closed her eyes on a room that was starting to sway around her. Perhaps she was coming down with something, as she often felt off like this just before a cold reared its ugly head. Or perhaps it was that extra glass of wine she'd had at dinner. The day had been good up till about an hour ago, spending the morning swimming at the local sports centre as she did most Saturday mornings, before meeting up with her boyfriend for an early dinner as he had to be up early the next day to travel to a works event. It seemed unusual to have a meeting on a Sunday, but she knew that the company he worked at often had meetings on weekends so thought nothing of it. It was just when she thought that the dizziness was starting to wear off that she heard a noise coming from downstairs. Her first thought was that she'd perhaps left a window open, and it had somehow come off the latch and was slamming back against the frame. Rather than have the pane break, she forced herself to get out of bed to go and close it. Walking a little unsteadily, she had to grasp the handrail to help get herself down the stairs in case she slipped and hurtled down them head first. The first room she went into was the kitchen, where she found all the windows closed and locked. She repeated this throughout the rooms on the ground floor and found all the windows were similarly shut. It was then that she thought she must have imagined it and turned to make her way upstairs again. It was then that she sensed someone or something behind her, but before she could turn a hand was wrapped around her waist from behind and a strange smelling cloth was thrust over her nose and held there. Within seconds her vision started to black out, and she felt herself crumble to the floor before losing consciousness.

When she awoke she had a throbbing headache the level of which she had never had before. She was lying on her back, and trying to sit up made it one hundred times worse. The residue of the smell on the cloth hung menacingly around her nose, and she instinctively knew that it must have been chloroform on it even though she was unfamiliar with its aroma. As far as she knew she was still on the floor of her house, but as she raised her head and looked around her she found to her dismay that she was not. She had no idea exactly where she was, but it didn't look remotely familiar to her. The small room was dark and looked like a very small bedroom or box room; a single bed with a duvet and pillow draped with simple plain-coloured covers with a bedside cabinet next to it were the only things in there. The walls were bare, and the one window had what looked like grey paint splattered over it to prevent looking out. It was dingy, cold and menacing, and she instinctively knew that she was being held captive in there.

Forcing herself to get up she walked unsteadily towards the window, head pounding with every step, and tried to open it but it was locked, with the key nowhere in sight. She then wondered how long she'd been out, as there was enough light coming into the room through the paint for it to be either morning or even afternoon, she couldn't tell, especially as there was no clock be seen or her watch on her wrist to inform her. As her attempt to open the window to see out or even shout for help was futile, she resigned herself to lie down on the bed, at which point her stomach growled at her angrily; she hadn't eaten since around seven on Saturday evening. Today could be Sunday, or even Monday, as far as she knew. As she lay there she heard a key turning in a lock and the door opened slightly, but before she could raise her head enough to see it was closed shut again. When she managed to sit up, she saw a tray had been pushed in and left beside it. On it was a plate with a pre-packed sandwich, and beside that a travel flask with whatever was inside. She'd take them both, whatever they were; she was starving.

It was while she was eating the second half of the sandwich that she started to think a bit more clearly now that she had some kind of sustenance inside her and her headache had subsided somewhat. Why on earth had she of all people been kidnapped, as that was obviously what it was that had happened. She wasn't rich, nor did she have rich parents to bail her out if that was the reason, so why her exactly? Then a chill went through her when her mind took her to the only other possible motive she could think of: The missing women. She knew from Tiss that the fifth anniversary of the phenomena that dated back twenty years was fast approaching, on the 23rd of the month, to be precise. Surely this couldn't be anything ... but, no, she stopped herself there; she couldn't let herself think that this was in any way connected to that. Could she?

***

At about the same time as Claudia was being chloroformed in her own home, Jeff was sitting in the bar of the Regency Club. He'd already met with the officials and had been finally welcomed as a fully-fledged member of their society, so now was the time to relax. But he wasn't just sitting there for the social aspect of it, nor was he relaxing; he was biding his time until he could take a look around on his own in the pretext of familiarising himself with his new-found surroundings. A few people came to speak to him to introduce themselves while he was there, one even bought him a drink, but at that particular moment he was on his own. Time to move, he thought, and as casually as he could muster. With a drink still in his hand, he meandered his way around the lounge and out into another part of the club. Fortunately, he remembered where every section was when he'd been shown around, from the dining room to the behind-the-scenes offices – and the latter was where he was now headed. If anyone stopped him he had already conjured up a contingency plan: he would say he was just getting his bearings, smile and say whoops, sorry, had he gone somewhere he shouldn't have? He would go for newbie ignorance rather than intent and purpose. But he hoped that it wouldn't come to that. He knew how to stealthily insinuate himself into a precarious situation, and hoped that this would be no different to the times he'd done it all before.

As he made his way to his intended destination, he stopped at various points on the route hoping that anyone who saw him would think he was taking special note of his surroundings, fitting in, as it were. By the time he got to the section where he could access the offices, he looked around before casually slipping in through the doorway. Fortunately, there was no one in the corridor as he entered it, and he made his way towards the office where he'd first met the board, slipping on a pair of nitrile gloves as he went. He'd noticed a computer on the desk when he was there and thought that to be a good place to start. Although the door had a keyhole it wasn't locked when he tried it. Once inside he locked it from the inside, giving the impression to anyone trying the door that the key would be required to get inside. Should that, heaven forbid, happen then at least he'd get a warning and manage to get himself out before whoever it was returned. But he was jumping ahead of himself. He instinctively knew what action to take if that were to occur.

Jeff sat down at the desk and turned on the hard drive and monitor. It was a brand he was familiar with so he knew he'd be able to do what he needed to quickly and efficiently and not take up too much time. That was the kind of job he liked. He searched and found what he was looking for, taking a flash drive out of his jacket pocket and slotting it into the

USB port on the side. The three files loaded quickly; he'd look at them as soon as he got home rather than stay there to read them now. After closing the computer down he quietly and swiftly made his way back to the main club lounge before heading to the bar. He ordered a single whisky and sat for a while chatting with the barkeeper just to keep up appearances before heading home to find out exactly what was contained in the files he'd manage to extract.

CHAPTER THIRTY

Jeff knew it was going to be a long night. When he got in at just after ten, the first thing he did was stick the flash drive he'd downloaded the selected files from the computer onto into one of his own devices. The files were enormous, containing data he knew would take more than a few hours to go through. Fortunately, as he had a free day the next day, he had nothing better to do than to go through them in the hope of discovering something enlightening about the disappearing women as he didn't for one moment think that they were entirely innocent in all that. However, as the night wore on, he began to realise that perhaps he'd been wrong. Nothing he found had any bearing on the women, or even hinted at them, which made him believe that the only connection to the club had been the fact that they'd last been seen somewhere in its vicinity. That in itself suggested a connection, but what if there actually wasn't one. His mind tried to process all the possibilities and connotations, thinking that if they had been kidnapped for whatever reason, maybe the person who did so had lured them to that spot simply for someone to register that they had seen them. By the time 3am came around, and after drinking what Jeff assessed to have been around six large mugs of black coffee, he reluctantly admitted defeat. At least defeat with those files he'd downloaded and viewed so far. He had one section left to check, but his eyes were starting to hurt him too much to carry on. He'd look at that in the morning, but if nothing jumped out at him then perhaps others in the club's system might offer him further information. If that was the case then he'd return there that night, but in the meantime he finally turned his computer off and headed up to bed to grab whatever sleep he could after the copious amounts of caffeine he'd just drunk. He didn't think he'd get much, but at least he'd try.

***

The longer Claudia was missing the more Tiss' anxiety intensified. Allowing the first twenty-four hours for initially reporting a person going missing had already been bypassed, mainly because DC James Woodhouse, working in conjunction with the cold case squad, was aware that any woman going missing at this time was worthy of an immediate follow-up regardless of the usual time constraints. It was a good thing that he had, but sadly, Claudia's whereabouts still remained unknown despite the area where her phone was still giving off a signal had been extensively searched without avail. She knew that the first seventy-two hours were vital in any missing person case, and the hours were ticking by far too quickly for her liking. In short, she was in a state, and she'd asked for a day off from work as she was unable to concentrate, and had been granted it. It was while she was still lying in bed at 9am on Tuesday morning that Jeff rang her. The first thing she said to him was that she was at home, and he replied 'ditto'.

'I've come across something I think you should know,' he continued before explaining to her the events of the previous evening.

'You were careful, weren't you?' she'd asked in concern. She kept saying it to him, and he was probably sick of her saying it, but the last thing she wanted was for anyone else to get dragged down into this if it all went to hell. She'd set the ball in motion in the first place, so any fallout had to be all on her shoulders.

'Yes, I was, but listen. I've discovered something about Frank Marshall's wife, Miriam.'

'Oh yes?' Tiss sat up a bit straighter in the bed, eager to hear what he was going to say.

'You know how I said the Regency Club was going to have what sounded like some Bacchanalian festival on the 23rd?'

'Well, you said it was going to be some kind of party with women invited, but you didn't mention the fact that it was going to be Bacchanalian.' It occurred to Tiss as she said it that the way it came out sounded like she was jealous. Was she jealous of the fact that he'd be going to an event where there'd be seemingly willing women?

'You're right, I don't think I did, but that's what it's starting to sound like. Anyway, guess who has been assigned to supplying the women?'

'Supplying, as in providing some kind of escort service?' Yes, *now* she was jealous!

'I think that's probably the correct way to put it, but yes. And,' he continued, obviously itching to tell her. 'You're not going to believe this, but she was once prosecuted for once having a bawdy house-'

'Bawdy house – as in house of ill-repute or a brothel?' Tiss interrupted, knowing what the term meant, but was amused by his rather archaic choice of word for it.

'Exactly that. And she was prosecuted for it ... by your mother back in 2001.'

'What?' Then it sunk it. Was that what she was doing going into the club that day with a younger man, going with him to plan all this? But wouldn't her husband already be aware of that if he was on the board of directors, so why did he come to her office that day just after Christmas saying he thought she was having an affair, wanting her to investigate? She aired her thoughts with Jeff.

'So it looks like he knew exactly what he was doing; probably targeted you from the start.'

'Wait, do you mean that he *wanted* me to get involved in this; to what end?'

'I'm thinking to possibly get back at your parents somehow.'

'For my mother prosecuting her? Perhaps if she hadn't broken the law in the first place,' she huffed before an horrific realisation sank in. 'Do you mean to say that I might have been personally picked out as the next woman to go missing?'

'I don't know, but the timing and all seems more than a little strange. That being said, I can't find anything in the files I downloaded last night that even mentions anything to do with a specific ceremony, but I'm planning to going back there again tonight. If Marshall *is* involved in any way with the missing women, then it probably means everyone at the club is too.'

'Please be-'

'I know,' Jeff interrupted. 'Please, Tiss, you don't have to say it again, believe me. I have no intention of getting caught.'

'Said by every criminal on the planet who ever gets caught,' she retorted. 'But if I was the intended victim then why have they taken Claudia?'

'Another way to get back at you; make it hurt even more.' He said coldly.

***

There were only a few days until the 23rd and Claudia had been missing for three. Tiss was distraught. Jeff had again broken into the Regency Club's files the following night as promised, but had found nothing. He, too, was likewise distraught. Seeing Tiss heartbroken by her friend's disappearance had broken him as well, although he managed to keep this to himself as best as he could while he tried to support her. He'd visited her each evening after work in an attempt to keep her sane even though beneath it all he was falling apart as much as she was. But he was there to support her; she needed it more than he did, so he kept doing it. Apart from all the worry, he knew he was falling hopelessly for her.

DC James Woodhouse was also distraught. After his abysmal failure of finding Claudia's phone, (his own words, not the Force's as they thought he'd shone for his quick action), he was left floundering. He *wanted* to find her, *needed* to for both his own and for Tiss' sake, and he knew what was behind it was the fact that he was becoming increasingly attracted to her. No clues or leads had emerged that would lead them to her discovery which he hoped would find her alive and well, but he knew the Spring Equinox was approaching in a few days, and for that reason it was vital to find her whether or not the two things were related. As far as he knew, Claudia had no relatives in the UK only a boyfriend, who had been immediately interviewed as soon as she went missing but had since not been considered a suspect. At a complete loss as to what to do next, he asked if Tiss and Ruby would meet him at Claudia's home in an attempt to see if they could spot anything amiss, something he and the forensic team could not and might require someone with a personal knowledge of the woman to spot. So he arranged for the two women to meet him that afternoon.

Starting on the first floor and working their way down, Woodhouse followed them as each woman ventured throughout the house looking for something which seemed out of place to them. They started in the bedroom, checking through each of the drawers, something Woodhouse had not being comfortable with doing, but they did it with the ease of familiarity. It was easier for someone who knew her personally to do such a thing rather than a stranger such as himself. After the bedroom offered nothing of interest, their visit to the bathroom was over with within a couple of minutes as all there was where her toiletries and towels. The second bedroom was merely a minimal space designed for overnight or weekend guests, with a bed neatly made and a printed duvet set in a colour which complimented both the walls and the carpet, and a wardrobe and set of drawers left empty for anyone to fill themselves. When they all came downstairs the kitchen was the next port of call, but despite the two women examining every drawer and cupboard, nothing emerged as having any significance to Claudia's disappearance. The lounge was next, the final room, and Woodhouse didn't hold out much hope for that either. The house so far was neat, far too neat, and said to him that whoever had taken her must have returned at some point to tidy everything up. So he was surprised to say the least when Tiss had an unexpected reaction to something she was holding up.

'What is it?' he asked as he crossed the room to see what it was. She seemed agitated and was met with a photograph in a frame being pushed forcibly in his face. He took it from her he looked at the image – a woman, who he imagined must be Claudia, together with two men. One of them had his arm casually slung around her, and another man was standing next to him on his other side. He hadn't interviewed the boyfriend himself, somebody on the team had already interviewed him while he was out trying to trace her phone, so he assumed he was the one next to her.

'This person,' she said as she tapped frantically on the face of the other man in the shot. 'I know who he is.'

'Well, if he's a friend then perhaps you have-' his response was cut short.

'No, not as a friend, I haven't met him as a friend, I met him the first time I went to the Regency Club. He was the relief manager who was on relief the day I went there with Miriam Marshall's photograph.

'Did you get his name?' a stunned yet excited Woodhouse asked. Stunned because he'd not expected anything, and excited because this could be the first solid piece of positive evidence that had turned up.

'No, he didn't give it,' Tiss all but shouted in frustration. 'He wasn't very pleasant with me, though, as I recall. The person who was on duty on the desk that day was an elderly man by the name of George; I'm sure he'll remember me being there.'

'Good, this is good,' the detective constable enthused. 'Okay then, are you okay to go there with me now?'

'Of course I am,' came the eager reply.

'And I'm coming with you too,' Ruby chirped in just as eagerly.

CHAPTER
THIRTY-ONE

Eyebrows raised when Woodhouse flanked by Tiss and Claudia entered the Regency Club doors. Two men standing talking beside the reception desk looked all three up and down disrespectfully but seemed to change their tune somewhat when the police officer brought out his warrant card to show to the man behind the desk. Tiss recognised him as the George she'd told Woodhouse about, and she only hoped that he recognised her as well.

'May I help you?' George asked unphased, showing no emotion as to the fact that there were also two women standing beside the police officer.

'I don't know if you remember me,' Tiss said before Woodhouse could even get a word out.

'Yes, of course I do, Ms Lawson. We don't get many women come into the club, and if I may be as bold as to say that your entrance was quite memorable, which is why I remember you.'

Tiss blushed a little remembering at how forceful she'd been at the time.

'Anyway,' Woodhouse moved forward showing George his ID, 'I'd like to speak to your manager.'

'Which one specifically?' came the reply.

'Which one?' the DC echoed. 'Is there more than one?'

'Actually yes, there is, there are two. We have a manager and relief manager. Whoever is in at the time is usually simply referred to as "the manager,"' George confirmed.

It was then that Tiss produced the framed photograph from her bag and presented it to him. 'Him there,' she said pointing to him in the photograph

'Ah, yes, Mr Wilson. I'm afraid he's not on relief at the moment though.'

'And what time is he in?' the detective asked.

George then turned around to pick up a ledger from a shelf behind him and open it up, quickly scanning through the pages to the one he was seeking. Was everything in the more conservative part of the club non-computerised? Tiss thought. There wasn't even a computer on the desk, something else she remembered from the first time, just the red signing in journal on the upper plinth. It truly was an old-fashioned establishment in more ways than she thought possible, apart from the more modern offices at the back which were kept separate. 'He's been off for a couple of days, so not until the day after tomorrow, I'm afraid,' he finally announced.

'Then I need to have his address,' Woodhouse continued.

'I'm afraid that's not possible, sir.'

'And why not?'

'You of all people must understand the law surrounding confidential information,' George said looking at the police officer with a tilt of his head and an entirely serious face. 'If you are seeking to obtain his address then it must be done with a search warrant as I'm not at liberty to disclose it.'

'Can I speak to the manager who *is* in then,' frustration with the situation clearly showing in his voice.

'You can, but I can assure you that he will say exactly the same as what I am telling you now.'

At any other time Tiss would have considered George to be badass, but her friend was missing and that would have been highly inappropriate under the circumstances. Saying that he would return presently with a warrant, Woodhouse turned to go and the two women followed suit.

Now Tiss would be the first person to normally say that she didn't believe in coincidence or fate or anything remotely like that, prior to this whole sorry mess that is, but as the DC was just about to open the door for them to go through it opened inwardly on them, and for once in her life she could say that maybe the whole coincidence thing was true after all. With eyes as wide as saucers Tiss stared at the person who came to an abrupt stop right in front of them. Eyes as equally wide as hers stared back at her before flicking to each of her companions in turn.

'Sorry,' Jeff Rawlings said to them before hurrying past and making his way to the reception desk.

'Ah, Mr Rawlings,' she heard George say as he greeted the new arrival, but was ushered out of the door by the detective before she could hear any more, and she didn't dare look around to see if he was still looking at her. She knew he was going to the club, he'd said as much earlier, but she hadn't expected to almost literally bump into him like that, and by the look of him neither did he.

Once outside Woodhouse asked her if she was okay. 'You look like you've just seen a ghost,' he said with a frown.

'No, no, it's fine; I'm fine,' she lied. 'I just didn't expect anyone to come barging in like that. It gave me a shock.'

'Right then, I'm going to ring the team at the station to get a warrant to get Wilson's address then I'm taking you both home.'

'You'll keep us informed of everything though?' Tiss asked hopefully, but already knew the answer to that. Woodhouse had already confirmed that he'd do just that every step of the way.

Woodhouse led them to his car and unlocked it. While the women got in he stood outside as he made the promised phone call. Ruby took the chance to quiz her friend further. 'What was all that about in there; do you know who that person was?' she asked.

'That was Jeff Rawlings, the guy who works with Lily Singer.'

Ruby looked at her in astonishment. 'The Jeff that's been helping you with the missing women cases?'

'The very same.'

'But what's he doing here? Did you know he was a member?' But then it seemed to dawn on her and the realisation began to sink in. 'Oh, Tiss, please don't tell me he's doing even more than just giving you files – like the two of you doing a little private investigation on your own together? Are you both nuts.'

All Tiss could do was to shrug. 'It can't do any harm to have somebody work the inside too.'

'To work the inside ... Tiss, this is dangerous stuff and you shouldn't be getting yourself mixed up in all this. Jeff is a PI, this is what he does.'

'Actually no, it isn't. He's a computer whizz who helps Lily out with that kind of stuff.'

'Well that's even worse then, isn't it. What if the pair of you get yourselves arrested, or worse?'

'Then I am a solicitor after all.'

'Tiss!'

But before she could add anything else to that Woodhouse opened the door and climbed into the driver's seat. 'Okay, that's done,' he said with a smile, even though it was only as a confirmation rather than the fact he was happy. While he drove away Tiss pulled out her phone and sent a quick text message to Jeff: *Sorry about that, will speak later. Can you find out anything about the relief manager, a man by the name of Wilson?* The reply came back almost immediately: *Of course.*

***

Although Jeff was dying to know what it was about, he knew that if Tiss asked him to do anything then it must be important. Perfect timing, he thought as he made his way to the bar – the place he found was a good stopping off point to assess where people were and to make sure the coast was clear for him to go off and do a bit of investigating. His sole intent was to go back to the computer and download the remaining files he hadn't downloaded the day before, but now he had another task: find out about Wilson, the relief manager. He assessed in the brief moment that he was confronted by Tiss and the two others that one was most likely her friend, Ruby, and the other was Woodhouse, the detective constable who was heading up her other friend, Claudia's, disappearance. So how was the relief manager involved in this? Doubtlessly, Tiss would tell him when he rang her later as promised, but in the meantime he would try to find out what he could for her.

One of the older club members came up and spoke to him as he cradled his glass of whisky – which he had to admit was one of the nicest blends he'd had in a long time, and he must ask the bartender what it was. The guy was a retired surgeon, and Jeff had to admit to himself that he recognised his name. They sat and chatted for a good twenty minutes or so before the gentleman excused himself saying that he had an appointment shortly. In that moment Jeff began to feel like the sham he was. He actually felt quite comfortable in this place, and in other circumstances might have joined somewhere like this just for the companionship. He had plenty of acquaintances but admittedly not many friends outside his line of work. He saw Lily as a friend in a platonic kind of way, and there were a couple of people from his university days he still kept in touch with, but a true lifelong friend had always eluded him as had a permanent girlfriend or partner. He hoped, really hoped, that Tiss might just say yes if he asked her out one day. He'd already mentioned the fact that he'd like to date her to Lily, but wasn't sure if she would make Tiss aware of that fact, and it wasn't said in the hope that she even would. So why had he said it? Perhaps he was just putting the feelers out, testing the waters, as it were, to see if he might have a chance. Nothing Lily had said made him think that he didn't, but that would only be proven by actually going ahead and doing it. In truth, he wanted it so much that he was scared to go ahead and do it in fear of rejection. Rejection wasn't something he could easily cope with, never had been.

After his drinking companion left he decided to make his move. Tuesdays didn't seem to be overly populated nights for members to be in attendance, something he was grateful for under the circumstances. So he downed the rest of his exquisite whisky and headed off in the direction of the offices, reminding himself to ask what the label was when he returned. He met no resistance when he slipped casually into the hallway leading to them; so far so good. He slipped on a pair of nitriles before trying the same door he'd easily entered previously, but found it locked this time. Fortunately, he'd brought his lock pick set with him this time. Once in he locked the door behind him again and made his way over to the computer and worked quickly to find what he wanted. Apart from the files he hadn't taken the last time he found the information Tiss had asked for and took a screenshot of it with his phone; he'd send it to her once he was back in the bar as he now wanted to get out of there as quickly as possible in case someone just happened along. He'd been lucky last time but didn't want to push his luck this one. As he headed to the door he took one last look over his shoulder to make sure all was as he'd found it before opening it to leave. It was just as he was opening it that he felt a force thrusting him back into the room and he fell flat on his back, the wind knocked clean out of him. Before he had time to move or even look up, a body was sitting on top of him with one strong hand pinning him down on the floor while another cloth-wrapped one was on his mouth. A pungent smell attacked his nostrils before the room began to sway and a blackness overcame him.

CHAPTER
THIRTY-TWO

Claudia was dozing on the bed as there was nothing else for her to do when she heard a scuffling outside the door of her cramped dull room. Her first thoughts were that she was being rescued, but that that was quickly dispelled when the door was harshly flung opened and a person was thrown bodily through it. The man landed heavily on the floor at the side of the bed and the door was shut behind him with a loud bang. She sat up and looked down at him as she heard him let out a painful groan.

'Are you okay?' she asked with concern, thinking the manner in which he'd been manhandled and landed must have been more than a little uncomfortable for him, surely causing at least painful heavy bruising if not small break if he was unlucky.

'Where am I?' the man moaned as he tried and failed to sit up. Claudia was almost afraid to try and help in case his injury was severe, and knew that moving him was the worst thing anyone could offer. Even so, she felt compelled to at least do something, so she got off the bed and knelt down beside him.

'I've no idea where we are,' she admitted as she looked him over. His face was bruised and he had a few cuts on it, but she got a whiff of that pungent smell she'd smelled on herself when she awoke, meaning that he'd likely been chloroformed just like she had before being kidnapped. 'I'm Claudia, by the way,' she said as a way of introduction, and was surprised to see his eyes light up in recognition.

'Claudia Romano?' he asked as he forced himself to sit up, causing him to grimace as another groan passed his lips.

'Um, yes?'

'Everybody's looking for you. Sorry, I'm Jeff, Jeff Rawlings, I'm a friend of Tiss'. I've been doing a bit of investigating for her, but it seems I wasn't as stealthy as I hoped I'd be.'

'Ah, yes, Jeff. I know who you are. You gave those files on the missing women to Tiss, didn't you?'

'That's me.'

'So why are we here?' she asked.

Jeff sat up sufficiently to swivel around and sit with his back against the bed. Claudia sat down on the floor beside him. 'Tiss and I both think that the Regency Club has something to do with the missing women, and I managed to infiltrated it as a member just to see what I can find out in their computer system.'

'Isn't that dangerous?'

'Apparently,' he said with a slight upturn of his lips and a shrug of his shoulders. 'Before I was attacked she asked me if I could find out the address of someone called Wilson who she said was the relief manager. I found it and was about to send it to her when I was jumped. Did you happen to see who attacked you?'

'No, but I can smell what I think is chloroform on you; they got me the same way in my home. Since then I've had meals pushed through the door on a tray, but whoever's doing it was wearing a balaclava as a mask.'

'So it could be anybody.'

'Yes. I get in a sense why they'd take you, but why me?' Claudia asked.

'I think it's to get at Tiss' parents.'

'Tiss' parents?' she frowned. 'Why them, and why me?'

'I think it could have easily been Ruby as you, but as she shares a house with her fiancé you're a better target as you're on your own. As to the why as regards her parents – I found out that Miriam Marshall, Frank's wife, the person who was seen going into the club with a younger man, used to have a brothel and was arrested years ago for it and prosecuted by Tiss' mother.'

'And have you told Tiss all this?'

'Yes.'

'So this Miriam Marshall has held a grudge all these years?'

'It would seem so.'

'But what has this to do with the missing women?'

Jeff let out a sigh. 'Well,' he began with a drawl, 'we believe that it's something to do with the spring equinox and the winter solstice, at least it was Tiss who drew that to my attention because of the dates when all the women over the last twenty years vanished.'

'So, it's what … it's something to do with magic or the supernatural?'

Jeff could only shrug. 'Or something based on ancient ritual, but I don't know to what end if it is the case.'

'And I'm an intended missing woman?' Claudia looked at him in horror, and he could only nod in return.

'I believe so, or at least it's possible. In all seriousness I believed that Tiss might have been the one who had been targeted as she fit the type perfectly: same age, hair colouring, overall appearance. But looking at you now I can see how you'd also fit the bill.'

'Dear God! So it's some kind of sect thing?'

'I honestly don't know. The strange thing is, though, all the stuff I've gleaned from their computer doesn't seem to indicate it. In fact, there's nothing at all mentioned about equinoxes or solstices, and the only mention to women is Miriam Marshall ferrying about a dozen of them in for the AGM on the 23rd – which coincidentally is when the spring equinox is, but I'm now not convinced that it's in any way related. I think it's more of a planned orgy than anything else.'

'Eww, disgusting. Then who is it that's kidnapped us, and is it even related to the missing women case?' Jeff could only offer a shrug in response.

***

When Tiss didn't hear from Jeff she became quite worried, worried enough to want to do something about it. Despite him telling her that everything would be all right, she knew the risk he was taking even being in there in the first place. There was always the possibility that someone would invariably find out the true reason for him wanting to join their secret band and they wouldn't take very kindly to it. Her anxiety had grown tenfold in the two hours that had passed since her texting him; with his skills finding as something as simple as an address should have been child's play, so in the end she rang DC Woodhouse to make him aware of her fears.

'He's done what!' he all but shouted down the phone after she explained how she and Jeff had been investigating the club in more depth than he already knew. 'Do you know how both ridiculous and dangerous that is? The files you showed me were bad enough, but this?' She had to admit to him that she knew both of those things, but the whole situation had demanded her full attention from the start. Some would even say it had become an obsession.

Woodhouse let out a groan that sounded part-sigh and part-defeat, but although she knew that he was annoyed, an understatement she was well aware of, she also knew that he understood where she was coming from with this as they'd discussed the case but not the true extent of her involvement in it. That was a revelation to him, but Jeff's welfare was important to her and that superseded anything unofficial they'd both done.

'Right … okay,' he said at long last after ruminating over all that she'd said to him. 'I've got Jonathan Wilson's home address and the search warrant has just this minute come through so I'm about to go over there now.' The line went silent for a moment as Tiss waited and hoped that he might be mulling over inviting her to come with her, but her hopes were dashed when he added 'You know I can't ask you to join me, don't you?'

'Of course,' she said half-heartedly, the sadness evident in her voice. She knew, of course she knew, but wanted to go, nevertheless. She could have always pulled her "well, he might need a solicitor" card, but if Wilson was guilty of having anything to do with this horrific case then she didn't want to represent him or in fact have anything to do with him.

'Look, I'll keep you updated with what I find,' he said as a way of softening the blow even though he was well within his rights not to tell her anything at all about what he was doing. After all, she was a civilian, he was a police officer, and the two just shouldn't mix when it came to investigating anything suspicious - regardless of the fact that they now were.

'Okay. Thank you,' came the reply. All she could do now was to sit and wait for news about the two of her friends who were now missing instead of just the one.

CHAPTER
THIRTY-THREE

D C James Woodhouse took two uniformed officers with him when he went to check the address of the club's relief manager. Like before when searching for Claudia's phone, the cold case unit had obtained a search warrant in record time for him, something he was more than grateful for. The address was an apartment building in the centre of town, one of the newer upmarket ones which had only been built in recent years and which was mostly inhabited by high-earning executives who wished to be closer to their places of employment. Quite the opposite to Woodhouse himself who, when off duty, preferred to be as far away from his work as possible. Even at his relatively young age, Woodhouse had seen enough to make most people quake in their boots; everything from property crimes and white-collar crimes to the more violent ones like assault and homicide. He'd personally borne witness to the savagery of death and the after effects crime had on an unsuspecting public. He'd also experienced first-hand how it had changed the lives of victims' friends and relatives, and the nightmare world of disbelief and forced acceptance it had driven them into. Each and every crime he'd witnessed were equally devastating in their own right and upsetting to anyone who had one iota of a moral compass. It was for this reason that when he clocked off from his shifts he wanted to find himself in a place of quiet and reason, distancing himself from life's cruelties, to be comforted by his friends and family, most of whom couldn't conceive the horrors of being a police officer even if they were being told about it. It was something that had to be experienced, to be seen to be believed, but he wouldn't wish that on anyone, not even his worst enemies if he had any.

There was a reception desk when they entered the building, just off to the right of the main entrance doors, but as there was nobody sitting behind it, it didn't seem to be a requisite that their arrival needed to be reported or announced to a resident. If that was the case, as it appeared to be, Woodhouse wondered why there even was one. Perhaps it also acted as a sales or rental desk for any potential future tenant or home owner, as that would be the only other reason to have one at all. As they approached one of the two lifts, a floor plan beside them indicated which floor they'd find Wilson's flat on: the fourth. All three officers entered the lift when it arrived with a ping, and Woodhouse pressed button number four to ascend. Wilson's flat was at the end of the corridor, and one of four apartments which appeared to be on each floor. If the external décor was anything to go by then the interiors of each properties would also be of the highest quality. As a relatively new build, he didn't doubt that they would have all mod cons and top-of-the-range appliances, probably reflected in the monthly rent or sale prices. Fortunately, they hadn't as yet encountered one living soul from entering the building to where they were now. Had they, they would have inevitably seen horrified faces as one of the two accompanying offices was carrying a battering ram with him in order to get into the property should nobody be at home. Luckily, after Woodhouse pressed the doorbell, the sound of footsteps within could be heard approaching.

'Mr Wilson?' Woodhouse asked when the door opened to revealing a smartly dressed man in his late twenties.

'I'm afraid not,' came the unexpected reply, his eyes flitting from one of them to the other as he tried to assess the situation. He eyes widened almost comically at the sight of the ram in the officer's hand. Woodhouse had seen that reaction so many times, and under different circumstances it would have appeared as funny as it was. But this wasn't a time for humour; a woman and now a man were both missing, which was no laughing matter.

'And you are?' the detective asked the shaken young man.

'Barry. I'm Barry Tomlinson. What ... what's going on; what's this about?'

'I'm looking for Jonathan Wilson. Do you know his current whereabouts?'

'No, I'm afraid I don't. Nate said he was going away for a couple of days with his brother, and I'm just here to feed his cats. I live a couple of doors down.' He looked stunned, and Woodhouse didn't doubt that he was who he said he was and doing as he said, yet he had to make sure.

'Do you have anything that can show your identification?' Woodhouse asked for some form of non-verbal proof before continuing, and waited at the door until Tomlinson went back to his flat for his driving licence. Once satisfied as to the man's identity he produced the search warrant from his pocket and handed it to him.

'Is there some kind of a problem; are they both okay? I don't understand!'

'Just let us in to take a look around, Mr Tomlinson, and we'll be out of your hair before you know it.'

Without saying a word, the man stood back to let them enter; it looked as if he was in shock. As they came in he stood looking at the warrant as if wondering what to do with it. Woodhouse instructed the officers to look around for anything they considered to be interesting while he continued speaking to the fearful cat-sitter.

'And do you know where they've gone; an address or even a telephone number?'

'I'm not sure where they're staying as he didn't say, but I've got his number if that's any help to you?'

'That will do just fine,' he responded as he retrieved his notebook and pen from his inside jacket pocket and offered them to him, adding, 'If you don't mind.' While Tomlinson was doing that Woodhouse strolled further into the flat, his eyes taking in everything he passed. As he was doing so his gaze settled on a photograph of two men, one of whom he now knew to be Claudia's boyfriend Simon and the other Jonathan Wilson. It looked like they were in a bar somewhere. No Claudia in the shot this time, though. He walked over and picked it up, then took it across to Tomlinson.

'These two men; how do they know each other?' he asked as the other man looked on.

'That's Nate, I mean Jonathan,' he said as he pointed. 'He's prefers to be called Nate.'

'And how does he know the other person in the photograph?'

'Well that's his brother, Simon.'

Simon was Jonathan Wilson's brother … who in turn was currently dating Claudia Romano? Woodhouse was stunned. Surely this was a little more than passing coincidence. Apart from that not-so-little bombshell, he and the other police officers found nothing that would indicate any kind of intent, and so they called it and left the flat. Woodhouse thanked the neighbour for his cooperation on the way out, hoping that Tomlinson would adhere to his demand not to get in touch with Wilson, but by the look on his face and the ashen colour he'd gone as he'd asked it, he suspected that he wouldn't. At least he hoped that he wouldn't. Once they were far enough away from the door and any chance of being overheard, Woodhouse rang through to his contact on the cold case team to give him Wilson's phone number. He knew that he'd know what to do with it. As long as it was switched on, under the Investigatory Powers Act the police could contact his phone provider to obtain the last know location of it, and once the location was found that's where he would be heading.

***

As neither of them were wearing a watch in order to tell the time, Claudia and Jeff had no idea how long they'd been held captive, or even what time of

day or night it was. Had they been wearing one
when they'd been taken, it was highly likely that it
would have been taken off them whilst they were
drugged and unconscious. Claudia thought that
perhaps a day had passed before Jeff had joined
her, but she really had no idea. At least they were
being fed, if a sandwich each and a bottle of water
a few hours apart could be counted as a nutritious
meal that is. It was far from perfect, but at least they
weren't being starved, which was something.
However, two people being confined to a small box
room with the only toilet facility being a shared
metal bucket was embarrassing to say the least, but
in the grand scheme of things that was the least of
their worries as the reason why they were there
was the main one.

At first, both found a common ground in Tiss,
talking about their connections to her, but after a
while their conversations began to expand to other
things. They talked about anything and everything
just to pass away the hours in an attempt to keep
the dread of what their captors had in mind for
them at bay. It seemed that if both stopped talking
they would retreat within themselves to think, and
if they started to think about the situation they
were in then they'd start to panic. At some point
along the line both of them fell asleep. Jeff had
insisted on settling down on the floor in order for
her to have the small bed to herself, claiming he'd
done it before and could do it again, but Claudia
wouldn't hear of it. She told him not to be
ridiculous; sharing the bed wouldn't be a problem
under the circumstances.

Like the time spend in the room, neither knew
how long they'd been asleep, but both woke
suddenly when it sounded like all hell was breaking

loose just outside their door. There was loud shouting followed by scuffling until it fell silent again. Jeff and Claudia sat up and stared at one another before directing their attention to the door, fearful for what was coming next. After a few moments they heard a key being turned in the lock before the door was flung open. Two uniformed officers with visored helmets and body armour appeared before them, the assault weapons clutched in their grasp momentarily aimed at them. Seeing the two terrified civilians before them the officers lowered their guns and gestured for them to follow them. Jeff and Claudia didn't waste a second getting off the bed to follow their instructions. As they walked somewhat unsteadily out of the room, they found themselves in a larger one, the living room of what looked like an old abandoned house which was scantily furnished apart from a couple of chairs and a threadbare sofa which had seen far better days. A few empty bottles of alcohol were lying scattered around on the concrete floor beside it. Several other officers stood milling around near the door with weapons nestled on their hips, watching as the pair were led outside and into the bright sunshine. The sudden glare was so harsh that they had to shield their eyes from it as hands guided them towards the ambulance parked up alongside an unmarked black van and a police car. Although they felt weak from their experience, they didn't think they required the need for hospital treatment, but allowed the police to carry out their due diligence by transferring them over to the waiting paramedics to be checked over. It was while they were sitting on the floor of the ambulance just inside the open back door and having both their blood pressures checked that a plain-clothed officer came across and made himself known to them.

'DC Tom Woodhouse,' he announced, 'and I believe you are Claudia Romano and Jeff Rawlings.' It was more of a statement than a question, and both nodded as confirmation. Woodhouse, of course, already recognised Claudia from her photo, but Jeff wasn't familiar to him, although, under the circumstances, there wasn't anybody else it could be.

'Thank goodness you've found us,' Jeff declared. 'How exactly *did* you find us?'

'There'll be plenty of time for that later,' the detective said as he laid a friendly hand on his arm, 'but in the meantime let's get you both checked out at hospital to make sure you're okay.'

CHAPTER
THIRTY-FOUR

'Oh, Claudia. Oh my goodness. Oh my goodness!' Tiss cried out as she came barrelling into the room where her friend was lying on top of the bed. 'Are you all right?' She sat beside Claudia and grabbed both her hands, holding them tightly in hers. Tears began to flow freely from both eyes as she stared at the person she thought she'd never see again.

'I'm fine, I'm okay, we both are. I'm not sure where they've taken Jeff, but he'll be around here somewhere too.'

'Yes, I've been told he's in the room next door, Lily's with him, but I just had to come and see you first. DC Woodhouse has told me all about it, about how he managed to find you, and it's quite a story.' She edged forward and moved a stray hair out of her friend's eye to hook it around her ear.

'I haven't spoken to him yet, not since he had a few words with us before the ambulance brought us here. Does he know why we were taken?'

'He said that he was going to start interviewing the Wilson brothers when he finished speaking to me.'

'The Wilson brothers?'

'Oh, of course, you don't know.' Tiss felt stupid; she'd jumped the gun. She forgot that her friend wouldn't know anything about her boyfriend and his brother and didn't really want to be the one to break it to her, but it seemed that wasn't an option now as she'd overstepped and would have to tell her. So she settled back with more than a degree of nervousness and began to relate to her as much as she knew.

'But I don't understand,' Claudia said at long last just as Ruby and Josh entered the room, and for a few brief moment Tiss had a welcome respite from telling her about how her boyfriend had been found at the scene. Once the greetings were over, she looked over at Tiss and insisted she continue with her story.

'And he, what, he kidnapped me?' Claudia asked incredulously after Tiss recommenced telling it to both her and now the two newcomers, Ruby and Josh.

'I still don't understand!' she exclaimed in frustration when Tiss nodded. 'Do you mean he's been conning me all this time? And why did he kidnap me, him and his what, his *brother*, did you say?'

'Yes, they're brothers. Jonathan Wilson is the relief manager at the Regency Club, and other than that, I'm still waiting to hear the reason for it all from DC Woodhouse. But we – we being the detective and Jeff Rawlings – think it all has something to do with the missing women.'

'You mean the two who go missing every five years, as in the files you showed me and Ruby?'

'Yes, the same.'

'But why me? And why Jeff?'

'Jeff's been doing some digging around at the club, even joined their secret society to try to get access to their computer systems. I don't know what he found when he was there last as I lost all contact with him, but by then Ruby had already alerted the police to you being missing.'

'The last thing I remember was going to bed early on Saturday night because I felt a bit dizzy after Simon left, and before falling off to sleep I heard a noise downstairs. I thought it was an open window or something, but when I went down to take a look that's when somebody put over my face, a cloth or a towel, I think, which I later began to realise must have been chloroform, and I woke up in an old house somewhere. I think it must have been the day after when Jeff joined me. It was difficult to tell the time in there, but although the windows were painted out, there was still the sense of dark and light. I remember it being light then going darker then at some point it was light again before he was thrown in there.'

'Thrown in, as in physically thrown in there?'

'Yes. I think he'd been chloroformed too as I could smell the same thing on him that was on me.'

'You two have been through the wringer, haven't you?'

'You could say that.' Claudia agreed, then she seemed to realise something. 'Oh, no, if he's involved, does that mean that Simon, slipped me something when he was there before he left to make me feel off?'

'I really don't know, but it's possible.'

Claudia leaned forward on the bed and put her head in her hands in despair, and Tiss reached across to grip her hand tightly in an attempt to comfort her.

'Try not to think about it as it won't do you any good to worry. Now you need to get your strength up again, you and Jeff both. I'm just so glad that you're both okay, and that's what matters now.'

After that interchange, Tiss excused herself and left Claudia with Ruby and Josh as she went next door to see how Jeff was. When she entered, Lily was sitting on a chair beside the bed and both looked over at her and smiled. Jeff had a blossoming bruise on his left cheek and a cut above the same eyebrow which had been dressed with three butterfly dressing strips. He looked a mess and she was immediately filled with guilt at having got him mixed up in this mess in the first place. Her face must have shown it as Jeff said to her that it was all right and he patted the bed for her to sit on it.

'I'm so sorry, Jeff,' she said to him as she felt a solitary tear trickle down her cheek.

'Hey, hey, it's okay, I'm fine.'

'No you're not, look at you.'

'I'm in one piece and that's all that matters,' he replied, reaching out and taking her hand in his.

'But I feel so guilty; it's all my fault.'

'No it isn't,' he insisted. 'I volunteered to do this and I could have said no if I didn't want to do it, so stop blaming this on yourself. If anyone, blame it on those two who kidnapped me and your friend. How's she doing, by the way?'

'She's fine, and looks far better than you do.'

'Have the two men been interviewed by the police yet?' Lily spoke up for the first time since she'd entered. She looked as exhausted as the rest of them and had probably had about as much sleep, or lack thereof, since the news of both Jeff's and Claudia's disappearance.

'I don't know. I spoke to DC Woodhouse very briefly when he told me he'd found both Jeff and Claudia, and he promised to let me know as soon as he had something to give me.'

'He sounds like a decent bloke,' Lily continued, tucking one leg under the other as she sat on the chair.

'Seems so. And to think that at one point I was beginning to have my doubts about him.'

'In what way?' she asked settling herself more comfortably. It seemed she was there for the long haul.

'I think I was beginning to suspect everyone, especially after hearing that Tom Davenport knew the Marshalls and was also a member of the Regency Club.'

'But Woodhouse is a police officer,' she argued.

'True, but even police officers can be suspect.' She shook her head. 'I don't know. Apart from Jeff here, I was beginning to suspect every man I came into contact with.'

'It's nice to know that you trust me,' Jeff tried to smile, but then grimaced as it affected his swollen cheek.

Tiss stayed for a while longer, alternating between the two rooms to check up on each of her friends. She was anxious to hear what was going on down at the police station; anxious to hear the reason why the Wilson brothers had done what they had, but she knew that she'd have to wait until Woodhouse contacted her, which she realised could be hours yet depending upon what they said or if they were even willing to talk in the first place. It was while she was still there that a text message came through from her work: everyone had been given the day off in light of the current situation, and all appointments had been rescheduled. She felt sorry for Diane having to ring around everyone before finally getting to go home herself. She'd call her later to check up on her.

The doctor who did the rounds said that he'd like to keep Claudia and Jeff in for a few more hours before finally releasing them. As she couldn't do anything else, she decided to make her way home, saying she'd be over to see Claudia as soon as she was settled in back at her own house. Lily said that she would stay with Jeff for a while once he was released, but Tiss said that she'd be over to see him too following her visit to Claudia. As she realised that she didn't even know where he lived, she had to ask him for his address.

'Then I'll stay until you get there,' Lily said, forcing back any objections Jeff began to make, brushing his hand away as he tried to reach across to her.

'But I'll be okay,' he insisted, sounding weak despite his determination. Tiss imagined he would be in a great deal of pain with his face looking the way it was.

'I'm sure you will be,' Lily continued giving him a frown, 'but best be sure, eh?'

Eventually he gave in and relented, bravado finally leaving him.

***

The call she'd been expecting from DC Woodhouse finally arrived at 4pm, much longer than anticipated. She had been sitting with Claudia, Ruby and Josh at the former's house since 2pm after she'd been released, and had to say that she was faring far better than expected, and definitely much better than poor Jeff was.

'I'd rather not talk about it over the phone,' Woodhouse said, which immediately piqued her attention.

'Okay,' she'd responded and waited for his suggested as to where they meet.

'Can you come down to the station?'

Saying that she could, she informed her friends of her intentions and excused herself as quickly as she could.

When she arrived at the station she made her way to the reception desk and said that the detective had asked to see her. After a quick phone call, Woodhouse appeared from one of the two lifts either side of the desk.

'Ah, you're here,' he said as he shook her hand before indicating that she should follow him. Once they were in the lift he pressed the button for the fourth floor. As the doors closed and it slowly began to ascend, Woodhouse began to tell her of what he'd learned in the hours since the Wilson brothers had been arrested.

'Well, it's not very much,' he admitted. 'But Simon Wilson has been way more helpful than the other Wilson, insisting he knew nothing about what his brother was doing.'

'And do you believe him?'

Woodhouse rubbed the back of his neck. 'Not totally, not one hundred percent,' he admitted, 'but I have to say I'm inclined to.'

'Why?'

'Just a feeling; call it a hunch, a professional one. That and the fact that he's happy to talk to me. From my experience, the more guilty a person is the more they shut up and demand a solicitor, but from a legal standpoint it will take more than just his say so or what my senses are telling me.'

'I hope that's not why you've asked me here, to act as a solicitor for them,' Tiss said a tad more harshly than she intended.

'Oh, no, no, that's not ... I'm sorry, perhaps I should have phrased that a little better. No, of course that's not why I asked you to come down here; I'm waiting for the duty solicitor to be able to come and see them both.'

'Thank goodness,' Tiss breathed a sigh of relief. The last thing wanted was to be asked to represent anyone who had kidnapped two of her friends, and who had also beaten up one of them. 'So what was it that you couldn't tell me over the phone?'

'Although he hasn't admitted anything, Jonathan Wilson said something very interesting while I was questioning him.'

'Go on.'

'He said that it was all his brother's fault, and left it at that.'

'What on earth did that mean?'

'No idea, which is why we're now waiting for a solicitor to come in to try to get him to open up.'

'So one's saying they are innocent and the other's blaming his brother.'

'Looks like.'

'And when will the solicitor be coming, do you know?' Tiss asked, something slightly off-putting going through her mind as she asked.

Woodhouse just shrugged in reply. 'It depends. There is only one duty solicitor, and they're currently with someone on another case.'

Tiss was quiet for a moment. 'How old exactly are the brothers, because I'm thinking about the other deaths twenty years ago. Would they have been old enough at the time?'

'I'm not certain. Maybe not for the ones going back twenty years, but five or even ten years ago is feasible.'

'A parent, perhaps? Keeping it in the family?'

Woodhouse grimaced at that. 'Well, that thought's not creepy at all, but I see where you're going with this. I really don't know; it's possible, I suppose.'

Despite her reticence, she forced herself to make an almost unthinkable proposition. 'Do you think it would be a good idea or not for me to go in there and speak to both of them?'

He looked at her and frowned. 'But I thought you said that you wouldn't want to; why are you thinking that now?' It was the last thing he'd expected; it was the last thing *she'd* expected, but once Tiss had an idea in her head he knew she felt obliged to go through with it.

'I know, I know,' she held both her hands up, acknowledging the ridiculousness of it, 'but hear me out. I'm here, and you're waiting for a solicitor. I'm a solicitor. I'm not planning to represent either of them, if that's what you're thinking, just use my position to try to get some answers out of Simon at least, especially if he's willing to speak.'

'But doesn't the Wilson who's the relief manager of the Regency Club know who you are?'

'If he remembers me at all he'll only know me as a solicitor.'

'Perhaps he knows you better than you think,' Woodhouse intervened. 'Claudia was taken and she's your friend, so surely he'll know that you're connected. And Simon,' he continued, 'surely he knows you from your connection to Claudia; knows what you look like from photos he's likely seen of you and she together?'

Tiss had to admit to herself that she'd overlooked that possibility. 'But it's better than nothing. And, as you say, you don't know how long the relief solicitor is going to be. At least let me try to get something out of them; and in any case, I'd speak to Simon first. I don't *want* to do it, but we can't just stand here and do nothing for hours on end. Please,' she begged.

Despite knowing that he shouldn't agree to this, Woodhouse reluctantly admitted that it would save them some time, but he made it abundantly clear that he wasn't happy with it in the slightest.

'I know,' she said sympathetically, 'and neither am I, but needs must. What about the club,' she added, 'what's happening there?'

'I secured a warrant to have it looked into. There are officers there as we speak going through everything they can find. Although,' he said, looking candidly at her with a raised eyebrow, 'I think your friend Jeff Rawlings has carried out a pretty thorough investigation of it himself.'

As Tiss cast him a shy sideways glance, he continued, 'Although I don't condone what he did, from what he's already confessed to me he seems to have done a good job and doesn't think they have anything to do with this, but if there's anything left to turn up that will connect him to the women's disappearances then the team will find it.'

'Are you certain?'

'Absolutely. The cold case team and the forensics division are nothing if not thorough.'

'There are only a few days before the 23rd, so I hope this will have scuppered any plans for this year.'

'If they *did* have anything to do with it then, yes, I sincerely think it will have,' came the reply. 'So, if you really want to do this and are ready, would you like to go down to the interview rooms?'

'Yes,' Tiss said, now feeling slightly better about being given the go-ahead to do so. 'It might be worth a try.'

CHAPTER
THIRTY-FIVE

Tiss felt nervous as she followed Woodhouse down in the lift to the ground floor where the interview rooms were. She'd spent years interviewing clients in her role as a solicitor, but this was so very different to that. For one thing, it was assumed that both men she was about to interview had kidnapped two of her friends and about to do goodness knows what to them, kill them at worst, perhaps. So yes, she was nervous. Simon was the one she wanted to speak to first. Although he was Claudia's boyfriend, (ex-boyfriend now she didn't doubt), she'd never met him as they'd only been together for a few months, but she knew that Woodhouse was probably right, in that he'd almost likely seen photos of her with Claudia. Was he part of this whole kidnapping thing or was he not? He'd pleaded his innocence to Woodhouse, and the detective was in a mind to believe him, but it could all be a ploy, she knew that, but she had to go in there with an open mind and listen to what he had to say. She couldn't let herself be judgemental because of an assumption.

Once out of the lift, Woodhouse took Tiss past the main reception desk, through a double door next to it, and down a long corridor to the interrogation rooms.

'I'm going to go in the next room and watch you through the glass,' he said as he stopped outside the second room down on the right. Tiss felt her heartbeat speed up a bit as he entered the room leaving her to go into the one next to it. You can do it, she thought to herself as she gripped the handle and turned it.

Simon Wilson's head rose when she entered and he actually looked happy to see her. 'I'm a solicitor,' she announced, making sure not to tell him any more than that, like she was the duty one. Woodhouse was being liberal even allowing her in the room, and she didn't like the idea of claiming to be something other than what she was. By citing "solicitor" she wasn't exactly lying even though it wasn't exactly the truth either, or at least not the way Wilson would be perceiving it. To her she *was* the duty solicitor. 'I've been told you asked for someone to talk to.'

'Thank goodness,' Wilson nodded as she pulled out a chair from beneath the table and sat down opposite him. Then she realised that she didn't have anything to write on to make it look both legitimate and professional, so she pulled out her phone and asked if he minded their conversation being recorded. He looked a bit puzzled, obviously expecting her to have a brief case along with a notepad and pen, but she improvised by saying that she'd been called in quickly – which wasn't a lie. It seemed for all intent and purpose that he didn't recognise her as being Claudia's friend.

'Do you know who I am?' she asked, thinking she may as well be truthful about this.

'Yes,' he said, looking her straight in the eyes, 'you're the duty solicitor.'

'I'm not, actually,' she reluctantly admitted.

He sat back in the chair so hard that it must have hurt his back in doing so. 'What? Then who are you? I asked to see a solicitor, more than happy to see one.'

Tiss half expected Woodhouse to come barging in at that point, but was glad that he didn't as that wouldn't have served any purpose at all. 'You really don't know who I am?' she asked again.

'Apart from me thinking that you are the duty solicitor, no. Why, should I?'

'I'm here because I wanted to know what happened to two of my friends,' she said as she stared back at him with the same intensity as he'd stared at her. But then as she kept her eyes on him he lowered his and his brow furrowed at what she'd said.

'Your friends? I ... I don't understand,' he stammered.

'You were found at the house where they were being held captive. You can't tell me you had nothing to do with it?'

'But I didn't!' he cried out desperately. 'I tried to contact Jonathan but I couldn't, he wasn't answering his phone and I wanted his help with trying to find Claudia. Then I remembered that I had a tracker on my phone and I put his number into in and found his location.' He stopped suddenly as he appeared to then realise who she was. 'Wait, are you Tiss?'

She didn't answer his question but instead continued with her own. 'Why were you trying to contact your brother?'

'I went to his flat but one of his neighbours heard me knocking and came out. He was a bit confused at first as he said he'd been told by someone that they thought Jonathan and I were away together for the weekend. I was confused too as I hadn't seen him for several weeks, that's why I went around, and we'd certainly not arranged to go away together.'

Tiss now felt confused herself. Simon Wilson looked for all intent and purpose that he was telling the truth, but she knew guilty people could look and sound innocent in order to save their own skin. But there was definitely something about him that made her think that he was perhaps an innocent party in all this, despite him been found at the scene of her friends' incarceration. Perhaps Woodhouse's intuition was correct after all, and he was as guiltless as he claimed he was.

'So, what do you make of all this?'

'I really didn't know what to think, and that's the truth. Nate's my brother and I had no idea what he'd done, that he'd kidnapped Claudia and that other man. I know I hadn't seen him in a while, but this is … this just isn't like him. I just don't understand it. Like I say, I managed to trace his phone; he showed me how to do it once and I forgot I could do it. When I got to where he was in the old building I had no idea what was going on. Why was he even there? We rowed, and then I thought I could hear other voices in the house, people talking quietly, and I asked him who else was there. He refused to say anything, which is when the police arrived on the scene and we were both arrested. So you are Tiss, aren't you?' he pushed again.

'Yes,' she finally admitted. It was pointless now not to. At least Woodhouse must be approving of what she was saying as he hadn't come bursting in to drag her out yet.

'Is she okay?' he asked, genuinely concerned. 'Please tell me she's okay!' his face draining of all its colour.

'She was taken to the hospital but she is fine; she's out and she's home now.'

'Dear God!' he declared, resting his elbows on the table and putting his head in his hands. 'And the other person?'

'Another friend of mine.'

'Ruby?'

'No, not Ruby; someone else I know.'

'But I don't understand, why ... why would he do such a thing?'

'That's what the police are trying to find out,' she admitted. She hoped that Woodhouse was taking this all in from behind the mirrored partition and cast a quick glance over in its direction, frowning as she did so. Then she remembered about what Claudia had said, that when Simon left her house on Saturday evening she felt a little dizzy. 'Was Claudia okay when you left on Saturday?'

'Yes ... why?' he asked in shock. 'Did something happen to her after I left; is that when Nate took her?'

Now that was a reaction Tiss felt nobody could fake. He looked so horrified by the mere thought of it, and it must have been how she looked when she first heard the news that her friend was missing. 'She said that she felt a bit peculiar and had to go and lie down.'

'I know she and I had perhaps a few too many glasses of wine, but apart from that she was okay.' 'The police thought that she might have been drugged judging by her description of how she felt.'

'And they think … No, I certainly didn't do that. I wouldn't … I couldn't.'

Tiss believed him. 'Look, I'm going out of the room for a while, but I'll be back, okay?'

Wilson only nodded a response; his head had ducked down even further as she got up and made her way to the door. 'Would you like a drink of water?' she asked before leaving and heard him utter a quiet yes.

When she was out in the corridor Woodhouse was standing waiting for her. 'What do you think?' she asked him and he rubbed a hand over the back of his neck.

'I'm not sure,' he admitted, looking defeated, 'but it certainly looked like he knew nothing about what was going on.'

'My thoughts exactly,' Tiss replied. 'But did his brother do this alone, and nothing to do with the Regency Club, or is he doing it on their behalf?'

'I won't be able to answer that until the club's been severely vetted and all their files and hard drives gone through. I'll reluctantly admit that Jeff Rawlings did a good job, albeit an illegal one doing it on his own-' Tiss tried to interject but he held up a hand to stop her and continued. '*And*,' he stressed, 'I'm now fully aware of what it is he does, so both of you need to be glad that I'm not pressing charges on this.'

'And what would you be pressing charges for if you were going to?' Tiss stood her ground. Yes, she knew that a lot of Jeff's work was potentially illegal

– or very illegal, depending upon how anyone looked at it – so what category could that fall under.

'Well, let me see. Possible espionage, for one, and illegal access to confidential material for another.'

'Espionage?' she asked aghast.

'I understand your man is available on contract to infiltrate certain areas.'

'Not my man for starters, and what do you mean by infiltrate?'

'Oh, come on, Tiss,' Woodhouse sounded exasperated, 'I've already told you I'm not pushing for anything despite I'm probably risking my job right about now by not reporting it. But I *do* know what Jeff does for a living, so as a future warning I think he should tread just a little more carefully if he doesn't want to get caught.'

'But you wouldn't have known anything about it if not for this case.'

'And I rest my case, madam solicitor. If I didn't know better I would think that you've temporarily forgotten about your legal obligations. You know that what you've both been doing is definitely *not* on the right side of the law, don't you?'

'Well, yes, but-' she blushed slightly at the insinuation which was, admittedly, true.

'But nothing,' he cut in. 'Come on,' he said reaching out and taking her by the elbow, 'let's go and get that Mr Wilson in there a bottle of water before you go in with all guns blazing to the speak to the other brother.'

Despite the serious conversation Tiss had just had with him she could now sense humour in his voice as he said it, and allowed him to lead her along the corridor to where a drinks machine was.

After slipping in quickly to hand Simon Wilson his drink, Woodhouse joined Tiss in the corridor to lead her to Jonathan Wilson's interview room.

'I don't think this is going to be as pleasant as the other one,' Tiss muttered as the detective came to a stop beside a door further down.

'Are you sure you're up to this,' Woodhouse asked in concern. 'He was verbally aggressive when he came in. Maybe I should come in with you?'

'You don't think I can handle myself then?'

'Oh, I know that you can,' he said with a slight chuckle. 'More than most people I know, including the so-called tough detective types.'

'Is that a compliment, detective?' Tiss asked with a smile, taking in the slight flush of his skin as she said it.

'All I'm saying is, you're one tough cookie, as our American cousins say; can't fault you for that, nor would I.'

Tiss felt flattered and preened herself somewhat at that statement. But for now she had to go into another room to question the other Wilson brother. Only this time, she knew that she was in for a rough ride.

CHAPTER
THIRTY-SIX

Jonathan Wilson looked at Tiss with a fierce and unfriendly expression, his face contorting into something akin to disgust. His gaze was unnerving, or would have been to many people, but as concerned as she was about this meeting, she didn't flinch or give him the pleasure of thinking he'd intimidated her; her training had provided her with the ability to overcome that. However, there was something else behind those eyes that Tiss couldn't quite determine: pride, toxic masculinity, fear even. Now why did she think fear? Perhaps he felt that she was personally responsible for him sitting there instead of it being the result of his own actions, she didn't know, but what she did know was that he was just as unpleasant as when she'd met him that one time at the Regency Club. She sat down without saying a word but held his contemptuous eyes throughout.

'And what do you want?' he asked sharply as he sat back in his chair and folded his arms over his chest. The tension in the room was palpable; you could have cut it with a knife.

'So you *don't* want legal representation.' It was a statement rather than a question. If he was going to be hard, then so was she.

He looked at her with a puzzled expression on his face before answering. 'I said I wasn't prepared to speak to anyone, not even the duty solicitor, and I'm guessing that you're not the duty solicitor.'

'Why do you assume that?'

'Well, you're not, are you,' he said defiantly, eyes blazing with fury.

'So you *do* know who I am then?'

'Yes, of course I do; I remember you coming into the club all those weeks ago and asking for the manager.'

'And is that the only reason you know me, from there?'

'Yes, of course. Where else would I know you from?'

Tiss wondered if he was playing a game with her, or if he genuinely didn't know that she was a close friend of both the people he had just kidnapped. She was about to say the people that *they* had kidnapped, but after hearing what his brother Simon had to say, that he didn't know anything about it, she was inclined to believe him. Maybe she shouldn't have assumed, but what he'd said to her rang strangely true, and she was usually right about how a person answered any of her questions from a legal point of view.

'Why are you in here if you're not here in an official capacity?' The man's anger was growing by the second, and although not fearful of his behaviour, Tiss was glad that Woodhouse was watching what was happening from behind the two-way mirror on the wall. If things were to get really out of hand, if he became physical, then she knew that he'd be in there in an instant.

'I've just spoken to your brother. He's keen to talk, has spoken in fact, and he tells me that he knew nothing about the two people you kidnapped.'

'Did he now?'

'He did.'

Tiss wasn't sure how much she was going to get from this conversation with Wilson, if anything, as he was certainly being hostile towards her. She'd experienced this kind of reaction from someone incarcerated before, but this was more personal to her, and she began to think that this wasn't such a good idea after all. Maybe she should leave it to someone unconnected and more detached. Taking that into consideration, she rose from her seat and made a move towards the door but was stopped by what he said to her.

'You know, there are still a couple more days until the 23rd, so I'd be careful if I were you.' It was said with such delight that it sent a chill down her spine as she hurriedly left the room. She was shaking by the time Woodhouse joined her out in the corridor.

'Did you hear what he said?' she asked in a cracked voice. 'Did he just threaten me?'

'I heard, and it did sound like it.'

'Do you think somebody else could be involved, someone from the club?'

'I don't know, it's possible, especially as both your friends seemed to think that there was more than one person in that house with them. It could have been someone from the club, but it could also have been another friend of Wilson's. But now that I've heard that I'll have to go down there and interview the board members and anybody else who is there, see what they say about Mr Jonathan Wilson.'

Tiss nodded; it had to be done. 'Has the cold case unit given you the go-ahead to do all this on your own then as you seem to be doing all of the work for them?'

'They have. My immediate boss transferred me over to them as his representative.'

'That's quite a recommendation,' she smiled, slowly getting over her confrontation with Wilson.

'Yes, it is,' he returned the smile. 'He's even said that he's recommending me to do the sergeant's exam, which is a big step up for me.'

'That's fantastic and I'm very pleased to hear it.'

'Okay,' he said going into business mode. 'I'm going to insist that you go home now and let an official solicitor handle this while I head off to the club. I hear that the team is still down there looking around so it will be best if I go now. Then there's both the Wilson brothers houses to check out, so I'll have to get some other team members to help with that.'

Tiss agreed, but as already pre-arranged, after leaving the station she headed off to Jeff Rawling's house. If there was someone at the club involved in all this, she only hoped that they'd find out sooner than later. She also hoped that they'd discover the real reason behind all this, why the women in the past had been taken never to be seen again. Tracy Dimmock seems to have been an anomaly as she'd been found dead, if she had been an intended missing woman in the first place, that is. Her disappearance and ultimate death had never been determined one way or the other, intentionally connected or a random victim of another crime.

Neither she nor Jeff could do any more investigating now that the police were on this one in force, but the clock was ticking, and the 23rd of March was fast approaching quicker than anyone liked.

***

Jeff looked worse for wear but comfortable when Lily let Tiss into his house. He was lying on the sofa looking through a folder as she entered the room, but put it down on seeing her. She hoped it wasn't anything to do with either the club or the case as his face was testament to what he'd been through. He began to lower his legs but Tiss stopped him.

'No, stay there,' she insisted. 'There's no need to make yourself less comfortable for me.'

He stopped what he was doing and smiled as he settled his legs back on the sofa. 'I was just being polite.'

'You needn't be with me.'

'So you'd rather I was impolite?' he asked with a laugh.

'You know what I mean,' she chided in return.

'Now that you're here I'll be getting off them,' Lily smiled at their interaction as she reached down to pick up her bag from beside one of the chairs, the one she'd obviously been sitting in waiting for Tiss to come. 'He's no bother; he just requires a cup of coffee now and again and he's happy!'

'Haha, very funny!' Jeff retorted with a twinkle in his eyes.

'Okay,' Lily continued. 'Now you take good care of yourself. Perhaps you should consider cutting back all your extracurricular activities for a while, and maybe your day job for a couple of days too. You can't be going in dressed up to the nines in a suit and look like you've gone a few rounds with the world's heavyweight boxing champion.'

'I agree,' he said somewhat unexpectedly, which made Lily take a step back and clutch at her chest. 'Well I never thought I'd ever hear you say you'd take it easy. What is the world coming to!' Having said that in a mocking tone, she walked up to Jeff and bent down to give him a peck on the cheek. 'Make sure you take good care of yourself,' said more seriously this time. 'You gave us both a scare that I'd prefer neither of us go through again.'

'I will,' he said as he took her hand in his. 'And thank you for all you've done today.'

'It was nothing.'

After she left Tiss sat down in the chair opposite and looked at him. 'You and Claudia gave us all a shock,' she said as she tried to keep the tears at bay. Despite her attempts they began to flow freely. 'Dammit,' she said as she wiped them away. 'I was trying to stay brave for you as well.'

'Hey, it's okay. I'm fine, and I hear that Claudia is okay too.'

'But it might not have been as both of you could have been seriously injured, or worse. This is dangerous work you do.'

'It's not usually like this; it's mostly all white-collar work, digging around in a computer from the comfort of my own home most of the time. It's not like I went out looking for trouble, it's just that it came to find me.'

After she made them both a cup of coffee, Tiss told him what was happening with the Wilson brothers, and how Woodhouse was personally going out to oversee what the rest of the police teams were doing at both the brothers' houses and at the club.

'He's really into this isn't he?' Jeff said as he sipped on his drink.

'And I think he's about to be rewarded for it. He told me that his boss has suggested that he study for the sergeant's exam, and I think he'll be really good at it if he decides to go ahead and do it. He has a nose for it.'

'Well, good luck to him then.'

'And what about you, Jeff, are you going to slow down your extracurricular activity and stick to your day job?'

Jeff gave her a look to say, "are you kidding?" and she laughed out loud at his expression; it was hilarious!

'No, I didn't think so,' she admitted whilst trying to control herself. 'Even looking like you've just lost against the top cage fighter in the country?'

'Sure, why not? After all the time I've spent both working with Lily and working with other clients I've never run into any trouble. There was I minding my own business when somebody sneaked up from behind and chloroformed me; that wasn't me being irresponsible. Not paying attention maybe.' Despite trying to sound serious, his façade soon broke when he saw Tiss trying to hold it together herself. 'Oh, stop it!' he declared, laughing himself, as he flung a cushion in her direction.

CHAPTER
THIRTY-SEVEN

DC Woodhouse decided to contact the teams currently at both the Wilson brothers' homes to see if they'd uncovered anything rather than go there himself. He didn't know why, but he had a feeling that if anything was going to be found, then it was more likely to be at the club than anywhere else. It was a hunch, intuition even, but he instinctively knew that's where something would be as there were endless number of places in there anyone could hide something if they didn't want it to be found. And there certainly appeared to be some mysteries in that place. Although he knew that Tiss, working with Jeff Rawlings, had discovered relatively little about the club and its history, the cold case team had actually been watching the place for years, that little tidbit being revealed to him only within the last twenty-four hours when it was brought to his attention that Tiss wasn't the only person to have a man inside – the cold case unit had one inside too. That had been a revelation, especially when he discovered who that person was.

After a quick conversation with the two teams, who reported nothing out of the ordinary so far, he made his way over to the Regency Club. As he approached the club he could see a police presence outside the building in the form of a two uniformed officers, each standing on the pavement at opposite ends of the steps leading up to the large wooden door. Woodhouse flashed his warrant card to each of them before ascending. Once inside, the place was full of activity with both uniformed and plain clothed officers milling around. It might have looked chaotic to the casual observer, but Woodhouse knew it would be well organised with each participant doing what they were requested to do. George wasn't on relief, but the elderly man who stood behind the desk looked fearful as he gazed at what was happening around him, probably never seen the like of this before, the detective imagined, and likely hoping that he never would again. Woodhouse made his way through the club to find his cold case unit contact, DS Patrick Dunbar, to see what he and the others had turned up. He found him at the back of the building, in an area separate to the body of the club and which contained several offices and what looked like rooms intended as private meeting spaces. Each had their doors open and police officers were working inside them. This had to be the offices Tiss mentioned Jeff had been in.

'Ah, you're here,' Dunbar greeted him warmly. He was standing next to a large desk, now covered with a wealth of box files and manila ones which were being closely scrutinised by two seated plain clothed officers. He moved forward away from them to shake his hand.

'Yes, I've just spoken to the teams at the suspects' houses, but they haven't found anything of interest that would incriminate either of them.'

'I've been informed of that, yes, but they're still keeping at it. We, on the other hand, have discovered something quite interesting, which I'm sure you're going to want to see.' Woodhouse noted the broad smile he gave him and knew whatever it was had to be significant. 'Follow me,' he said, leaving the two officers to continue their search.

Dunbar took him further down the corridor which looked to be a dead end, but as they got closer to it he took a sharp right, bringing them into another more hidden area.

'What the ...' Woodhouse began as they walked into an entirely separate section. He'd never seen an optical illusion like it before, and he had to admit that it was a clever camouflage obviously designed to hide something from people's eyes.

'I know, right,' Dunbar smiled over his shoulder. 'We didn't even realise it was here at first, but when a key was found in the manager's safe we knew it had to open a door somewhere, and this is what it opened.'

The old, heavy wooden door looked completely out of place at the end of the pristine white walled corridor. It looked ancient but well preserved and taken care of, with odd inscriptions engraved into it. Woodhouse swore some of them looked almost satanic. Dunbar leaned forward and grasped the wooden door knob and twisted it. When it opened, what Woodhouse saw before him made him gasp. In front of him was a cavernous room painted in a deep aubergine colour, looking more like the set of a horror film than anything else. Strange paintings covered the walls, flourishes of red and black sweeping across the canvases without shape or definition, giving them an eerie look which drew the viewer in. Were these the paintings Tiss said her friend had been commissioned to paint? Woodhouse was brought out of his astonishment by Dunbar speaking to him again.

'Weird, right? At first we thought perhaps it was what you're most likely thinking now, in that it has something to do with devil-worship, but I don't think that's it, at least not now anyway. Maybe at one time it was when the club first opened, I don't know, but for now it's more aligned with debauchery than anything else and, believe it or not, human trafficking.'

'Human trafficking?'

'We've found evidence to prove that's been happening for quite a number of years.'

'The missing women you told me about?'

'I would bet money on it.'

At that point a person Woodhouse knew entered the room: Tom Davenport.

'Oh, James, this is DS Tom Davenport, and he's been working undercover at the club for quite some time now.' If Woodhouse hadn't already been made aware of Davenport's involvement he would have been stunned by the revelation. In fact, he *had* been stunned when he'd initially learned of it.

Davenport offered Woodhouse his hand and he shook it. 'I believe we have a mutual friend,' he said casually as he let the other man's hand go.

'Tiss?'

'Yes, Tiss. I'm sorry that I couldn't say anything, but as you will appreciate we had to keep this under wraps.'

'Yes, of course. But perhaps it might have been pertinent if I'd been made aware that someone was working on this from the inside?'

'Sorry about that, James,' Dunbar put his hand on his shoulder in a friendly manner. 'We just didn't want this one to get away from us.'

'I'm sure I wouldn't have jeopardised anything for you.'

'No, no, of course not; I wouldn't have thought that for one second. Nobody on the team knows about Tom being one of us other than me – and now you too.'

'Well, thank you for including me in on that.'

'Okay then, fill him in on what you've found out,' Dunbar said to Davenport as he stepped back slightly.

'We're lucky to have found this,' the undercover detective began, indicating the room they were in, 'but once that key was found we knew it had to belong somewhere. And it was an old key, nothing that would have fit any of the locked doors in the building, so we figured it must be out of the way of the main members' areas.'

Davenport began to move towards an open door in one of the corners and the other two men followed. When Woodhouse found himself to be in a kind of old-fashioned waiting room, the other two men stopped and Davenport continued. 'The door out of here,' which he indicated, 'leads out into the alley behind the building. Like the corridor that led us here, nobody would even realise it was there unless they knew about it.' He then walked over to and stood beside a desk where an old, red leather-bound ledger sat open. 'There's a lot of information in here,' he said pointing down towards it. Woodhouse moved in closer and turned a few pages seeing lists of names and dates, taking note that all the names were those of women. 'What is all this?' he asked, but suspecting that he already knew.

'From what I can figure, they're the names of all the women who have visited the club over the years for less than honourable reasons, such as club members wanting escorts for the evening.'

'And they've kept a record of them all?' Woodhouse was astounded as both men nodded.

'We also note that many of the women who have gone missing without trace are also in the book, which is why we're thinking human trafficking. There is a sub-section which lists sums of money, so yes, that appears to be the obvious answer, that and prostitution.'

'This is horrendous,' Woodhouse muttered, his eyes scanning the current page in front of him and saw Tracy Dimmock's name written down. He pointed at it. 'I thought she was a decent woman who was about to get married; what on earth was she doing mixed up with this lot?'

'Goodness knows, but I've come across five familiar names so far and I'm expecting to find more.'

DS Dunbar then joined in the conversation. 'We also found out that the wife of one of the board members is central to this, Miriam Marshall. Only we know her by the name of Miriam Southland, her maiden name, and she was prosecuted for running a brothel twenty years ago. She married her husband, Frank, a few years after coming out of prison, but it looks like she's gone back to her old profession again.'

'Do you think Frank knows about her past history?' Woodhouse asked, finding it more than a little difficult to believe that he wouldn't. He already knew about it, of course, through Tiss and Jeff Rawlings' little investigation of their own, but he wasn't going to tell them about that.

'I don't know as I've yet to speak to him, but chances are he does as she's the one who appears to be hiring these women to come in.'

'And also causing them to disappear to the trafficking trade,' Davenport added.

Woodhouse let out a long whistle. The day had taken a turn for the unexpected. 'So, what about all that demonic imagery out in the other room?'

'I'm assuming it's all for show,' Davenport said. 'I can't find anything to link it to what's happening in the club now. The building is quite old, a couple of hundred years I think, so who knows what went on back then. Marshall and his brother have connections to a club in town called *Lux*, which is all dark and mysterious inside and has the same kind of paintings on the walls, so I'd say it's perhaps just a kink of his and nothing more.'

'How long have you been working inside the group?' Woodhouse asked Davenport, curious to know if he'd been undercover when he first met Tiss. If that was the case, why had he honed in on her?

'Since last September,' he admitted. 'The cold case unit were going through old case files and the Regency Club's name popped up more times than we liked with some of the missing women last been seen near it or at least on the same street. It raised a few red flags.'

'And quite rightly by the look of things.' Both men nodded at his response.

'Which is why we thought getting someone in the inside might be beneficial,' Dunbar said.

'But how didn't you know about this room before now?' Woodhouse asked a pertinent question.

'Because I was there to investigate Marshall and his wife primarily, especially with her past history with women.'

'Yes, that makes sense when you know. And the key to this room, it was just in the safe all with everything else?'

'It was in an ornate box with Jonathan Wilson's name on it.'

'But wasn't that a bit risky? There are two managers, aren't there, what if the other one found it and asked what it was?' Woodhouse realised just as he said it that he mentioned the fact that there was a relief manager, someone Tiss had told him about and he wasn't officially privy to that. Fortunately, neither of the two other officers seemed to pick up on the comment, and if they did they didn't react to it.

'That's something we thought of and we need to ask. Someone is on their way to see him now.'

'So he could be involved as well?' Woodhouse asked, thinking that if it was a shared safe then anyone would be curious as to what would be in the other person's wooden box, especially if it needed to be kept in the safe.

'We'll just have to wait and see,' Dunbar said to him.

After a moment's thought Woodhouse just had to ask. 'You mentioned Tiss Lawson before,' and Davenport nodded. 'You befriended her so I'm wondering why you did so; was it something to do with the case?' He stared at him expecting some kind of confrontation.

Davenport just shrugged, saying that he knew she had been to the club and had also acquired the help of both Lily Singer and Jeff Rawlings, and also admitted that he wanted to get close to her to see what she had found out. He was worried that her apparent unofficial investigation might hinder his, but eventually deemed that it wouldn't.

'That's a bit unethical though, isn't it?' Woodhouse retorted.

'Am I stepping on some toes there, detective?' Davenport asked with a smirk. 'It was purely professional, nothing more I can assure you.'

'Okay, well perhaps you should tell her that. From what I know about Tiss I think she believed there was something there.'

'Then I shall have to tell her the truth when this is all over,' he said without emotion, which angered Woodhouse no end, an expression of disgust openly evident on his face, enough for the detective inspector to butt in.

'Okay then,' Dunbar clapped his hands together, seeming to sense the tension that was rising in the small room and wishing to defuse it. 'Let's see what else we can find in here and in the next room.'

After that minor incident all three men worked meticulously, going through files, documents and ledgers as well as examining the larger purple room for anything incriminating. Woodhouse thought that the appearance of it was incriminating enough, but personal thoughts sadly didn't qualify as evidence. As he looked around and took in more of the details, it looked to him more like a film set than anything else. If the Regency Club had taken part in supernatural practices in the past, there was very little evidence of that today beyond the way it was decorated. He knew that the black and red canvas oil paintings had been fairly recently painted by Tiss' friend Anita Jazmin, and as for the rest of it, he believed it was nothing more than for the enjoyment of one or more of the members who wanted to indulge in a little BDSM or other kinds of kinky roleplay. The handcuffs fastened to the walls and other items scattered about here and there, along with an old wardrobe filled with a variety of role-related toys and outfits, seemed to be testament to that. However, with the room being as well hidden as it was, it would appear that access to it was via Jonathan Wilson as he had the key kept securely in his safe. Did that then mean that only a select few people even knew of its existence? Again, something to find out for certain, and he had no doubt that somewhere in the files and ledgers there would be the names of those who partook in what the room offered.

CHAPTER
THIRTY-EIGHT

Things were starting to look bright again for Tiss Lawson. She finally discovered why Barnes had been discussing her with someone on the telephone all those weeks ago, and it wasn't as she'd thought. At the time Diane had overheard him say that Tiss was "the key to everything in the future, the key to their success", and it had been worrying, especially in the midst of everything else that was happening. However, it emerged that Barnes, along with Sanderson, had been considering elevating Tiss' position in the company at the time, such was her value to them, and they'd now promoted her to a position of a higher ranking and income.

Four weeks had now passed since the kidnapping of her two friends, Claudia Romano and Jeff Rawlings, and the uproar it had caused in the community with the families of the previously missing women demanding to know what had happened to their relatives. The police had their work cut out for them in no uncertain terms. The Regency Club had been temporarily closed down pending further investigation, and a firm of police-appointed forensic accountants had been brought in to look into both the legal and illegal side of the business. DC James Woodhouse was in permanent communication with Tiss, bringing her up to date on anything and everything they came across, and regardless of her and Jeff's somewhat rogue detective work, he was quietly glad that they'd brought the whole sorry mess to the attention of the police. It may not have been in his remit to do so, but he did it nevertheless as he felt she deserved to be kept in the loop under the circumstances. Despite this, the previous month had been a struggle in itself for her as she couldn't rest until the perpetrators of the crimes had been brought to trial. Only then would she feel that she could get her life back again.

He knew that she wanted to, but Woodhouse advised that Tiss not attend when the trial was fast tracked to the courts. He would be attending and promised to give her daily bulletins instead. He knew how much the whole thing had got under her skin and what it had taken out of her; he couldn't let her go through any of that again when it wasn't necessary, and he knew she needed a break from it all. He said the same to Claudia and Jeff, especially the latter as he'd come out of it battered and bruised.

When the trial commenced, a total of ten people in total had been taken into custody: Frank and Miriam Marshall, Fred Marshall, and Simon and Jonathan Wilson, along with three other members of the club who had participated in the procuring of women for activities in what the police now referred to as "the purple dungeon room". Frank Marshall claimed on the stand that he knew nothing about his wife's part in it, nor about her former life in the escort business, which both Woodhouse and the cold case team doubted him on but the final decision on that was now up to the jury. His brother Fred, on the other hand, was not seen as being so innocent. Information from the found files had proven beyond a question of a doubt that he and Jonathan Wilson were the brains behind the whole BDSM dungeon set-up, along with a few other high-ranking pillars of the community club members who had been arrested along with them. Further information showed them to have paid a pretty penny to partake in their extra-curricular activities. As expected, Miriam Marshall had been charged and was on trial for procurement for sexual gratification, and seeing that she'd already been charged for the same thing in years gone by and served prison time for, it didn't stand well for her. As for the Wilsons, Simon had been seen by the police as an innocent party in his brother's work with Mrs Marshall, but again, that was up to a jury to decide. In their opinion though, Jonathan Wilson was irredeemably guilty and he didn't even attempt to deny it when he eventually questioned. His conviction should be an easy one, especially as he'd eventually confessed to it.

Some of the older ledgers the police had found which dated back to the early part of the twentieth century provided more unsavoury information regarding the room and the mindset of some of the members. At that time, when the club was a genuine Freemason lodge, some members had taken it upon themselves to use the club as a meeting place for their darker interests, mainly black magic and satanic rituals. It was revealed, as Tiss herself had originally suspected, that they held ceremonies at certain times of the year, namely the spring equinoxes and winter solstices, ceremonies which required sacrificial offerings to some nameless entity for whatever reason which ultimately led to a woman's death. The names of the women who went missing over the twenty year period were also found in the newer ledgers. All the ledgers were entered as evidence in the trial, and Woodhouse hoped that once on trial Mrs Marshall would reveal how she'd managed to persuade otherwise normally upright and apparently clean-living women to partake in such a thing, because at the moment both he and the other police officers involved in the case found it profoundly baffling.

As somewhat expected and hoped for, Frank Marshall, Miriam Marshall and Jonathan Wilson were convicted of their crimes and sentenced to prison, a huge win for Woodhouse and the cold case squad. Regarding the reasons behind the road Jonathan Wilson had taken, upon learning about the existence of the room it had brought on deeply hidden thoughts he'd held at bay within him since childhood, namely an interest in the supernatural, and penchant for cruelty and the demeaning of women. His sentence was by far the strongest. Simon Wilson was judged to be an unfortunate bystander and any all against him dropped. The three club members were given suspended sentences, but Woodhouse suspected that their upstanding roles in the community would now be forever tarnished. He wasn't upset by that. The only unanswered question in all of this was the death of

Tracy Dimmock, as everyone convicted claimed they didn't know anything about her or her death. Woodhouse felt that under the circumstances her death should be investigated further, and it was something he would put to his superior officer.

Once everything was back to normal, or as normal as it now ever could be, and when Jeff Rawlings had got over his rough treatment at the hands of Jonathan Wilson and had shaken off all his cuts and bruises, he'd officially asked Tiss out on a date, and she'd happily accepted. They were now three weeks into their new relationship, three happy and contented weeks for both of them, and Tiss had finally found that one thing she never knew she'd either missed or wanted. But now that she had it she was determined to make it work, and somehow she knew that it would.

Printed in Dunstable, United Kingdom

63981704R00198